Ea

LIVE A

'I had two intimates, ever with me, my past and my future.'
But as the *Albicore* sailed slowly on towards Africa's infamous slave coast, his past and future seemed equally grim
to young Edward Mansell.

Condemned for a crime he never committed, hanged,
cut down for dead, and saved at the last moment, his hopes
of becoming a famous doctor had almost vanished, and all
the hazards of Africa lay before him. The terrible, fascinat-
ing continent to which Ned's fate had led him was to jolt
him out of the despair he had sunk into. First of all, he had
to outwit a plot, hatched by the ship's officers, to sell him
into slavery. Then he was to discover the land of the
Kranois – a mysterious race of white Africans – take part
in their war against the fearsome M'gai tribe, and prove
himself a truly courageous man of action. And one day,
far in the future, he was to return to England to find out
whether the shadow of the gallows still hung over him . . .

This fine tale (slightly abridged from the original) by a
master storyteller is the sequel to *Dead Ned*, also published
in Puffins.

For readers of twelve and over.

John Masefield

Live and Kicking
Ned

A Continuation of the Tale of Dead Ned
Abridged by Vivien Garfield

Puffin Books

Puffin Books, Penguin Books Ltd, Harmondsworth, Middlesex, England
Penguin Books Inc., 7110 Ambassador Road, Baltimore, Maryland 21207, U.S.A.
Penguin Books Australia Ltd, Ringwood, Victoria, Australia
Penguin Books Canada Ltd, 41 Steelcase Road West, Markham, Ontario, Canada
Penguin Books (N.Z.) Ltd, 182–190 Wairau Road, Auckland 10, New Zealand

—

First published by Heinemann 1939
This abridged edition published in Puffin Books 1975
Copyright © John Masefield, 1939

—

Made and printed in Great Britain by
Hazell Watson & Viney Ltd,
Aylesbury, Bucks
Set in Monotype Garamond

To
My Wife

Live Ned, or The Reef-Tackle

While at sea, I noticed a fitting on a sail, and asked a seaman what it was.

He said; 'A reef-tackle.'

I asked, 'What good is it?'

He said, 'In reefing, it takes up the weight of the sail, so that you can pass your ear-rings.'

I have called this volume of my story The Reef-Tackle *because it takes up the weight of my life during a blowy and anxious time. How I passed my ear-rings will be matter for another tale.*

I F you have not read my story, let me tell you, that I am a doctor, the son of a famous London doctor. Just before I came of age, I was accused of the murder of my benefactor, old Admiral Topsle Cringle, of Hannibal House. I was innocent of the crime, but my luck was out; I was condemned and hanged for it.

On the dissecting table, my medical friends restored me to life. With some trouble, and with much danger to myself, they contrived to get me to Liverpool, as surgeon to the slave-ship, *Albicore*, then bound for the Slave Coast in Africa.

Let me tell you of my ship and shipmates.

The *Albicore* was a small, full-rigged ship, commanded by one whom I shall call Captain Paul. He was the youngest brother of the famous Captain Valentine, who had been hanged for piracy many years before. Paul, although not a pirate, was still a credit to the family stock. As I entered Newgate, I saw him discharged, for want of evidence, for the atrocious murder of a seaman. On the night before our sailing, in the efforts of securing a crew, he had killed another man; for this murder a warrant had been issued against him and had nearly been served. His chief officer was a man named Pegg; his second mate was a Mr Tulp. We were now at sea together, with a fair wind, and piling sail to make the most of it.

The sun set early that evening. I was on deck, watching

the yellow sky all tossed about with menace, and wondering at my escape, when Mr Pegg asked me, if I would go to have a look at the Captain in the cabin.

'What is the matter with him?' I asked.

· 'The usual,' he answered. 'He's got the Wraith on him.'

Now this was a phrase that I had learned in Newgate, where it was believed, that murderers are beset, soon after their crimes, by the wraiths or angry spirits of those whom they have killed. The talk in Newgate ran much upon this point, and agreed, that while the Wraith is on a man he is incapable of wise decision. That it is so, I have no doubt.

I went at once to the cabin, where I found the Captain at table. On one side of him sat the Black Mantacaw, his negress; on the other sat Mr Tulp, plainly much scared. The Captain had his case of bottles before him, and clutched a pan containing rum. He was swathed up in rugs, although it was not a cold evening. In spite of the rugs, he was shivering; his teeth chattered and he was mumbling curses or snarling.

'What do you want, Doctor?' he asked.

'I'd like to take your pulse and see if a dose of bark won't help matters,' I said.

'It's not a case of bark,' he answered. 'It's a case of bite. It's that fellow's wraith on me. He's on me like irons. He says he won't let me set a course.'

'Nonsense, sir,' I said. 'There is nobody here but ourselves.'

'You can't see him,' he answered. 'He isn't on you. He's on me, with the side of his silly head bashed in. Ah, you grinning devil, for all your speed, you did not get the beaks in time. And you say I can't set a course but will lead me to destruction?' He leaned forward as he said this and spoke across the table to Mr Pegg's empty chair. I am sure that he did see the wraith and that the wraith was there. 'You were a Popery man,' the Captain continued, 'and you wouldn't this and you wouldn't that. And now I've fixed you so you can't, even if you want to. Don't think you'll stop me setting a course that'll be good. I've got ways of finding a course that'll be good.' Here he turned to the Black Mantacaw. 'Listen you,' he said, and made her look at the empty chair. 'You tell him, you know some stronger than he knows. You know Old Master.'

The Mantacaw was scared, but she answered: 'I know um.'

'Yes, you, Barney,' the Captain said, still staring at the empty chair. 'She know um. She bring um, too: she drive you some place. They'll tell me a course to set where there won't be destruction. Now, you, Judy; you go call um.'

She was scared. She said: 'Old Master, he not come.'

The Captain took a gulp of rum and said: 'Get to your den and put on your scarlet and your crown. You fetch um. Go on with you.'

She would have argued, but the Captain's last words were not to be disobeyed. He had an inflection in some of his speeches, which made everybody feel that any hesitation in obeying would be visited with death. She went into her den, for all her scare. The Captain said: 'Hoodoo'll tell me a course to set. It'll take more than Barney to go against hoodoo.'

Mr Tulp, being only a junior officer, usually said nothing in the Captain's presence, unless he were spoken to. To my surprise he spoke now.

'It won't do you any good, sir, on the Coast, nor on board here, to work hoodoo. The hands'll know it, and the natives'll get to know of it, and they'll steer clear and ruin you. You'd best not try it, sir; it's a bad thing.'

'Cock,' said the Captain. 'If he ain't a psalm-singer.'

'No, I'm not a psalm-singer,' Tulp said, and it was a gallant thing to stand up to the Captain in that mood, 'but bad as your luck may be, hoodoo is asking for worse, and so you'll find, sir.'

'You are an ignorant common fool,' the Captain said.

'I know I am, sir,' Tulp answered.

'If you give me any insolence,' the Captain said, 'I'll cut your throat just like a pig's over a pig-bucket.'

I said, 'Sir, he has used no insolence. You are suffering from a strain and an over excitement. Let me give you a sleeping draught. In the morning, after a night's rest, you'll be able to set any course with a clear head.'

Perhaps he would after that have cut the throat of one or other of us, but at that instant the door of the den opened, and the Black Mantacaw came in, dressed in scarlet and wearing a gold crown. She had a mad look in her eyes and was swaying from side to side; plainly she was up to some devilry, which rather scared her, but to which she was much looking forward; she had trodden that path before.

The Captain took a glance at her, and said, 'That is the way; you fetch um Old Master.' Then he turned to us, and took a gulp of rum. 'On deck with you,' he said; he was talking hoarsely, and had to repeat it, 'On deck with you. I've got to prepare here.'

'Sir,' Tulp said, 'it'll be the ruin of you.'

'I'll be the ruin of you, Tulp,' the Captain said. 'Get back on deck or I'll shoot the pair of you.'

Tulp, who knew the danger-signals better than myself, leaped for the ladder and went; I followed. I turned to watch the Captain, wondering, had he gone mad, and ought we to disarm him. I saw him lean across the table with his two pistols, and speak to the imagined wraith. 'Will you threaten me?' he said, and fired both the pistols through Pegg's chair and the bulkhead beyond it. The cabin filled with drifting smoke. He stayed to charge his pistols, while I went on deck.

I found that Tulp had already told Pegg all the news. The helmsman was listening with all his ears; pistols in the cabin meant something stirring.

'What on earth is hoodoo?' I asked.

'Their sort of god,' Pegg said. 'They consult him when they want to know a thing.'

'Does the god tell them?' I asked.

'Of course he tells them,' Pegg said rudely. 'Surely you know that. But it makes this ship a hoodoo ship.'

'It's a shame,' Tulp said, 'it's a shame; that's what I call it; and the first night out, too.'

'It's a damned shame,' Pegg said. 'Now we'll have nothing but trouble, you'll see trouble with the hands, foul winds, trouble with the Coast; and a lot of slaves with vomito. You'll see, Mister.'

But at this point, the Captain appeared on deck, breathing hard and beset by the wraith. He was bareheaded, and had slung on his pistol-slings, so that he had six pistols in quick reach, dangling down his chest. He was a terrible-looking man at all times, mad, dark, sideways and murderous, but he looked appalling at that moment.

'Get you forward out of this,' he shouted. 'All the lot of you, get forward. You, too, Misters; I mean you, too. Don't any one of you come aft again till I call.'

The officers had sailed with him before, and all hands now knew enough, to obey when he bade them. They leaped to the order; I leaped, too; for one had not to know much to know that in that mood a murderer will murder. The Captain went to the helmsman, took the tiller from him, and told him to get out till he was called for. The man slid away, quaking, and joined our group in the waist, where I think we all quaked.

There in the glare of the sky, our Captain stood and steered, now looking at the upper sails, now bowing from dread of the wraith and snarling. Below him, somewhere in the cabin, that black Witch of Endor in scarlet and gold was asking her god what our course was to be. To say that the seamen were scared is to put it too mildly; to them it meant destruction. They had shipped in one of Hell's packets, they knew that; but now, Satan was being called in to command.

After a long time, the Black Mantacaw crawled on deck in the last of the twilight. She was completely exhausted. Her face was all grey, and bitter smoke followed her through the hatch. She tottered towards the helm, where Paul was steering. She no longer wore a crown; the odd hair-dress which she always wore, of her frizzled black hair worked up to a cone with grease and wooden ornaments and then transfixed with daggers, had all fallen sideways; all her scarlet was now foul. She crawled up to Paul, holding on to anything that could support her. Tulp was at my side; he heard what I heard: there can be no doubt of it. We heard the Mantacaw speak in a cold, clear man's voice, not her own voice at all. We heard her give a position in latitude and longitude and the course, by compass, that would bring us there. It was spoken very clearly, and beyond any possibility of mistaking.

Tulp, who was crossing himself, whispered, 'That's her hoodoo speaking; Big Master, as they call him. Now he'll tear her and go out of her.'

And indeed, something seemed to bend the Black Mantacaw as though she were going to be snapped in two; she fell down with a cry and lay senseless. However, hoodoo had spoken; the Captain had learned what he wanted.

I have here in my study a fine globe shewing the oceans and the continents. In the blue expanse of the North Atlantic Ocean I have put a minute speck of red ink to shew the spot to which we were directed. To that speck our ship's head was turned, and to that point we sailed, with a wind which took us at once away from England and arrest, and then gradually died, so that we crawled on a stagnant sea.

I was in a world new to me, it was now my world and, it behoved me to become useful to it; to win the confidence of its citizens, and learn its ways. So, on the morning after the witchcraft, when we were out of sight of land, I rose up, determined to learn. I knew that I had little sickness on board to occupy me. The Mantacaw had recovered from her exhaustion; one man was still sick from some drug or drugged drink which had been given to him; five others had been cruelly hit, kicked or clubbed; still, all of these could make some shew of working. My day was like to be idle, unless I made occupation for myself. I had been expressly told, moreover, by Captain Paul, that my job was to watch the slaves, who were worth money, not to pamper the hands, who weren't. 'No man goes sick aboard me,' Captain Paul had told me, 'not till he's dead, and then he won't need to.' I had detected in Pegg a kind of dislike of myself and my office. To him, I could see, I was a sort of landsman and idler; a kind of passenger, who ate and was yet worthless and did not pay his passage. I thought, 'Perhaps, if I turn to and learn to be of use, he may change this view.' I had already surprised him by not being seasick; 'now,' I thought, 'I will surprise him more by becoming a sailor.'

It was a praiseworthy resolve, but in my ignorance I went the wrong way about it.

As soon as possible, the ship settled to her sea-routine; all hands were put to quarters, and especially to the exercise of the guns, for the Channel was not safe then from privateers and worse. Both in the forenoon and afternoon, the watch on deck had to exercise at the guns under Captain Paul's supervision. We had a Gunner on board, but Captain Paul took the first drills. He was a grim teacher, impatient and very savage, with a blow, a kick or some other devilry for any stupidity or slowness in any man. In the forenoon, when the guns were first cast loose, I went to the Captain and asked, if I might learn the exercise. I said, that I knew that in action I should have to tend the wounded, but that if we were hard-pressed I should like to know what to do.

'You can learn if you like,' the Captain said. 'Catch hold of that piece of string and heave on it.'

I was a willing pupil, and did not do badly. I knew too, that I pleased the Captain, for he said, 'It's something to have one of a gun's crew who knows what a thing is for. If you'll go to Puggy, the Gunner, after knock-off time, and take him a pannikin of rum, I daresay he'll tell you what you want. It's pointing and charging you ought to learn, not this handspike and tackle part of it.'

I said I would try to learn both. Pegg said something about a new broom always sweeping clean, and that I might not be so ambitious by the time I reached the Coast. However, after dark that night, I did take some rum to Puggy the Gunner, and made my lot the worse by doing so.

Puggy lived with the Sailmaker in the 'tween-decks. He was a short, elderly, powerfully built man, with a nose flattened by a blow, and yet pierced right through from side to side. He wore ear-rings, like so many of the men, and was very fond of rum.

'Guns?' he said to me. 'You want to learn about guns? You come to the right shop and I'll be proud to learn you. Bullets and Christianity are the two great gifts we bring the blacks, if you ask me.'

I learned something of the theory of gunnery from Mr Puggy Crackers, as well as much of the world. He had had extraordinary experiences. Like most sailors, he did not know that they were extraordinary. On our second evening, he told me, that he had lived as a native at a place called Milindi on the Coast for eleven years, and that the hole through his nose had been pierced there for the skewer or nose-plate, which a native always wears, from puberty till death. I asked him at once, if he would teach me some of the native languages. This was a mistake.

'Oh, no, sir,' he said. 'I lived native; that's one thing. I was married to Samba, and in business. But I had to keep White Man's Face. A white man doesn't lower his Face by learning the native gibberish. That would be pampering them. That would be putting 'em above their boots. We've not sunk so low as that, I hope. No, sir, what I talk to them is Palaver, and that's what you'll have to speak to them. I'll learn you that with pleasure.'

I thanked him, and said I would be glad indeed of some lessons. So I sat on there for some half-hour more, learning how to speak to natives without endangering the White Man's Face. Now, Palaver is a jargon made up of all the European tongues spoken on the Coast during the past three hundred years; in the main it is probably always the tongue of the speaker. It is spoken forcibly, so that there may be a minimum of doubt of what is meant, and it is emphasized with signs and gestures. The natives are naturally shrewd and have by this time clear perceptions of the simple greeds of white men. I began upon this tongue with interest, for the simple sentences of the lesson taught me something of the Coast where it is spoken. I gathered from the talk, that on the Coast life was easy, and death easier still; that life was the satisfaction of greeds, and death a dissolution by vultures, ants and crabs. Thirst was the enemy and cruelty the occupation.

From Palaver, we turned to some of the practical parts of gunnery. I had never seen gunpowder made. Puggy Crackers, like many of the older sea-gunners, still made at least his priming-powders. He promised to shew me how to make it; I could help him, he said.

In the morning, after breakfast, when my examinations and reports had been made, I joined the Gunner on deck, to make some priming-powder. He had rigged up a set of screens of wetted canvas in a quiet part of the deck. Within this shelter, with buckets of water beside us, he set out his ingredients, blended them and milled them, a little at a time. I had never done it before; it interested me very much.

I was busy, thus, with the Gunner, thinking no evil and enjoying myself, when I heard Pegg, whose watch it was, say to one of the Boatswains:

'He signed as Doctor, but he seems to be Gunner's Mate by the look of things.'

The Boatswain sniggered. I knew, then, that I had committed a sin against sea-custom in working thus with the Gunner. Still, I had done so with no ill intent, and with the Captain's approval. A few minutes before noon, I went below, to find Mr Tulp, who was then dressing to take the afternoon watch.

'Mr Tulp,' I said, 'tell me, have I done any wrong to Mr Pegg in taking lessons from the Gunner?'

He was a secret, sad young man, Mr Tulp. He always

spoke in a whisper, after looking about for listeners. I judge that he had had a terrible life of suppression and tyranny from which rum and knowledge had been his sole ways of escape.

'Yes . . . No,' he whispered. 'But he thinks you do it, to shew that you despise him.'

'What rubbish,' I said; 'what utter rubbish.'

'He says, "A chief officer ain't good enough for my lord Doctor; none but a Stink-Pot Maker is good enough for him".'

'But, good Lord,' I said, 'I'm only trying to make myself useful on board.'

'That's what he says,' Tulp answered. 'He thinks you may be starting a party against the officers.'

Now, this seemed to me so crazy, that it took my breath away, but I remembered how my old Master had always warned me against the enormous power for evil in injured vanity.

'Thank you,' I said. 'Do, please, always warn me, if I make more mistakes like this.'

Eight bells were made at that instant. Mr Tulp went on deck to relieve Mr Pegg, and the Boatswain piped to dinner.

Before I had left my cabin, Mr Pegg came down to the saloon, pitched his hat upon the table and cried in a loud voice to the Captain. 'Sir, it's not what I've been accustomed to. This Doctor of yours finds this mess not to his liking. Every word we say here gets reported to that Gunner. If we're not good enough company, let him mess with the Gunner. But we're the Deck Department, and in every ship I've been in, the Deck's been a lot more important than any Bangs. Yes, and a lot more important than a whipper-snapper sangrado, if it comes to that, what's just done drawing teeth at Bart's Fair. If this

Doctor can't stomach us, but must have the Gunner, let him go there, or turn me forward where I won't have the gall of it.'

All this was spoken in a loud voice under an open skylight. Every word was heard, not only by the steward, but by the helmsman at the tiller just above us, and by half a dozen men of Tulp's watch who were working on the mizen-rigging. It was, of course, meant that I should hear it. I came into the cabin at once and said,

'If there's any complaint against me, I ought to hear it.'

When vexed, Pegg had a snorty way of puffing himself out and blowing with his lips; he did this now.

'Come on,' I said, 'what is the trouble? You don't like my going to the Gunner? I go to him with Captain Paul's permission, in order to learn things which may be useful for a ship's doctor.'

'A ship's doctor minds the sick; that's his business,' Pegg said.

'I do mind what sick there are,' I said. 'Why should I not try to make use of my time, when that is done?'

'Because it lowers the cabin in the eyes of the men,' he answered. 'Because the men see you go direct from the cabin to consort with the Stink-Pot Maker.'

'What is done with the Captain's approval cannot lower the cabin in any way,' I said. 'But come, Mr Pegg, this is early in the voyage, and I am green to the life of the sea; you must make allowances for me. I want to learn how to take my part in the life of the ship, and I hope that presently you will teach me some of your mystery. If Captain Ashplant will permit. I will ask for a punch to settle this matter. What do you say, Captain?'

The Captain was an odd savage; one could generally count on a rough answer from him. To my astonishment, he was helpful.

'The trouble on board this damned privateer,' he said, 'is this damned leak that's coming in. I don't wonder you're vexed, Mister. It's enough to send anyone to the Gunner, or to Satan's self for that matter. Come on, now, steward, fetch a punch, and let's hear no more of this. Now, Mister, you and the Doc, there, drink.'

We drank, and for the time that matter ended, but I knew now that Pegg was a jealous and evil little man, with a set against me. It was the first time that I had heard of any leak. I asked about it, as soon as we had settled to our meal. It was coming in somewhere amidships, Pegg said, somewhere right amidships, and on the port side, which was perplexing, because she had been tight enough in Liverpool. However, it was nothing yet; they could clear it easily; perhaps the Carpenter's gang would get at it.

That evening, the wind which had brought us so proudly and swiftly clear of the Channel and Soundings fell light and became flighty. We went on slowly towards that red speck upon the chart to which some evil power had directed the Mantacaw. Presently, when we were thereabouts, the wind drew ahead, and settled. It was not bad weather. It was settled fair weather, miles from the usual course of the slavers bound to the Coast. There we slowly beat and floundered, against a light, hostile wind, which the seamen said was a dead muzzler. We beat against it for a week, and at the end of it had gone no farther on our way; the drift was against us, and wiped out what we made. After a time, the wind failed; we were becalmed; then gave us a brief lift and died away. All said, that they had never before known calms like that in that season. They said, that that came of bringing the Devil on board, yes, and having him on board, too, for who could doubt, that he was now within the Black

Mantacaw, living in the cabin. She came on deck sometimes. When she did, the men made the sign of the cross
upon themselves. I heard men muttering on deck in the
night watches, that they would get no fair wind, nor
come at the leak till that Black Judy was put over the
side. It was hot, fair, hazy weather, with multitudes of
flying-fish all about us.

When the calm set in, the Captain tried to find the leak.
We shifted the weights to one side and worked very hard
to come at the place. I worked with the others and enjoyed
the effort and the hope of success. After a time, we did
find whereabouts it was: I heard it. All the space of the
hold was full of gurglings and complainings; odd stretching creaks and whickering cracks went across slowly
from side to side as the ship gently rolled back and to.
Water washed and whimpered away from her bows outside and clucked and splashed in the bilges. Among all
these noises was a noise as of a small steady teapot being
poured; this was the leak.

'It sounds like a trunnel,' the Captain said.

'Either that or a bolt, sir,' the Carpenter said.

'It's not likely to get any worse,' the Captain said.

'No, sir,' the Carpenter said. 'But it's best to keep the
sea on its own side the fence; I'll hope to get at it tomorrow.'

As there was a dead calm on the morrow, they tried.
They took a lot of trouble, and hove the ship well up,
but the place was not to be reached. The verdict of the
Carpenter was that it was coming in below where it came
through. They gave it up, after that, saying that on the
Coast they could heave the ship right down, and strip
her copper off. It was not yet a serious leak; still, it added
to the work and to the worry.

I continued to take lessons from the Gunner. I learned

to mill priming-powder and to handle big guns, and could recite the charges for all known shot. Pegg growled and was rude about it. I told him, that it was no concern of his, how I passed my time, and that he might take notice, that I did not interfere with him as Mate.

'No,' he said, 'and you'd best not try, neither.'

'I have no intentions of trying,' I said. 'I keep to my own business.'

'You don't,' he answered hotly. 'Gunning ain't your business. Keep to your flap-doodle and rags and that, them's your business.'

We had many petty bickerings of this sort; usually we patched them up over rum-punch, which we drew now as a daily ration. All slavers, I had learned, took in great quantities of rum in the West Indies, where nearly every planter made rum. I suppose, that a third of the death and half of the cruelty usual in the trade were due to the rum. Rum only made a truce between Pegg and myself. After drinking, he would go off, snorting and vexed, to mutter against me to all and sundry. 'There goes our precious Doctor, to his crony the Stink-Pot.' However, I learned, that on the whole, I was liked, and Pegg disliked; and that sea-custom prescribed, that the Doctor was not under the Mate, and could do pretty much what he chose, provided he did his doctoring. What doctoring I had to do, I did successfully.

I had hoped, that we might make a swift passage to the Coast, so as to fill with slaves and be away on our Middle Passage before any letter about us could come from England. This hope was now gone; no ship could have made a worse passage than we were making. We had done what the Devil had bidden, and here we were, lost in the mid sea, where we might perhaps stay for days to come. By this time, it was plain, that even a slow ship with an average passage, standing on the usual courses, might have reached the Coast even if she had sailed a fortnight or three weeks after us. The men growled, that it was the Captain's fault. This was what came of bringing the Devil aboard; this was the foretaste and the earnest of it; presently we should have the full due paid. As the days passed, it began to be said, that we should lose our season. We should come to the Coast too late, and find all the slaves already shipped. I heard a man say, 'Here we are; here we shall rot, and the Devil will have his own. That's what we asked for.' But it was the Captain, the man responsible for the asking, who cursed our fortune loudest. Like most Captains, he was proud of his ship's speed, and had made famous passages in her. Now he would walk the poop, snapping his fingers and rolling his grim yellow eyes. 'See, now,' he would cry to me, or Pegg, or the helmsman, 'see, now. I stood to the West, as this damned Witch of Endor told me from her Obi or her Hoodoo; and here I am in a calm, which won't even give her steerage way.' Then, in his rage, he would go to windward, or to which ever side happened to be northerly, and whistle for a wind. This, to myself, seemed only silly; to the crew, it was like tempting God. They all crossed themselves when he did it, and turned quite white.

'You must never whistle for a wind, sir,' the Gunner told me, when I asked about it. 'I don't know why, so don't ask me; I only know you mustn't. Only Finns and damned fools whistle at sea.'

Perhaps time has mellowed my memory of the Captain. I know that, at first, I was shocked by his appalling presence, and by the knowledge that he had murdered two seamen. After a few days, I found myself admiring some of his qualities; and I admire them still, though I say now, at the end of a long life, that he was quite the murkiest savage I have ever met.

Let me state his qualities. Pegg had described him as the finest captain in the trade, bar none. He was certainly that. He was at all times diligent in his business, if ever man was; no man could have served his owners with more zeal, nor with shrewder brain. He had affections, of a kind. He loved the *Albicore*; he was sometimes gentle to the Mantacaw; and he was devotedly fond of his father, now a very old man, who kept a little shop and repaired boats upon the Mersey shore. He often talked of this father, who suffered much, it seemed, from swollen legs. Often the Captain would tell me of these swollen legs and ask me about possible causes and remedies. He would listen to me with deep attention; finding that I had knowledge and sympathy in these matters, he was very civil to me.

His appearance was frightful. In the slave-trade, perhaps, his face was his fortune; it struck terror wherever he came. I suppose bile, gall and liver were all affected in him. To this day, I cannot think of his face without a shudder. It was pale, and tinged with yellow. The whites of the eyes were injected as well as yellow. He looked at you downways and sideways, with a lifting upper lip that shewed his yellow hyaena teeth. He had a way of snarling before speaking; his words followed on the snarl like a bite. This habit he had cultivated, to terrify his crew. They were very rightly terrified of him, because as the bite followed the snarl, so the blow followed the bite; and this often with little or no cause. If the man answered a question, he might be beaten or half-choked, for what the Captain called 'Coming the old soldier on me.' If the man were too terrified to answer, he might be half-choked or beaten for what he called 'Coming the sullens.' The men knew him very well, you must remember. They had not sailed with him before, but his name was infamous throughout the sea-faring world; now that they were with him for a round voyage, they trembled, and were wise to tremble.

We in the cabin were usually free from personal violence from him. I was always free, because I told him at the beginning, that I had letters to the Governors in the Indies, and would not tolerate any insolence of the kind, so let him beware, since the Governors should surely call him to a strict account.

He was all that is evil, yet I think of him always with some tenderness, because of his father's legs, and because of his liver, which was the cause of half his crime, I suppose; I might perhaps have treated that liver and left him almost human; but he was not one to submit to medical treatments.

He became worse, more cruel, and by much more dangerous as the passage lengthened, because it was now certain that word for his arrest must have reached the Coast. He punished the unhappy hands for this. He said that it would not be safe to make for any well-known port, and cursed his luck for it. I, who had my own reasons for fear, was thankful for it; but I was full of dread. I thought that they might have sent a cruiser to watch for us as we made the land. I should hear perhaps the oars of a boat, and the hail of some official voice. 'You have on board an escaped felon under the name of Edward Torrance. In the King's name, deliver him.'

These thoughts filled my mind as we stood-in to make our landfall.

Remember, that the Coast of Dead Ned (as men called the Slave Coast) is a peculiar place, easy to get into, for the wind blows you in: difficult to get out of, for the wind still tries to blow you in. As the wind there blows from west to east all the year round, the westward end is called the 'windward,' the eastward, the 'leeward.' No ship-captain goes to leeward if he can help it because of the difficulty of getting back.

Now Captain Paul had told us, that he was going to a little-frequented place rather far to leeward, called Great Momboe. That place in most seasons would have been as safe as Alsatia to him; but we had been so long at sea, that he was now afraid of going there. He let it be known, that he meant to ask at Monos Grandes if even secluded Momboe would be safe. If word had come that the *Albicore* was to be stayed, it would be talked of at Monos Grandes, and with a warning, Paul would go still farther to leeward for slaves, where he would be safe indeed.

It had sounded perfectly safe, to go to a Portuguese port, to ask for news; but as we drew nearer to Monos Grandes, it sounded less safe to me. I began to dread again. Still, Captain Paul proceeded like the coy virgin; he went with caution, keeping far out to sea, and avoiding every sail. When we stood-in, to make the land, I stayed on deck, staring, watching and scared.

Now that we were there, we became very coy. Paul said, that he would sail to the port entrance after dark and send Pegg ashore in a boat. Pegg would go to a certain agent known either as Perheira or Old Gutsache, well-known to both of them, and find out very privately, yet exactly, what was known about the *Albicore*, and how hot a search was being made for her.

Pegg shewed some hesitation at the task set for him.

'What are you growling at?' Paul asked. 'Monos is Portugee. You're English. You aren't in any trouble. There's no danger to you, just going ashore and asking a question.'

'I like that,' Pegg said. 'Probably, they've got thief-takers waiting for us there, and they'll take me, instead; you'll see. I like my freedom as well as another man. I'm not going to be a chopping block for your meat.'

This was sound sense in Pegg, but as like to mutiny as the Captain wanted. He leaped at Pegg, tripped him and flung him, then dragged him along the deck and bent his head back over a bucket. 'Not go?' he said. 'If you won't go, I'll cut your throat right now, just like a pig's over this bucket.'

Pegg exclaimed, that there was no need to talk like that; of course he would go. On being allowed to stand, he put on an air of injured pride. 'Come, Captain,' he said, 'there's no sense in talking like that. That's not decency nor manners, nor what I'm accustomed to.'

'Right then,' the Captain said. 'I'll send you in to-night, and with a case of claret for the Governor. But you won't meet with any trouble.'

However, it was quite clear that both he and Pegg expected trouble, and I knew too well, that I should share in any that was coming.

It was at about nine at night when we came off Monos Grandes, and lay by, while the boat made ready, to go in. It was there that I first heard the noise that I must always associate with Africa, the solemn, long, lapsing and rising roar of a great surf. It was always the voice of the Coast. It was sometimes lulled, sometimes louder, but never silent. At night, it spoke like the lamentation of the Continent for the curse that man had brought upon it. By day, it was full of threat.

Paul made no farewell, except: 'Well, Mister, you know what you have to do. Don't stay long.'

Pegg said, meaningly: 'I hope I shan't be made to,' and went down over the side and shoved off.

I could see the lights, and hear the bells of a church and a noise of singing, I think from some anchored ship. Paul had the nettings rigged in case any officer came out to serve a warrant. He also had the guns loaded and pointed, and after giving the hands a dram, made them lie down by their guns. He explained, that for all we knew England might have gone to war while we had been at sea, and that we might be attacked by an enemy. I knew very well, that it was nothing of all that, but a determination to kill anyone who tried to take him, and then to turn to the seas, like his brother, as a pirate from that time forward.

We waited for a long time, watching the Coast, listening to the surf, and seeing the gleams in the water as swells lifted or sharks rose. The ship lay by idly, with creakings and tuggings of her gear. Paul talked about the surf. 'It's a grand noise,' he said. 'I never tire of hearing it; but I wish this Mate of mine would come. It's not being certain that I dislike.'

I said, that we should soon know. Mr Pegg must be coming soon.

'He's a damned vain man, Pegg,' Paul said. 'He is always shewing off before these ladies. If old Gutsache has had in the girls for him, we'll be all night here. I can't go without the boat and the boat's crew. I wish I'd sent Tulp. What do you think a judge counts as evidence?'

I said, that a judge counted as evidence whatever is sworn from personal knowledge, but that he often made mistakes. I had reason enough to think so, God knows.

'Would he go by heads?' he asked. 'I mean, if five said they saw me hit that man in Liverpool, and you and Pegg and Tulp swore I was never out of the ship that night, would the judge go by the five or by the three?'

I said, I thought that most judges would test the three and the five, to try to find if either spoke the truth.

'Ah,' he said, 'well, I could bring in the Steward and the Boatswains, as well as Sails, and the Gunner. With all those, it would have to be brought in "Mistaken Identity".'

We saw a boat at this time.

I said, 'There they come.'

His eyes were more used than mine to searching dark waters at night. 'That's a fishing canoe,' he said.

Indeed, in a few moments, I saw that she was. We heard the bells of the Portuguese church from time to time.

'It's close to the church that Gutsache lives,' Captain Paul said. 'Gutsache has given him a dram and had in these girls, and the fool has stopped to dance.'

He named one or two bright stars to me, and said, 'There was a black girl down the Coast at Malindi when I was young . . . I'd have married her if it hadn't been for losing face. You lose face with both sides if you do a thing like that. Still, I've often wished I'd married her and gone bush. She was a Mata, too; a proud judy; not like that black hag in the cabin. I'd ought to have married her.'

He fell silent, thinking of his wasted life.

'What became of her?' I asked.

He did not answer. I could not see his face, but I do believe that he was weeping. The church bells ashore struck and chimed here, in a very sweet peal; after that, he said suddenly, 'There are oars; that's a ship's boat. On deck there, stand by your guns. Blow on your matches, there.'

The men sprang to their feet and stood by their guns. I saw the gun-captains blow on the smouldering matches, so that face after face along the decks glowed red for an

instant. I heard the grunt of rowlocks, and soon saw a
boat advancing from the harbour.

'That's Pegg,' the Captain said. 'He'd be well advised
to come slow.'

I saw that the boat was heading directly for us. I
thought, 'Now for it. Has Pegg betrayed Paul? Has word
come, that we are to be stayed? Is there a thief-taker in
the boat?'

Paul turned his night-glass on the boat. After a long
time, he swore, and said to me in a low voice, 'There's
another man in the stern-sheets. Pegg's got somebody
with him.'

We watched and listened till the boat was within hail.
Pegg had been warned that he would be fired at if he
tried to board us without hailing. He now rounded the
boat to, so that she lay broadside on some fifteen yards
from us. I could see the second man. Was it a thief-taker,
sent out from England for Paul and myself?

'Ahoy, the *Albicore*. Is Captain Ashplant there?' Pegg
hailed.

'Who's that you've got with you?' the Captain
answered. 'Who is he? What does he want?'

'He's all right, sir,' Pegg shouted. 'He's a dealer who
wants a passage. He's Perheira's son-in-law, sir. He's
given ten pieces for the passage to Momboe.'

'Is he English?' Paul asked.

'No, sir; doesn't speak any English; he knows the
Palaver.'

'Well,' the Captain said, 'trice those nettings clear.
Secure your guns. Come alongside, Mister.'

During the talk, he had had a good look through his
night-glass and seemed satisfied: all the same, he drew his
pistol. The boat drew alongside and Pegg jumped aboard.

'He's quite all right, sir,' he said to the Captain in a

33

low voice. 'He's perfectly all right, and Perheira sends a dozen of port with him. He's sort of a white nigger, sir, and won't give any trouble.'

At this, the passenger came aboard. He was a slim, well-made, youngish man, white, as far as I could see, rather good-looking and with charming manners. He bowed low to the Captain and to myself, and spoke to us in Portuguese. I answered for us both in French. The man at once spoke French, and asked if he might express his thanks to the Captain for permitting him to come with us? He said, that he much wished to get to Momboe. Since we were going there, he hoped that he might come, too. His goods were passed up out of the boat. The boat was hooked on and hoisted; in a minute more, we were under way again.

I heard Pegg say, 'They have had no word here about you, sir. It has been a bad season, in all these windward places, not a slave in any of 'em, but they are said to be coming into Momboe. Old Gutsache thought we should do nicely there. He said that King Jelly Belly made a great raid to leeward and took a lot of people.'

Paul looked at the passenger, turned to me, and asked, 'What the hell does he call himself?'

I asked the passenger if the Captain might know his name. He said, 'Kamansh.'

'Perhaps, Doctor,' the Captain said, 'you'll see to Mr Smask and tell the steward to fix him a berth.'

He then turned to Pegg and said, 'So Gutsache had heard nothing of the Liverpool trouble?'

'Not a word, sir.'

'That's the best news,' the Captain said. 'I can drink on that. I was anxious about it.'

The next day, when I saw Kamansh in the light, I found him a good deal older than I had thought. He was over thirty-five, he said. I asked him, if he had been to France and had learned the language there.

He said, 'No, I have never been in France; I am not Portuguese.'

Presently, when I asked him what he was, he said, '*Je suis* Kranois; or as you might say, Kranish. We are a white race, who live in the interior; some say, that we are Greeks, but I do not think that, because of the language.' It flashed into my mind at once, that perhaps the Admiral had been right, not out of his mind from fever or sunstroke, as I had often thought, when he had spoken of a white race in the interior. Possibly, this was one of them. Possibly, there was still some French man of genius like that Edmond Quichet of whom the Admiral had told. I looked at this Kamansh with the keenest interest.

He was of European stock, certainly; he had straight hair, a fully-formed nose, and thin lips; he was a white man, with sallow skin and black hair. I had seen no Greeks to speak of, save a few sailors who had come for ointment in London. He did not seem to come of any of that stock; to me, he looked more like a Spaniard.

I said, 'I heard once in London of a white race in Africa; a race which builds cities and boats in the European ways. I heard that the race had as many as seven cities?'

'We say that we had seven once,' he said, 'but now we have two; a big one and a little one.'

'And are they far from here?' I asked. 'Could I go to them?'

'They are far from here,' he said; 'far to the east, and far inland. Many days. You could never get to them; nor will any white man get to them, ever again.'

'Yet you go there?' I asked.

'No. I do not go there,' he said. 'I am exile. I have not been there for nine years. I shall not go there again. They are stupid, ignorant people.'

'Tell me,' I said, 'if it be not a rude question; did you learn French in your city?'

'Yes,' he said. 'Oh yes; the French have penetrated there.' He looked at me with a certain anger. I saw that the topic was distasteful, and asked him no more.

We talked then of other things. He had a low opinion of the Coast natives, and felt that they all should be enslaved, but not exported to the Indies or the Americas. 'That is folly,' he said. 'Why send them all those thousands of miles away, losing from a third to a half in the process, when the land here will grow all that they will be set to growing there? It is not sense.'

He had a clear (and to me very awful) hope of a vast slave dominion along the Coast, ruled by white men, with lots of Face, for the benefit of whites in Europe. After some years, he thought that slaves might be bred there in large numbers, for export to the Indies and the Americas. 'There is no reason,' he said, 'why this should not be done. If we had brood-mare women-slaves and good buck stallion-slaves, we should soon find a strain that would export well. It is a well-known fact, that children stand the Middle Passage better than adults. It stands to reason that they must. The tender and the young do not have to be packed and chained. You can allow children liberty on board. They arrive in good health, and do not fall sick and die of the sullens, as so many adults do. Very well, then, let us breed thousands of children here, and ship them west as soon as they are fit to travel. It is simple sense. It will make the fortune of any man who first does it.' I confess that it made me sick to think of it, so I strove to turn to other matters.

'Sir,' I said, 'it is most interesting to me to think of descendants of the Greeks in Africa. You said that the language is against their being Greeks. I know not very much Greek; just enough to enjoy Homer very much. Would it be too much to ask of you, that you should teach me some of your tongue, so that I might perhaps resolve the point.'

He had a most winning charm, although he gave me the impression of being a very hateful creature. 'Sir,' he said, 'I will most gladly teach you the Kranish speech. But I am sure that it is not Greek.'

Well, the ship went slowly on, in light airs. When my work gave me leisure, I spent my time with Mr Kamansh sitting in the draught of a sail trying to learn his tongue, which was unlike any tongue known to me. At first, I wondered, if Mr Kamansh were not making it all up; but, no; that was not possible; it was a language. It had no literature other than some songs and genealogies; it had no alphabet, and no native system of writing. A certain number spoke French and wrote in the European fashion, so he said. They had a religion, too, so he said, but very stupid and ignorant, well worthy of them, in fact. What they were I could not guess. So we leisurely dragged along, in great heat, in a good deal of anxiety, and with a leak which varied very little, yet tended, as a leak usually will, to increase as time went on.

Sometimes we saw Africa as a haze or cloud away to the north, sometimes we were right out of sight of land. We stole on, in sweltering heat, through a grey and steaming sea. In addition to my sea-companions, I had two intimates, ever with me, my past and my future. My past was grim enough with fact and with surmise. I had been hanged for a crime; who had done the crime? Had anyone been hanged since for saving me? Who had murdered that old Admiral for whom I had been hanged? My future was grim enough with the same two figures. The Law was after me; would the Law catch me? And if it did not so catch me, what were my prospects? I was an unvouched-for doctor in a slave-ship, a man, that is, almost beyond the human pale and tinged with the infamy of the traffic. If I were lucky and escaped the Law, what future should I have? I might land and live native like the Crackers brothers, and perhaps marry a black woman with a skewer through her nose; or if I escaped into the Indies or the Americas, I might live secluded in some glen and come to town for market days to let blood and draw teeth at sixpence a patient. That seemed a poor life to one who had hoped to be famous through Europe.

As we were now upon the Coast, we had prepared for the trade there. We had rigged up a trade-room below; and had set out in it the brightly coloured beads, pots and copper-pans which the Captain traded for what little gold or old ivory the natives might have to sell. We had also prepared the chains and shackles with which our Captain hoped to secure some hundreds of victims presently. Slaves were not paid for with beads, pots or pans, but with other currencies, such as rum, gun-powder, and what were called trade-guns; but the main coin paid for slaves by men of our race was bar-metal. Flesh and blood was reckoned with great exactness in these things; and as little else was discussed at meals, I had come to know how much to offer or to abate for the stalwart or infirm man, woman or child. I was also well advised as to the diseases to look out for in the offered wares. Presently, we began to draw near to our port of Great Momboe. There was the land, still swathed in the heat haze, but with clearly defined hills above the cloud. Presently, the haze went; I could see low-lying land with curls of white roller running along it. Soon I made out that the trees were of a rank, harsh green, and seemingly closely packed. They looked like a kind of green sheep gathered to oppose our passage, but indeed, we seemed to have no passage, only a green hill barring our way. The Captain had come on deck; someone had reported a sail in sight.

I looked in the direction in which the Captain looked. With my unaided eyes I saw only a tiny smudge, dark grey against the paleness of the mingling of sea and sky. I saw that the Captain's face changed as he looked at her through the glass. Presently, he shut the telescope, slung the glass behind his back and said to me and to those within hearing, 'In these waters it is always well to know who your next neighbour is.' He slowly went aloft to the main-topmast cross-trees, where he looked long at the Coast to which we drove, and a lot longer at the distant ship. When he came down, he seemed relieved, as though that particular danger were over. I had shared his fear all through this time; now I shared his relief. In another way, he was a changed man that morning; he loved action. After the long inaction of the voyage, so full of calms and set-backs, he was about to be busy, bartering for slaves and seeing them on board. It is said that the devils in hell can never be glad; but perhaps they feel as the Captain felt that morning, rather proud, that a lot of new damned may soon be under hatches.

I asked him what the distant ship was. He said, 'The Station frigate, bound to the windward; she won't trouble us now.' He rubbed his hands and said. 'I believe, Doctor, the heat would do my father's legs good; what do you think?'

I said, that it would be a great change of climate, and that old plants were difficult to transplant.

As we were now within four miles of the Coast, the hands roused up from below two breakers or casks of what they called dolly. It was the custom to give a drink of dolly to all natives who came on board to trade. I had seen this poison brewed the day before by Pegg, who was a master-maker of it. The foundation of it was bad ship's beer touched up with rum and rinsings; the whole flavoured with the juice of boiled rank tobacco leaf and seasoned with red pepper, to make it fiery. I had seen Pegg taste it and spit it out, with the remark, 'The best dolly I ever made. Kicks like a mule and leaves a scar all the way down; something as'll take the paint all off; and cheap too. No man could drink more'n fourpence worth and keep his reason.'

But by this time, the Coast that had seemed to have no passage had opened up. In front of us was a river mouth all whitening and rolling for half a mile and more. To the left of this was a wooded hill, giving shelter; to the right was a shallow bay in which a multitude of birds, nearly all white, fished and clamoured, in a beauty unspeakable of light and grace. And now, as we headed for the river, at least thirty canoes shot out to reach us. In front of them came one with a lug-sail, going very fast; she had on board a big black buck with a scarlet handkerchief about his brow. After him came all the rest with straining shining bodies and flashing paddles and rags of sail of all the colours of the rainbow. There were shouts and cries and the shining of enormous teeth, with cries of, 'You gib him dolly. You gib him nicee dolly. Dolly for de black, he makee jumpy-jack.' In a minute the canoe with the big black buck had run alongside, and the buck was on our quarter-deck, saying, 'Good day to Capn Ashyplank. Me pilot take you to de pool.' The other canoes boarded us as they came up; all there were slavers or slave-guards; all demanded dolly; all cried that Capn Ashyplank was de good boy, we lub him. With shouting, swearing, yells, blows and muddling we shot across the bar and slowly stood on to the pool, with our upper sails hanging in their gear and sail after sail coming off her. Canoes ahead of us beckoned us the way. Women ashore held up their children to see us. All the port seemed awake to welcome us in. We came into the pool of Great Momboe, and at the word of our Captain let go the anchor, and fired a gun in honour of the local King. I asked Tulp the name of the King. He said, 'Old Full-Bottomed Wig-Wig,' and pointed out the royal palace, a big open hut, thatched with palm-leaf. Almost at once the pipes sounded as Captain Paul went down into his boat to wait upon His Majesty with a gift of dolly, to ask about the prospects of slaves. We were in Africa.

In all the noise, drunkenness and yelling, the pilots and their friends had been able to give us news. The Station frigate had been visiting the leeward ports and had called at Great Momboe only three days before; we had just missed her, and need not expect her again, for she had lost many of her hands from the fever and was bound back to Cabo to refit. This was good news, to us, who had reason to dread her visits. There was no new war, as far as was known. But as for slaves; well, the season was one of the worst known. There were slaves in the slave-sheds ashore, oh, yes, but the pilots let us see that they were not quite the kind we were accustomed to.

'Dey not so good,' the pilot said. 'Dey not so good. Him die. Him go cluck-cluck.' The place was pretty big; there were many huts. About a hundred canoes lay about upon the beach. The town swarmed with skinny fowls, long-legged pigs, mangy goats and odd dogs. We were the only ship in the port. A schooner lay on her side in the mud not far from us. I could read her name, *Two Brothers*, Bristol, painted on her transom. Her crew had all died of 'the fever' some years before; Wig-Wig had then sold her masts to a Dane, and nobody since had bothered about her. All this Tulp told me.

It was a savage-looking place, perhaps, but full of interest and beauty. Wherever I looked, I was amazed by the energy of the life. All the natives, if they were doing anything at all, were doing it with zest and shouting; they had a song for everything. Most of them were fishing now. They brought piles of fish aboard for us, in the hope of getting dolly for them, but the free dolly had now claimed its tribute of human membranes; no dolly was left for trade.

However, I had not much time for thinking of these things; the boat came alongside with word for the Doctor to come ashore in her, since the Captain wanted me in the palace. I took my bag of instruments and was soon at the beach, where a big negro carried me out of the boat to a litter. The palace was only a bare thirty yards from where we landed, but we had to save the White Man's Face there; it would have lost us Face had I walked. At the Palace, Captain Paul said, that he wanted me to come with him to the slave-sheds.

'There are slaves,' he said, 'but something's wrong with them. Perhaps you can tell me how bad they are, and whether they can be shipped. Have they told you anything about them?'

'Yes,' I said, 'they say they are dying and going cluck-cluck.'

'What disease would that be?' he asked.

'It sounds like some kind of cough,' I said, 'but one little look is better than any description.' Our bearers stopped outside some long open huts thatched with palm-leaf. There were eight of these, each being about twenty yards long by four broad. Each hut had the same simple design. The thatch sloped down on each side from a central ridge, so as to screen a long, double, raised shelf on which the slaves were lying. The place stank intolerably, with the stink of Christian Newgate. Any doctor within scent of it could tell, that here were plague, pestilence, famine, poverty and cruelty. The air was rank with disease, and the smell of death, not the smell of death past or present, so much as the warning smell of death coming, such as I had known dogs to howl at in England. These were the slave-sheds, where the victims lay till some ship's captain bought them. A good deal of noise came from them; the jangling of chains, the moaning of misery, a lot of monotonous singing, in which three or four voices would join and then tail off from weariness, a lot of excited, silly jabber and even more foolish muttering, which came from delirium, and above all, a persistent, dry hacking hiccough, from at least twenty patients. I knew from the sound that those who went cluck-cluck on that note, day-in day-out, would very likely die.

'These men are very ill,' I said. 'Will you come in?'

'How ill are they?' he asked.

'Very ill; but I will see. Come in.'

'Not I,' he said. 'I'll keep to windward here, thanky.'

He swore in the Palaver at his bearers, who sheered away from the sheds to a tree with a dark bole and foliage some dozen yards away. Here they halted. The Captain, with some trouble, ·lit himself a roll of tobacco-leaf.

'I'll keep the infection off here,' he said. 'Be as quick as you like, and let's be away.'

He called something in Palaver to the agents of King Wig-Wig, who were at the sheds waiting to shew their wares.

The chief agent was a playful mongrel, who began thus: 'Him a fine lot of boys, only dey got de cold, see? Him got cold in de head; make him cough. It go in one day, two day.'

'Let me see this cold in the head,' I said.

We went under the thatch together. In that shed, chained and tightly packed together, in the frightful heat and filth and stench, amid clouds of flies, were eighty-seven men, women and children, prone on the benches, some of them not visibly infected, some of them perhaps recovering, but most of them in high fever and visible agony. Some were dead, one was dying as I entered; and those who were ill were frightfully ill, and some few of them delirious to the point of mania, in a bodily anguish that made them scream. The chief symptom, however, was the hiccough which tore their poor bodies and took away their strength; it was a very distressing symptom. What was wrong with them I did not know, but a glance told me that it was a malignant fever of an appalling kind. I knew little about yellow fever, but this looked like what I had read.

'Him got cold in de head,' the agent said. 'But him be well in one day, two day. Him a fine lot of boys, him buccra boys, good for dig in de ground, oh so strong. Oh, how him lub to dig de ground for white mans.'

'These men will die,' I said. 'Who is looking after them? Who is here to give them water? Fetch plenty water quick. Give um drink.' He stared stupidly. I said: 'They are dying for water, for drink. Give um drink.'

He laughed and spat. 'Not such damn fool,' he said. 'Dey get de good drink when him go to bed.'

'They'll die, can you not see that?' I said.

He repeated: 'Him a cold in de head; him good boys; soon be well. Now, see, you tell de Capn dey soon be well; you make de Capn buy dem, we be your very good friend, see, gib you a wife while you here; she lub you dear.' I told him to stop trying to bribe me, and to try to help to make the men well; then I would tell the Captain to buy them.

He spat again and said, 'Dey get well by deirself.'

I had by this time taken a pulse or two and seen evidence that some at least of these sufferers had yellow fever; two symptoms, which I had read of, were plainly present on them. I went out into the air, for although the sheds were open, any place away from them seemed airy.

I called to the Captain, 'Sir, half these men are down with yellow fever as far as I can tell. Will you send me a couple of hands ashore, so that I can set to work to try to cure them?'

'Yellow fever,' the Captain said. 'Send hands ashore? Are the slaves fit to ship?'

'Sir,' I said, 'they are desperately ill, but we could save some of them, perhaps most, for they have good bodies and may throw it off.'

'You're not a slave-doctor, but my ship's doctor,' he said. 'If they're not fit to ship, that's enough. We'll get back aboard.'

'But, sir; we could save these lives . . .'

'I'm not here to doctor niggers,' he said, 'nor did I ship hands to nurse 'em. We will get back aboard. But don't come any nearer, thanky . . . I don't want the infection. Keep your distance, and when you come aboard, keep clear.'

We went back aboard, but I was not allowed to sit with the Captain in the boat. He went aboard and sent the gig back for me; when I reached the deck, I was told that I should have to live on deck for the next three days, as I had been exposed to the infection. I heard the Captain swearing, that the damned doctor had 'asked me to send hands ashore to nurse 'em,' which was a good joke to all who heard; nursing slaves who weren't even well enough to be slaves was not how our Commerce was fostered, by a long way.

When I came on board, I found that Mr Kamansh had gone; I missed him and his lessons in Kranish; and I also missed my position in the cabin. I lived now as a pariah under the awning on deck, thinking of those afflicted and dying men ashore.

However, I was not shut from the knowledge of what was happening. It appeared that the Captain had counted on finding an English agent named, or nicknamed, Peter, at Great Momboe. This agent was not there, but 'up the river, at Bimbi.' Peter was sorely wanted, for only through men like Peter could slaving captains learn of consignments of slaves. I could hear the matter being discussed below.

'This Wig-Wig has only got a set of corpses. I'll have to go up to Bimbi and see Peter. I must find out if slaves are coming or can be expected.'

Pegg said, 'Peter won't have gone to Bimbi unless he's expecting a gang of slaves there from up Malondo way. He'd never leave here in the season except for that. That's what it must be, sir. He's gone up to dash the Kings for it.'

'So I think,' Paul said, 'I'd better take some trade and go up there in the boat to help him.'

They talked thus at dinner, while I ate my own dinner in my quarantine just above them. I gathered from what followed that Bimbi was an important place in the trade, because two much-used slave-trails led there to the Momboe river. In the afternoon of that day, after a siesta, and the loading up of two big native dug-outs with trade,

Captain Paul set forth with native paddlers to talk with Peter at Bimbi.

Now, it may seem strange, but I had come to like Captain Paul; when I saw him setting forth, my heart sank. I wished, that he would offer to take me with him, for I did not relish being left in the ship under Pegg. However, he called to me as he went to the waiting boat, 'I'm sorry I can't take you along, Doctor, but a doctor must stay by the ship in all ports on the Coast. That's the rule of the trade. The men may fall sick at a moment's notice. This is Dead Ned, this place. I'll be back, let's see; not tomorrow, nor quite next day; say, the day after, to make sure. You'll oblige me by keeping aboard till then.'

I said that I would obey orders, but that I thought it inhuman, to let those unfortunates die in the shed ashore.

He seemed about to fly at me, but answered quietly, that he had neither the men nor the drugs to start nursing niggers, and that in any case he had his orders and I mine. He went down the side, to the sound of the pipes of both boatswains and their mates. In the boat, he called up to Pegg, 'No one is to go ashore, Mister, on any pretext whatever.'

Pegg replied, 'Very good, Captain Ashplant.'

The Black Mantacaw now went down into the boat. She was dressed in a scarlet gown with purple trimmings, and wore a big hat with an orange plume. She made a great impression on the natives, and no doubt added to the Captain's Face. I watched the boats dwindle up the river, till at last they were round the red rock and out of sight. You may not believe it, but my heart was doleful to see him go. He was the nearest approach to a friend that I had in that world, and now he would be away for three days.

After he had gone, I watched the city of King Wig-Wig, which now took on a strange beauty, as the myriad little oil-lamps began to twinkle. Fire-flies, which I had never before seen, flitted in thousands among the huts; the stars began to burn, and belts of mist, some grey, some white, almost like snow, formed and slowly glid about the hill. Against their dimness a few dark trees or parts of trees stood out, were merged, and then stood out again, almost as though they were living persons in a kind of dance. All was strange, and terrible yet alluring. I had a sense of the mystery and vastness of the land. This was Africa, the unknown, the untrodden; it stretched for thousands of miles from where I stood, in forest, mountain and river, full of savagery, full of life, containing, perhaps, the pygmies who fight with the cranes, and the giant snakes who killed the Romans. Perhaps, within a thousand miles of me, the cities of the Kranois still stood, with Edmond Quichet in command. I had so often thought of the African shore; now here I was, almost where the Admiral had been.

A lot of native drums had been beating, ever since the sun went down. Some men came out of the huts together, singing a song which hadn't much tune, so that anyone could join in it. They sat presently by a fire near the beach, smoking tobacco in their little funny pipes, and going on with their song. Sometimes it was the same for a minute at a time; then one of the singers would invent something new, perhaps a funny thing, for they would all laugh and repeat the successful line until somebody invented another. Tulp too, was listening to the song, no doubt with envy, for who would not rather be a happy savage than a miserable slaver's second officer? I have seldom seen a man who hated life more than Tulp with less power to change it. He had a kind of dumb, hopeless endurance, shot with occasional sorrowful drunkennesses. Yet he had so much interest in native ways that his knowledge was considerable and full of colour.

I called to him, 'What is the song? Is it a story?'

'No,' he said, 'it's about us. They always sing like that the first day or two. If another ship comes in, they'll sing about her. It is only silly stuff.'

'Can you understand it? Can you translate it?'

'Some of it,' he said. He listened and then said, 'This is the kind of stuff it is:

> The Captain is a great man, he beat
>> everybody on the head.
> 'Why not bring me more slaves?
>> I hit you,' bang, bang.
> Now he goes up the river away to Bimbi.
> 'You row me well, you rowers,
>> or I hit your head,' bang bang.
> Bimbi is very far away, oh, a long way,
>> the rowers get very tired.
> But the Captain he hit them on the head.
>> He say, 'You row,'
> By and by all come back from Bimbi,
>> the Captain glad.
> He give nicee dolly, oh so good,
>> and then we all be glad.

'They always sing a lot about the Captain,' Tulp added. 'You see, he's like one of their own chiefs. They like him for that.'

Captain Paul did not come back on the promised day; he was a day late. He came alongside after sunset, and told me to come down into the cabin with him, as he wanted a dose. He was looking ill, indeed, his look was frightful; his eyes were scarlet and had a frantic, mad look. He complained of agonizing headache, like 'some-

one driving a jemmy between my skull and the brain.'
He was in considerable fever; and his skin had a most
strange tingling heat. I gave him some calomel and a
sweating draught, and caused him to lie down and drink
cold water in abundance. He would not have obeyed me
had not the pain in his head been so acute. He lay tossing
for an hour or two; then said that he was something
better, and would come to table. His walk to the table
was that of a very old, weak, tottering man. My quarantine, I may say, was now reckoned to be ended.

At table, he said that Peter was down with fever at
Bimbi, and that the slave season was the worst ever
known. Some scoundrel or fool from 'up Malondo way'
had had a lot of slaves and had sent them by malice or
mistake not to Bimbi or Momboe but to Little Massa;
and that if we hurried to Little Massa we should get there
about the time they arrived, and have a chance of buying
them. 'Apart from these,' he added, 'there isn't so much
as the smell of a slave in all Dead Ned.'

For a few moments he seemed to throw off the disease.
Action was always a great spur to him. 'It's no good stay-
ing here. Peter is sure there'll be no slaves here,' he said.
'We'll unmoor, if you please, Mister, and get down to
Massa for them, *muy pronto*.'

'Now, sir?' Pegg asked.

'Yes, now; this instant.'

'Very good, sir,' Pegg said, and left the cabin to give
the orders. The boatswains of the watches at once called
all hands to unmoor and had them at it within the minute.
Pegg returned in a few minutes to say that he was sure
that he could take her out without a native pilot. Paul's
reply to this was, 'I hope you can, since a sucking child
could.'

The pain returned upon him, suddenly, across his eyes,

his loins, and down his spine. He muttered something about the Matablancos.

Pegg said, 'But they're a leeward tribe; they don't interfere here.'

Paul glared at him and with some effort said, 'If you can only use your throat to talk punk, cut it.' He glowered again, breathing hard from the agony in his head and joints. At last he said, in the Palaver, 'Peter he a sick feller at Bimbi; him go cluck-cluck.' After another long pause, he added, 'Paul a sick feller; a damsick feller.' Presently, he said, 'The Matas have done what I always said they would do; they've come west, into the windward. All their old lands are threatened by the M'Gai.' He glared at us, ready, in his usual way, to swear at anyone who spoke; then, as no one spoke, he said, 'The M'Gai are moving. They mean to kill the Matas and kill the Whites, and have Africa for the black man.'

We looked at each other and said nothing. We all judged, very rightly, that the M'Gai were some conquering tribe, who had come out of the darkness killing and killing and would presently die by the spears of others or of themselves.

He slipped from his chair to the deck babbling something that I could not understand about rigging, and writhing from the pain. As he was no longer conscious, I was able to take charge of him as a patient, and had him in his berth. Pegg had to leave me in charge, for he had to be on deck; the ship was already out of her berth and slipping down the stream. I asked the steward for the Black Mantacaw. The steward said that she had not come aboard with the Captain; she had gone to see friends at the palace. He added that she would come off in a canoe before we left the river. I believed this, but perhaps she or her friends were too merry and missed their chance.

When I left the Captain and came on deck, we were over the bar and at sea, bound for Little Massa; the Black Mantacaw had been left behind.

I had no doubt that the Captain had a fever far worse than the usual intermittent fever of the tropics; he was frightfully ill, of something that I had never seen and did not know how to treat. I told myself that it was neither typhus nor plague. Could it be yellow fever? I found that I could allay his agonizing pain with cold compresses, and lessen his fever with a cold sponge. There was no thought of feeding him; he was violently and frequently sick. Abundant cold water was his food.

Pegg assumed command, of course, and now showed that he wished to keep it. If Paul had been well, he would have stood out to sea, to avoid any meeting with a Government vessel sent to ask about us. Pegg stood along the shore. He said that we must lose no time, but drive her all the way, so as to have a chance of these slaves. I knew very well that he did not care twopence about the slaves, but that he hoped to meet some Government vessel and have Paul removed from our midst, so that he, Pegg, might be confirmed in the command.

The wind was very light inshore; we went slowly, in stifling heat. I fell very foul of Pegg on the first day out.

On the Coast of Dead Ned, a ship's surgeon surveys the whole company every morning. We had no men really sick, but half a dozen were ailing; I judged that they could not stand the intense heat. I, therefore, suggested to Pegg, that these sick might, at least, be kept out of the sun for a few days, and given some quiet work under the awnings till they settled down to the climate.

He said, 'The best cure for sickness is work, to work it out of you.'

He promptly gave orders for stages to be rigged over the sides, and turned my half-dozen into them with orders to scrape and paint the topsides in the full blaze of the midday. As he plainly did this to show that he was furious at the suggestion that a doctor's opinion might be wiser than the practice of a brute and a bully, I spoke up to him; we had a hateful dispute in public on the poop. I said that if the men died as a result of his orders, he should be made responsible in any port we came to. He won the dispute by saying that he was in command, and would put me in irons if I said another word. There was no doubt that he won. Unfortunately, my speaking proved to be fatal.

A man, named Harry, was in Pegg's displeasure. He was a quiet, decent man, not very bright in his wits, but a fair seaman and sober. By and by, I went to my cabin for something and heard a man just outside the cabin say, 'Lend us your wisp of yarns, Harry,' and knew that he was working just outside my cabin, abaft the main rigging.

Almost at once, Pegg's voice rang out. 'Put your back into it there. Do your work.'

There was a moment's hesitation, then Harry answered, very gently and honestly, as I will swear, 'I'm doing it, sir.'

I will make oath that the words were uttered with no taint of insolence, by a gentle, quiet and rather stupid man who always did his best. It was, of course, ill advised of him to utter them. Sailors usually stand mute to abuse, and let the storm blow over. They know, too well, that 'answering back' may be called mutiny and punished as such.

To Pegg, now, Harry's quiet remark was 'answering back,' and the very chance he had longed for. He swore at him, and bade him 'Get off that stage and come on deck.'

There was utter silence throughout the ship as Harry clambered up the side. I feared that Pegg meant to murder him, so I ran up on deck to stop him. Perhaps by doing so I let poor Harry in for much cruel misery. Pegg saw me come on deck, and did not commit that savage assault for which he had prepared. Instead, he said, 'I'll teach you to answer back when I bid you mind your job. I'll teach you manners, my fine lad. Get forward there.'

When forward, he bade Harry take two of the windlass-bars, put one on each shoulder and then march up and down for a while. Harry shouldered the bars, not without difficulty, for he was rather clumsy with his hands, and such bars are clumsy things.

'Now march,' Pegg cried. 'You'll be sorry you answered back before I've done with you. March, my British Grenadier. Right. Left. Right. Left. That's about all you're fit for, to march with the rogues' battalion.'

All this was on the hottest day of which I had any experience.

I felt the indignation of the crew all about me. The ship was soundless. I knew how near the men came to rising and flinging Pegg overboard; however, law and long obedience triumphed; the boatswains' mates and other warrant officers suddenly damned them for not bending to their work; they ceased to listen, and bent to their painting, while poor Harry trod up and down with the heavy bars at his shoulders.

Knowing that my presence would exasperate Pegg to greater savagery, I went below, wondering how I could save the man. It was almost noon: I resolved to speak to Pegg when he came down to dinner.

In a few minutes he came down, saying that he was as hot as hell; he pitched his hat into his berth, dipped his hands in a pan of water and wiped them on an old sail.

He took the Captain's place at table, and as the steward lifted the lid from the pot, said, 'I'll make that man sick that ever he answered me back.'

'Mr Pegg,' I said, 'you be careful that you don't kill him.'

'Kill him be damned,' he said.

'If you do kill him, you will be damned,' I said. 'Come, sir, I speak as a doctor. To march a white man in the sun like that, bearing those weights, is a certain way to kill him.'

'I'm in command here; not you,' he said.

'I'm responsible for the health of the crew,' I said. 'It's my duty to warn you that if you're not careful you'll kill that man; and that'll be murder.'

He looked at me very evilly.

'Come, sir,' I said. 'Give him a caution and let him go, to drink and rest.'

'I'll give him a caution, all right,' he said, and went on deck. We heard him call one of the boatswains and give an order. After a few minutes, he came below again. 'Well, there you are, Doc,' he said; 'that's that. I've sent him below, and now I hope you're satisfied.'

'That is well done of you, Mr Pegg,' I said. 'I am grateful to you. Let us shake hands.'

We shook hands, without any enthusiasm from him, however. The meal was over, and Pegg went to turn in, but paused to ask, 'How's the Cap?'

I said, 'Desperately ill, still. You can see.' I showed him the sick man, who was delirious and babbling. 'He's in high fever still.'

'Is it catching?' he asked.

'You know as much as I do,' I answered. 'I believe this is yellow fever; no man knows how it spreads, but it seems to come from places more than people.'

'I'll run no risk with yellow fever,' he said, and moved away from the door.

During that afternoon, I ordered the carpenter to get a scuttle opened in the deck above the Captain, so that a small ventilator could be rigged to blow a draught down upon him. As the carpenter worked, I kept sponging the burning, dry skin, with a cold sponge. I knew little enough of fevers, and had never seen anything like this fever. I remembered my old Master, Dr Copshrews' quiet remark, 'We fight fire with water. Nothing can be better.' I sponged the dry, hot, restless, moaning, babling body and devised a way of getting him to swallow water. When the air began to blow down upon us, I felt for the first time, that I might save him. Mind, he was a cruel, terrible savage who had murdered two men, one of them in cold blood. I didn't care about that. I know that I would have given my life to save him. There was something about that fearful creature that I could love and pity. I watched by his cot all through the evening and then far into the night. Sometimes, when my patient drowsed, and lapsed into muttering and restless tossing, I, too, drowsed, and had some confused muttering, restless sleep. At other times, I was at work, and often at desperate work, for my patient, whatever his weakness, was often violent. In his paroxysms, he was always leaping up from bed, and flinging away his bed-clothes, or trying to tear them. I had not much light, save the battle-lantern. I would see the restless, moaning, swearing, puking figure gathering for an outburst and be ready.

After two in the morning, he was quieter; and this quiet presently turned into what seemed a restfulness. He was less burning hot; there was even a moisture on his wrists. The pulse was weaker. In another hour, he was fairly asleep; in a good, quiet sleep, which I should have welcomed, but for the marked drop in the pulse. I watched him quietly for a time, hoping that the rest would last for some hours.

It must have been a little before dawn when I fell into a deep sleep. I was wakened by the steward creeping in with some hot infusion of camomile. It was light but not yet broad morning. I knew that the steward must have been up long before, to get the fire lit and this infusion boiled-up. He was a cowed, broken, pathetic man, who had lived so long in fear of blows, that he no longer dared to speak without looking round, to see who might be listening.

I said, 'That is good of you, steward; well done. You must have lost your beauty sleep, to brew him this.'

I took the tisane, and contrived to get the Captain to drink some of it. I noticed, on turning round, that the steward was shaking.

I said in a low voice, 'Do not be afraid, steward. If this is yellow fever, as I believe, it probably is not catching from the patient.'

He looked at me piteously; then he whispered, 'Harry's dead, sir. Mr Pegg killed him this morning.'

'What?' I said.

He repeated his words, shuddered hard, with chattering teeth, and then began to cry.

'Now, come, steward,' I said. 'Help me to get the Captain into clean things; you can talk as you work.'

I did not get the whole story from him; it reached me in pieces at odd times, in the course of the day. It was the most dreadful thing.

When Pegg went on deck, as I thought to release Harry, he did not release him, but sent him to march with his bars in the heat of the 'tween decks, which are always so much hotter and closer than the open deck.

He made him march there, without rest or drink, till he prayed for mercy. Pegg had then gone to him, and asked, would he sing, to be released? Harry, who had a sweet tenor voice, as all on board knew, said, 'Yes, sir; gladly.' Pegg, therefore, made him sing, and this without the refreshment of a drink of water, till he could sing no more. You must remember that this was at four in the afternoon, and that Harry had been on deck, doing hard work, with no food, since eight that morning. When from thirst and exhaustion he could sing no more, Pegg had said, 'I'm not going to let you off for a song like that. A sick cow could sing better. Pick up them bars and march again.' He had obeyed and had marched till perhaps five o'clock, when he had knelt to Pegg and begged him to flog him, or anything, but let him rest, even for five minutes. 'Ah, so you'd rather be flogged?' Pegg had said. 'Well, you shall be.' He then ordered the boatswains' mates to lash him to the windlass and beat him with the ends of ropes, which they did. Harry had expected, that he would be set free after the beating, but Pegg made him pick up the bars and go up and down again, till at last he fell. 'Ha,' Pegg said, 'would you rather have another beating, than walk?'

Harry answered, 'I can do no more, sir.'

'You shall have another beating, then,' Pegg said. 'Seize him up again, you.' This time they beat him till he was senseless and did not release him. They left him lashed to the windlass, and Pegg said he would like to see the man who would presume to let him go. He would show them what mutiny led to aboard a ship like the *Albicore*. The crew, cowed as all slavers' crews were, by constant tyranny and brutality, did nothing. What could they have done? The officers and petty officers were ready for them, and had the law on their side; any protest was mutiny; any effective action, piracy. They just had to watch and listen.

Harry was kept seized to the windlass during the night. In the middle watch, one of the boatswains told Pegg that he thought the bastard was dying, so Pegg went to him, spoke, and getting no answer, kicked him 'for being sullen.' Harry roused a little at this, and asked for his mother. 'He asks for his Mammy,' Pegg said. 'A little cold water will serve as mammy for you, my lad.' He had then dashed a bucket of salt water over him. However, this gentle treatment came too late; Harry quivered a little and died.

Pegg then told the watch to throw the body overboard, which the boatswains' mates did. There was no prayer, no word of burial, though some of the men wept openly. 'Now,' Pegg said, 'now you'll know what you'll come to, if you set up for captains and answer back.'

That is the story of Harry's killing. Judge of our feelings, cooped up in a ship in which those things were done.

You will not believe how deeply I loathed my life and my race. I had had a glimpse of the blacks, now. I had not seen them uncontaminated by the whites, it is true; but even so, those whom I had seen at Momboe were healthier and happier than any people whom I had seen in Europe. Yet savages like Paul and Pegg were driving poor men like Harry to misery and death so that those blacks might be driven to misery and death. Paul and Pegg were guilty, no doubt; but what of the proud and grasping soul behind them, who urged them on, who stayed at home and bribed Parliament to support him. His emissaries bore the heat, did the sin, shed the blood and broke the soul; he took the rich reward. He did not see, as I saw, the poor men of the crew, in the mercy of a brute like Pegg, creeping about their work with bent heads, some of them weeping. Do not imagine that deaths like Harry's were rare.

What with this misery, the heat, my restless night, and my anxiety, I was nearly exhausted. But I had some consolation. Paul had come very much to himself. He looked, and said that he felt much better. The fever seemed gone, though it had left many marks on him. His pain, in head and joints, was gone; his thirst was gone; his skin had lost that tingling heat which had so impressed me; it was now cool and moist, though it had come out in tiny red spots on arms and chest. The distressing hiccough and sickness had gone. I made him as comfortable and cool as our means allowed; and noted that a soft pillow gave him intense pleasure, this in a man who was as indifferent to bodily ease as man can well be. He asked for food.

I said, 'No; no food; try to sleep. Your stomach is in a very tender state. Let it have some rest, while nature restores its tone. You try to sleep a little.'

He growled, that food would restore his tone, but that he would like to sleep, as he had been very uneasy. I left him composing himself to sleep, and being deadly weary myself should have done the same, had not one of the boatswains' mates asked to see me, complaining of pain and fever. I saw the man, and noticed at once that his eyes, which were slightly tinged with yellow, had the bright, mad look that had been so marked a symptom in the Captain. The man had often had fever; he asked for bark.

I said, 'I'm going to give you some calomel; it's better than bark.'

He seemed uneasy, and said that he had been one employed to beat Harry, and was afraid that Harry was after him. I told him to put any such thoughts from his mind, to take the calomel, and go to his berth. I would see that Mr Tulp excused him.

He said he was sure Harry was after him. I told him not to think of such folly any more.

He said, 'Ah, sir, what's folly in England isn't folly here. Harry has done his ju-ju on me.'

I said, 'Get you below to your berth and say your prayers. They will put your fancies out of your head, and the calomel will put the fever out of your guts.'

He went away a few paces, then returned, to ask what prayer might be best. I said that the Lord's own prayer was the best. He asked which Lord, and what prayer that was? I took him forward, to explain, and on deck passed the murderer, Pegg, who glared at me, as I at him. I took the sick man to his berth, taught him what few words of prayer his racking head could retain, and saw him into bed.

I suppose that by this time it was ten in the forenoon. I was so very weary that I did but glance into the Captain's cabin. He was sleeping quietly, which seemed by much the best thing he could do. Having crept from his door, I went to my own berth and was almost instantly asleep. I was awakened at about three in the afternoon, by the steward, who asked me to come at once to the Captain. I turned out as I was, and reached his cabin in an instant. I found him in a state of desperate sickness, his face dusky, yet suffused with yellow, his chest speckled with tiny red spots, his consciousness gone, and all the fatal symptoms hung out like death's flag upon him. He was dying.

'How long has he been like this?' I asked. 'He was asleep at ten.'

'Yes, sir,' the steward said. 'He was very well at dinner-time. He woke and said he felt quite well. He asked for food.'

'You did not give him any, I hope?'

'Yes, sir; he made me fetch him food.'

'What food?'

'A soft-boiled egg, sir; one of the eggs we bought at Momboe.'

'Any drink?'

'Yes, sir; some brandy.'

'There it is,' I said. 'I told him that he was not to have food or brandy.'

'Yes, sir. I heard you tell him, sir. But I have to obey the Captain's orders, sir.'

'I wish you had called me instead of letting me sleep. Why wasn't I called?'

'Mr Pegg said he called you, sir.'

'Called me? But I wasn't called.'

'He said he called you, sir.'

I knew something of the heavy sleep of the sea. It was well possible that Pegg had called me, and that I had answered, yet not roused. It was also well possible that Pegg had not called me, hoping that the Captain would die. I knew that no patient recovered from the symptoms shown by the Captain. He was doomed; nothing could save him. He fought on, in an unconscious gabbling way till sunset, then died quietly; just as men came aft to ask me to come to Doggy, who was now desperately and ragingly ill, in acute pain, and saying that Harry was waiting for him.

By midnight that night we had buried the Captain, and come to know that Doggy would not survive. As soon as the Captain was over the side, Pegg said that he wasn't going to have me in the cabin again, infecting everybody. I should keep on deck, and deal only with the sick. He ordered all the Captain's bedding and clothes to be flung overboard. This was done by the boatswain, who, how-

ever, tied a line to the bundle in the dark, let it tow overboard and later retrieved it. For myself, I went back into
my quarantine; I lived again behind a screen of canvas
rigged for me under the awning, and all my things were
placed there. In a way, I was thankful for this, it saved
me from contact with the appalling Pegg.

The man Doggy, before going on to the sick-list, had
had a very evil influence upon the crew. In his babbling
he had impressed them with the belief that the wraith of
poor Harry had 'worked a ju-ju,' as they called it, upon
him which would not be satisfied till vengeance was
exacted. He had a way of shouting, 'Harry's waiting by
the windlass,' which rang through the ship and terrified
everybody. Pegg was terrified, as he plainly shewed. He
even asked me if I could not give Doggy something
which 'would put him out of pain like that.' I said that
he must know, that in such a disease the stomach brooked
no remedies.

It was a hot doldrummy night, with violent rain-squalls.
Sleeping under my awning, I was frequently wetted and
wakened by the rain, which I did not mind; it was so fair
a refreshment in the heat. I slept ill, and often in my
worry and misery wondered if the seamen were not right.
Why should they be wrong? Why should not poor
Harry's wraith wait by the windlass, calling for vengeance
upon his killers? A frightful deed had been done against
an inoffensive man; why should not judgement follow?
All along that frightful Coast of Dead Ned and Sin
millions of wild black men must have wished evil intently
upon their wrongers, the whites. The soul of poor Harry
had but to cry, to turn all that mass of hatred against us.
With these thoughts I bothered myself to sleep.

I roused at about half-past three in the morning. I
cannot say why I roused, but I started up, thinking,

suddenly, that I had heard Doggy cry 'Harry'll come for me at four, he says.' This I had heard him babble several times during the afternoon, and had thought it only nonsense. I did not think it nonsense now. 'I'll go down to Doggy,' I said to myself, 'so as to be near him before four.' On my way, I met one of the better seamen, to whom I mentioned what I was going to do.

'That's kind of you, sir,' he said. 'If you bring him past four, he'll be all right, no doubt. It's fancies and giving way to them that kills folk on the Coast here. When he finds it's fancy, he'll be ashamed.'

I stood talking with this man for some minutes. The ship was slipping along quietly in the hot, hazy night. We seemed to be shearing through swathes of wool which, as we drove into them, streamed aside into rolls of flame, that broke into spangles and died again into wool. I could hear the sick man on the deck below babbling and muttering.

'You hear him, sir?' the man said. 'He's a lot better now.'

I asked, 'Has Captain Pegg chosen another officer?'

He said, with some surprise at my not having heard, 'Yes, sir. Mr Staggers.'

Staggers was known to me as a young, truculent boxer of great physical beauty; he had been in the ship in the previous voyage; during this present voyage, he had been Sailmaker's mate. I had seen him about the decks and had disliked his look.

At this moment, there came cries from below, with a noise of scuffling; the man, Doggy, came rushing up the hatch tearing off his clothes. He fell exhausted on the deck close to me. Even in that light, I could see that he had become dusky in the face, like a mulatto. He babbled, 'Leave me. The boat's coming at four. Harry's sending the boat for me at four. Eight bells. And there'll be a man in the boat I won't want to see.'

I tried to raise him, but he struck at me.

'Come, Doggy,' I said, 'let us get you back to bed.'

'Leave me in the cool,' he said. 'For God's sake, leave me in the cool.'

The watch gathered about, coming not too near, but gazing with fascination and terror. It seemed to me that Doggy was at the point of death. I said to the men, 'I believe he's dying; do not touch him.' They would not have touched him. Doggy was babbling something. I knelt just over him, knowing that he might be saying something coherent of importance to someone in far-away England. He began to mutter the compass, 'North quarter east; north half east; north three-quarter east, nor' by east.' After a minute of this, he said solemnly, in a little voice which only two or three could have heard:

> 'Dead by live.
> Dead three-quarters live.
> Dead half live.
> Dead one quarter live.
> Dead.'

When he had reached this East Point, he said, 'There's the boat hooked on, and there's Harry. Oh, Harry, don't go against a shipmate. Tell the gentlemen, I had to do what I was told.' Then he cried, 'The gentleman's got his bonnet over his face. Oh, keep him off, Doctor.' He struggled a little faintly and died, just as the helmsman made a long arm and struck the bell eight for four o'clock.

So Doggy died, and was promptly buried, without any prayer. One of the men began to sing a hymn, which began, as I well remember:

> 'Sweetly sleep, dear saint, in Jesus.'

He stopped after this line as he could not remember what followed. Long afterwards, I found the whole hymn in an old book, and read it through with thoughts of Doggy, whose real name I never knew.

The night before we reached Little Massa, I went aft to my screen, to sleep. The cabin skylight was open. I could hear Pegg and Staggers in the cabin playing a simple card-game, of which they were very fond. It is the game called by children 'Beggar-my-Neighbour'; they called it 'Check.' I heard him crying, 'Check,' continually and then fell asleep.

I did not sleep long. I was wakened by hearing them creep cautiously on deck, as I suppose in the hope of catching someone asleep in his watch on deck. I heard Pegg say in a low voice, 'Is the Doc asleep there?'

Staggers tiptoed close to me. I lay still, for I did not wish to talk with them. He said 'Yes, dead-oh. He can do with his all-night-in, the Doc.'

They moved aft a few feet from me. I heard Pegg repeat: 'You're sure he's asleep?' and Staggers repeated, 'Dead-oh.'

They stayed there only about five feet from me. They could hear that the watch was busy at a job forward, and see that the helmsman was wide awake. Pegg had a look at the compass and returned to Staggers, who began at once thus:

'In the *Almeria*,' he said, 'under old Cap. Scratch Toes, the Doc kept watch and watch, all the time, when no slaves were aboard.'

I knew that this was designed to suggest to the Captain that I, too, should keep watch and watch. Any reply to it would also show to Staggers just how Pegg regarded me.

'And a very good way, too,' Pegg answered. 'Why

should a Doc live easier than any, when no sick are aboard? I've half a mind to try the same here.'

'Why not?' Staggers asked. 'You're Captain.'

Pegg muttered in a low voice, 'He may not be quite safe.'

'How d'ye mean? You're Captain.'

'Yes, I am Captain. But he's got letters in his chest to the Governors of Jamaica and Carolina. He may be a bigger dog than he seems.'

'He don't seem much of a big dog to me,' Staggers said. 'He wouldn't come in a slaver if he were much of a big dog. He came like all the other docs in the trade come, because he wanted to lie low a bit.'

'How d'ye mean, lie low?'

'Docs get into trouble by giving the wrong dose and that. This man came aboard at the last minute, with a lot of ready-made slops. All his things were new and marked new. They've been forward to be washed, and we talked of it there. He didn't bring one old thing to sea. That's odd to begin with. Generally, when a man comes to sea, he brings the oldest he has. Even this man's trunk was new. And that's odd, too, for one who says he was brought up in France, as they all say he says he was. I mean, you'd expect he'd have a trunk that had batted about a bit and shown the marks of travel and that.'

'Yes, he says he was brought up in France,' Pegg said, 'and he has a French book or two. And it is odd, now you mention it . . .'

'What is odd?' Staggers asked.

'He's got no papers to show he's a doctor; no parchment; no licence. I've been through his things to see, and can't see one anywhere.'

'Maybe he's got it on him,' Staggers said. 'He very likely keeps it on him.'

'I suppose it would be small,' Pegg said. 'It would go into a pocket-case, folded up. Are you sure he's asleep?'

Though he trod softly as a cat, I heard Staggers creep to me and examine me. I am not much of an actor, but I can act being asleep with anyone. Staggers looked and crept back.

'Dead-oh,' he said. 'It's what he's best at.'

'There's a mystery about him, that's sure,' Pegg said, 'but there can't be any doubt of his being a doc, because he cured the steward's leg, and he sets about anyone the right way. He set about Paul; a London surgeon couldn't have done him better; give the devil his due. He's a doc, all right. But, God, don't he make me sick, with his airs and college-talk. And he's only a kid, when all's said. I'll tell you my view of him. Mind, I don't want Tulp to know or to suspect.'

'I won't moot it to Tulp, nor anyone else,' Staggers said.

'Well, my belief is, he's a spy. There's lots of talk in England now by cranks and that, about this trade. It's being inquired about. A lot of skypilots were up and down Liverpool, you'll remember, asking about how the poor slaves are packed. My brother says they're at the same game in Bristol, all prying and peaking in anybody's business but their own. They've got men to ask about it in Parliament, too. They want to find out what goes on out here and in these ships. It's my belief, they got this kid, who's very likely a French spy when all's said, to come out here to report. That's what my belief is.'

'God, that's a dirty trick, ain't it,' Staggers said, 'to eat the trade's bread and then complain of the flour?'

'I'm not quite blind,' Pegg said. 'I've seen him close to and had time to figure on it. If he ain't that, what is he, this French lad? But I've made up my mind that he don't get past Captain Pegg.'

'What d'ye mean to do, then, Captain Pegg?'

'I'll just have a look-see if he's as asleep as he gives out.'

Pegg came quickly to me, and in a low voice said, 'Are you awake, Doc?' I moved in my sleep and flung myself over, as though about to wake, then settled to rest on my other side.

'He's asleep all right', Pegg said. 'Well, what I'm going to do is to sell him the day we make Jamaica or the Carolines. You may have heard what Paul did the other time with Doctor Tim? Hey? As a white slave with no papers and a knowledge of medicine this man or any other doctor'll fetch seventy-five to a hundred pounds on any big estate. He'd be worth more than that; double that.'

'But with those letters to the Governors,' Staggers said, 'there'd be trouble; big trouble. It don't do, to stir up Governors.'

'There won't be any letters to Governors by the time we make Jamaica,' Pegg said. 'There won't be any letter to anyone, nor any certificate round his neck, nor anything else. You mark my words, that kid is not Edward Torrance. He's here under an assumed name. He's here under false pretences. He'll be sold as a creole slave with a knowledge of medicine, and of the name of Edward. If he's not a creole slave let him prove it. He'll find it hard enough to prove, when once he's become it. Now I've opened my mind to you, Staggers, I shall look to you to bear a hand when the time comes. You shall not be a loser by it. He may make us sick enough with his airs at table and that, but he's a living bank-note for as much as a hundred plunk. If you stand in with me, you'll find there's a good deal to be made in this trade on the side. We'll talk of another matter later.'

Staggers went below. Pegg stayed a while, creeping softly about, probably to spy upon Tulp, or to hear what the watch on deck were saying. He looked closely at me, to make sure that I was asleep. I judged that he was going below to my berth to have another look for my certificate, which I was now carrying, much as they had surmised, in a little oilskin case hung round my neck. My letters of introduction were in this case with it.

After he had gone below, I did not sleep too well. I now knew what Pegg had planned for me; I must say that it terrified me. Dick had said, 'They'll sell you, if they get half a chance.' They would have a chance. What was to stop their chance? I was not sold yet, but I found no answer to the question. And another question also ran in my head; how many of the *Albicore*'s surgeons had already been sold?

Well, in time we drew in to make the port of Little Massa, about which I had so often thought. Edmond Quichet was famed to have burned it; now here I was, about to enter it. From the talk that had gone about the decks, I knew that it was a safe harbour, but dangerous above most ports at the coming-in and going-out.

At Momboe our approach had been the signal for a race of eager blacks, in canoes, dug-outs, rafts and other contrivances. We had been cheered by a hundred glad savages, and piloted in by a master pilot. At Little Massa, nobody put out to us. I could see black people on the beach ashore; not one was going to venture out, nor was I surprised, for the surf in front of us was frightful and seemed to worsen as we neared it.

I said, 'The surf looks pretty bad.'

Pegg snorted and said, 'Surf's nothing, so long as you

know the marks and keep your head. That ain't a bad surf! not what I call bad.'

However, Staggers and the boatswain did not like the look of it; plainly they did call it bad; the boatswain asked, 'Shall I signal for a pilot, sir?'

'Pilot? For Little Massa?' Pegg said. 'I can take her in, I hope; a place as easy as this.'

Like many vain men, he was ready to do a desperately silly thing to attract attention to himself. I took some of the despair from the faces near me. I could see into the lagoon or harbour now. It was exquisitely still and blue; so blue, that I have seen nothing bluer. It was so blue that it made one cry aloud from delight. But to get to it, the way to it was through the Clashing Rocks and a rage like Brynhilda's fire. Pegg had been in and out of it before; he knew, what I did not, that the entrance, though narrow, was well defined, well marked by guiding marks, and without bends or any sunken rocks. If you aimed straight and had wind enough you got through.

By this time, he was taking her in, and we had a nearer view of the surf, which had a rage and a roaring that would have frightened a saint. It broke with an untellable fury on a big rock to the west of the passage we had to make. As we were coming close to this violence the wind began to fail; I saw the sails crumple and empty, steady to the full, then crumple and flog. I knew that without power we were ruined. I gave the ship up as lost, for we were in the catch of the outer rollers and seemed to have lost all power of independent movement.

I could see that the crew expected the ship to strike. I saw them get over to the starboard side, to be away from the shock. Then suddenly, before Pegg, who was as white as a sheet, had found any order to give, if any order would have been of use to us, we felt the ship plucked, as though by a terrific force, and spun away in the back-wash, in a current that ran us as a mill-race runs a forget-me-not blossom. We went spinning away in the rush of this current, a nine-knot current, so one of the men said, without any means of helping ourselves, for the sails were flogging loose, and we had no sweeps out. To be brief, we went smash into a rock, which flung us for an instant on our side. Something crashed and ground below me, and certain light things came down from aloft. Then we were clear of whatever we had hit and were swimming gently into shelter, across that exquisite blue calm, where we anchored near the town.

'Just where I was in the *Jonas and Silas*,' Pegg said. 'Just the very same berth. What were you dogs quitting station for, just now? Have you never seen surf before?'

The Carpenter and his mates had gone below at the first crash of our hitting. They came up, now, to say that she'd been hit pretty hard in the old place, and that the water was coming into her; not much, but you could not tell yet.

Little Massa was a pleasanter place than Momboe, being so much more open. There was no sinister bush; there were no brooding hills. The town was on both sides of a river, which was nearly as blue as the harbour. It had an aspect almost gay from the profusion of scarlet flowers growing there.

When we had entered the harbour, the native canoes rushed out to greet us, as at Momboe. However, Pegg called to the hands to rig out boarding nettings, as he wasn't going to dash a lot of good dolly till he knew what he'd get by it. He was going to see what slaves there might be, first of all. If there were slaves, then dolly. If no slaves, not a drop of dolly. It was strange to see what a change for the worse power had made in Pegg. Change from generosity to meanness is a sad and bad sign. It was a bad sign here, and bad for us, for the blacks were furious at not being treated, and held up the fish and fruit which they had brought for us, so that our men might see what we were losing. However, a Captain commands, and hands obey. Pegg and Staggers went ashore to see about the slaves, while we remained on board, with orders to let no black aboard.

Down below, our carpenters worked at the new leak, and presently called to Tulp to rig the pumps and free her, so that they might know what the new leak amounted to. The men pumped the ship free. After this, the carpenters came on deck completely exhausted, and said that they couldn't come at the injury without shifting the water-casks, which would need the Captain's orders. They said, that the ship had probably been holed, and had broken off the rock that holed her. They advised Tulp to try to get some blacks to dive down to see what and where the trouble was. But by this time, the blacks had abandoned us, calling us various things in songs. Tulp translated some of them to me:

> 'They do not give their friends anything,
> They are like dog with bone; they say.
> "I eat this. No other have some."
> They are like the mangy buffalo. They
> smell and not know how bad they smell.'

We had lost Face.

Pegg and Staggers came back hot and cross for dinner. Both were cursing their luck; and let it be known, that the slaves of whom Peter had told us, had been at Little Massa only two days before, and that the agent had sent them back to Bimbi and Momboe, thinking that a mistake had been made.

'They've sent them back, if you please,' Pegg snorted. 'Four hundred Samboes and Talliks; enough to make our voyage. They've sent 'em back, all that way by road, where a hundred of 'em'll die. Now they're forty mile up country, and we won't get 'em at all.'

'And are there no slaves here, then, at all?' I asked.

'Yes, there are; but that damned black King is sour because I haven't crossed his palm. He asks forty-five pound a man. He'll not get that from me never. Not for any cock, let alone Matablancos.'

It was the custom of the Coast to bribe the Kings before trading. The Kings expected it and exacted it. Pegg knew this very well; but having made up his mind not to pay the toll, he was stubborn on the point.

The natives were now furious with Pegg for his meanness, and the King gave orders that we were not to be served. The divers would not examine the ship's side, the fisherman and fruitsellers would not trade with us. Pegg went ashore daily, to speak with the King. He was insulted, kept waiting, and put off with lies. All the time, the ship lay in the port, leaking from both leaks, neither of which could be reached by the carpenters.

The only consolation was the very poor one, that the Matas were still to be had, some seventy odd, but it was not to be denied that shrewd slave-captains refused to have anything to do with them. The Matas had a bad name. Nobody had enslaved them yet; they died rather than submit. Still, there they were, and no other slaves were being offered or were likely to come in.

It was decided that I should come ashore next morning, to have a look at these men. Pegg judged that they might be a sickly lot, as well as sullen; I had better have a look at them. If I approved them as healthy, he would buy them.

Just as we were deciding this matter, there came a hail from the port:

'Ho, the *Albicore*. Is Captain Ashplant aboard?'

Tulp, who was on deck, in charge, called, 'No; he's dead,' and a minute later came down and said, 'It's old Billy Crackers, sir; Puggy's brother. He'd like to come aboard, if he may.'

'That old fraud,' Pegg said. 'Yes, let him come aboard. He may know of slaves.'

'He's just come from the leeward, sir,' Tulp said.

'Well, he will know what's doing there, at least,' Pegg said.

We all went on deck to see Billy Crackers. There he was, talking to Puggy. He was dressed as a native. He was burned and stained almost black from exposure to the sun and the constant use of oil in which nut-ash had been mixed. He wore a sort of feather-kilt, no other garment. His hair had grown long and had been worked up with clay and oil, into a head-dress which served instead of a hat. He had a long ivory skewer thrust through his nose. It was sharp at both ends and stained scarlet. He looked extremely healthy and cheerful. He was the only white man present who seemed to be either.

'Why, why, if I don't see Captain Pegg,' he began. 'Well, sir, welcome to the Coast and congratulations on the command. Here we are again, you see. Good old Billy Crackers; you can't kill him with an axe. Why aren't you slaved? I can smell you ain't.'

'No slaves to be had,' Pegg said shortly. 'They're very few and dear as love.'

'Not to be had?' Bill said. 'Well, that's a state of things'll soon be cured. The M'gai are moving. You go along to Sixteen Peaks you'll get all the slaves you want, and dirt cheap. Hundreds of 'em. The M'gai are going to root out all the Coast tribes and live there. Slaves? You will bless the name of William Crackers when you see the cargo you'll get there. And you'll be the first to open trade with the M'gai. They'll give you any slaves you want for powder. What's this old thief here in Massa asking for slaves, cock and hen?'

'Forty-five pounds for a cock; he hasn't any hens in store,' Staggers said.

Bill whistled. 'Never knew prices like that,' he said. 'But you get along to the M'gai, and you'll get your account. They'll give you any cock you like for two pounds of powder; and a hen for a half a pound of bullets. They'll ask you to take the slaves as a gift, they've got so many.'

'Look here, Billy,' Pegg said, 'is this the truth?'

'Of course it's the truth; the truth and me's brothers born. I've been in Tsika, and seen 'em. But it's no good you're going there. That was twelve days ago; no; I lie; it was a week more. You go to Sixteen Peaks; that is where they'll be by the time you get there. Then, if you don't slave right up to the hatch, you call me the son of an unmarried merry female, what liked her own way best.'

'Have you been in Sixteen Peaks? What sort of a place is it?'

'Very good. It's deserted; has been for years. There were French pirates there once; not now. The M'gai are going there now, and that's where you'll find 'em.'

'Yes,' Pegg said. 'But will they trade?'

'Boy, they're panting for trade. What they want is powder. You give 'em powder and they'll lick your boots. On that I swop my solemn sam.'

After this, Pegg and Staggers took Billy below, to give him a drink and also to trade beads and small wares for some gold dust. During their talk, it was arranged, that Billy and I should go ashore the next morning. I was to look over the Matas who were for sale; Billy would bargain with the King for them. If Billy could beat down the King's price, and I could pass them as healthy, Pegg would buy them, ship them, and sail for the Sixteen Peaks. There, he would probably find a big settlement of M'gai, with hordes of slaves. He would be able to careen the *Albicore* in the harbour, find and stop the leaks, ship the slaves and make a fortune.

The next morning, the ship's boat took us in. I had a sort of what shall I say? oddness of feeling, about sitting next to a nearly naked savage, with tusks in his nose. It was an odd feeling, in one who had been in Newgate Hold, and in the hangman's cart, yet I had it. There was no trace of unease in Billy. His eye was bright and his wicked old mouth merry. He made me remember a remark made by a Frenchman to my father; 'So you ask the good God for wisdom and for guidance? Perhaps. But I ask him only for a good digestion and no memory.' Billy had a good digestion and no memory at all for anything unpleasant. He talked all the time. As the boat took us in, a shark drew up to look at us. Billy said, 'That's a slave-shark. You can tell 'em by the white snout. He knows your ship's a slaver, even though she's got no slaves aboard. The smell stays. They've got the noses of bloodhounds, sharks; they smell Death coming days before. They won't look at fish after tasting man; cannibals won't, either. Old Captain Voyal said he often had sharks follow him all the Middle Passage just for the slaves that went overboard; he would get to know them by sight, and always knew from them when a slave was going to die.'

As we were carried to the slave-sheds in litters (Billy

had a way of getting this done for us, which Pegg would certainly not have done), I asked him why he took to the Coast, which most white men hated.

'I like it,' he said. 'I did from the first, when I came here in the *Hannibal*, Captain Cringle. I said, "This is the life for William Crackers," and it has been. I like the sun, I like the life. Where would I get the sun and the life in England? No place. In England, you're always doing this or that because it's done, or because, if you don't, you're marked at once. Here I do what I please, which is what I always wanted to do. I like natives. They're a great deal better lot than white men, take them on the whole; and man for man, there's no question. It's my belief, they'll boot us out of the Coast, and that within the next twenty years, no, in the next ten. The M'gai won't have the white man here, depeopling the whole land. They'll boot the white man out, and a good job, too; it's a dirty job, this slaving. Not but what the M'gai may be a problem in themselves,' he added. 'They're very free with their spears; him likee blood too much.'

But by this time, we were at the sheds, where the King's slave-master was waiting for us. He was spoken of by Pegg as 'Old Pilly Pepper-pot,' goodness knows why. He was a short, squat, fat pock-marked savage, grey in the face, being some kind of a mongrel, and walking with a waddle. His greyness made his face like a mask, in which his little astute eyes were the only living things. His nose had a golden moon hanging from it. He wore an old scarlet uniform coat over his loin-cloth, and had a cutlass at his side.

'Ha,' he said, with insolence. 'Why not Pegg come? You only common mans. I not show good slaves to common mans. I save my Face.'

'Don't try it,' Billy said, 'or you'll get it trodden on.

78

None of that with me. Let's see these boys, and less talk about it.'

I have described the slave-sheds of Momboe. These were much the same, except that here there was no fever. There were many bold brown hawks cruising about for garbage. The slave-smell, of dirt, poverty and misery, which clung about the hold of the *Albicore*, was sickeningly strong all about the place.

'That's the House-flag of the trade, that stink,' Billy said.

As we came into the shed, every man turned to us, and fixed us with a stare. I knew from the quality of the look that these men were very different men from the wrecks who had lain dying at Momboe. These men were warriors, with hard, clean-cut faces. They had been trained to be indifferent to suffering, to endure all things and to show no trace. The flies swarmed about them; they must have been in desperate discomfort, but not a sign shewed on any face that they felt anything but at peace. These were the Matablancos of whom I had heard. I must say that my heart went out to them, not in pity so much as in admiration.

'Dey fine boys,' said Pilly Pepper-pot. 'Dey work, ho how dey work. De best boys ever to work. Dey worth any money. What you gib? Hey? What you gib?'

'These are Matas,' said Billy Crackers. 'Dey no good. Dey bad boys. Dey go killy killy. You take shoot dis lot. You give him sharkee; you bury. Dese not work. No can make work. Too bad boy. No white mans gib penny piece for all him.' He turned to me, and said in a low voice, 'Just go over 'em, Doctor.'

I turned to look at the slaves in turn. They were magnificent men; they had no fever, nor any visible infection. I went down the line slowly, then slowly returned, gazing hard at each man. At my first coming into the shed, I had noticed a man about half-way down the line. He sat or reclined in a way unlike the posture of any other. Dr Copshrews had always urged me to look with attention at that person who was at all or in any way unlike his fellows; I therefore, had noticed this man.

When I had gone down the line and returned, I went to this man, whose eyes were steadfast upon mine. I had made up my mind that he sat or lay in an odd position not from genius, but because his irons had chafed him and the chafe had ulcerated. This I found to be the case.

'Mr Crackers,' I said, 'get some brandy for me. This man must have this chafe washed and bandaged, or he'll have a fearful place here, which may suppurate and kill him.'

Crackers came forward, examined the chafe and, spoke to the man in Mata; the man replied in Palaver, that the sore would surely kill him, but what matter? If he died, he would die.

Finding that he spoke the Palaver, I spoke to him, and told him that I could ease his suffering. With Crackers' help, I was able to wash and dress not only his chafes, but those of a dozen others. I found that the unusual man, the man who had drawn my attention, was called 'Deray' or 'de Ray,' which meant, roughly, 'the King,' the leader of the party. He was a young man, but was no doubt a fine fellow. Nearly all the party had one or more white, raised scars at the sides of their brows. Billy told me that this was their 'man-tally,' and that a warrior put one such mark on himself for each man he had killed in battle. Now Deray had seven of these, although I suppose he was only about twenty-three.

When I had finished washing and dressing the chafes, this Deray spoke to me in the Palaver, using a kind more full of French than our sort. He asked me, 'What will they do to us?'

I told him, 'They send you in ship far to the west. Perhaps sell you, and try to make you dig.'

About a dozen of the slaves asked him what I had said. When he explained, a kind of derisive laugh passed along the benches. They were laughing at the thought of being put to dig, the warriors of the Matablancos, whose women dug for them. The very thought of being put to dig was joy to them. A spade was some sort of a weapon, and to use it they would have to have their hands free. Let them but be put to dig, and somebody's skull would be the first thing dug. These men were going to be dangerous till they were dead. Surely Pegg would not buy them? If he did, what sane planter in the West would buy them? These were terrible fellows, hard, scarred, tattooed and awful. Every man of them had more than one white 'man-tally'; one man had nineteen. I looked at old Billy Crackers, who was considering them with thought.

I said to him, 'Surely these men will never be slaves.'

'I never knew men buy Matas before, or have the chance to,' Billy said. 'If once it's known that English men have bought Matas . . .' He shook his head, leaving the sentence unfinished.

We went back aboard with our report. I said that the men were seemingly sound, without visible infection. Billy said, that it would be not only money thrown away, but just wicked foolishness to buy Matas. It would be known all over the Coast at once. The Matas would never forgive it; they would at once join the M'gai and wipe out every factory from Cabo to Tsika, and cook and eat every white man in the trade. 'No man buys Matas,' he said. 'You take a wise man's advice; have nothing to do with it.'

'I'm not going to leave seventy able-bodied men to be bought by the next comer,' Pegg said, 'in a bad season like this, with all the West Indies just rotting for the want of slaves. I'm going to take what offers.'

'God help you, then,' Billy said.

'He helps those who help themselves,' Pegg said.

'I'll tell you a thing,' Billy answered. 'It would pay you a thousand times over, to buy these Matas, and take 'em straight to leeward, to somewheres near their people; Sixteen Peaks or so. Tell 'em from the first that you're going to take 'em home. Treat 'em good and take 'em home. Let 'em go scot-free; even if you pay fifty pounds a man for 'em. If you make friends with the Matas, you'll get all the slaves you'll want till the day you die. If you try to slave these boys, you'll pay according, and white men for a hundred years'll pay. I've been among Matas; and I know how to deal with 'em. I tell you true.'

'Well, now you tell us something else,' Pegg said.

Billy was vexed at being insulted by one whom he considered as a foolish boy; he went aboard his sloop and shoved off, and we saw him no more. Pegg bargained all the afternoon with the King for these Matas, and at last bought them and paid for them. They were, no doubt, hoping to escape while being brought on board, but great pains were used to check them. Only one man got away; and though they put dogs upon his trail at once, he was not recaptured. The seventy-three others were brought in bonds on board, and laid on the shelves in the lower hold in the airless, stinking heat, in heavy irons. Newgate Hold was fairyland to that hold. What Pegg paid for them in the end we never knew. Probably it was some big price which he felt ashamed to speak of.

'Any man with legs and arms'll fetch his weight in gold

this year,' he said. 'And you, Doc, understand that these blacks aren't like white patients, to be fawned on and pampered. They're property, to be kept marketable, whether they like it or don't.'

'If you wish them to be kept marketable,' I said, 'you'd better have them out of the hold to begin with. They're used to the free air.'

'They're used to murder and plenty else they won't get again,' Pegg said. 'They are blacks; they'll stand the hold very well. Some'll die, of course; some always do; they wouldn't be human if they didn't. Your job is to watch 'em. When any of 'em comes out sick and spotty, say so; and we'll have him overboard before he infects the rest. That's the doctor's job; stop the infection.'

Well ... we sailed from Little Massa, despised and mocked by the blacks, to whom we seemed stingy and without Face, for giving so little 'dash,' and also crazy, for shipping Matas as slaves. Our crew was scared of our cargo; the Matas were dreaded everywhere. Still, when men are chained prone upon shelves, so that they can barely turn over, and are then battened and barred-in for the night, and the only possible exits are two narrow, closely guarded holes down which loaded swivel-guns are pointing, their chance of being terrible is diminished.

On leaving Massa, with great difficulty, I got the slaves the afternoon privilege of a quarter-pint of water, and begged that this mercy might be continued every afternoon, in the worst of the heat. It was only granted when I said that the men would surely die of heat-stroke without it, and then only on the condition that I myself pumped the water and served it. Pegg thought that I should be too proud to do this, but I did it. He mocked me for doing it.

'Here's one of these Friends of Africa, going round

bottle-holding to a lot of stinking savages. This is the
way to keep the white man's Face, I must say.'

However, on the next day, the slave-guards, the trusty,
tough boatswains' mates, reported while we were at
breakfast, that the slaves had got the 'sullens,' that is,
they were in a conspiracy, not to eat or drink.

Pegg asked, 'Are you sure? It ain't their religion
coming out?'

'No,' the mates replied, 'it's the sullens. They took
their chop and slabber last night; but this morning we
found it all spat out.'

I said, 'Very likely they're seasick.'

'Seasick,' Pegg said with much contempt. 'We know
when a slave's seasick, I hope. No. It's the sullens; their
cursed black froward natures. You get up the three who
seem to be chiefs; we'll start Jouncer on 'em at once.
Christianity says you ain't to kill yourself, nor let
another kill hisself. I'll give 'em good Christianity from
Jouncer.'

He went to a locker and produced some grim iron
appliances.

'These are Jouncers,' Pegg explained. 'Put one of them
in Juba's mouth, with the spikes and that, then you've
only to turn this screw to heave his jaws apart, and then
the chop has to go down and the slabber on the top. If
they don't know their good, I do. We'll have up the two
or three what get the respect. When they've had nicee
chop, we'll see if we can't persuade 'em to dance a little
to show they like it.' He was watching me, and saw my
disgust. 'We don't go to college,' he said, 'to learn how
to doctor slaves. If they lose appetite with us, we make
'em eat, and if we find 'em sullen, we make 'em dance. A
good cut or two with a cat'll make a big black Mantacaw
dance like Harriet Lane, and a turn with the Jouncer'll

make a rabbit eat like a wolf. Sense is what we go by here, let me tell you.'

I said that from what I had seen of the men in the hold, his methods wouldn't succeed. 'They'll die,' I said. 'Those men are a tough lot. You won't bend them; they'll die.'

'We'll see that,' Pegg said. 'I rather think we'll win. Iron is stronger than most things. Iron and pain'll make a lot of difference to even the proudest Juba. You might remember that, too, for your own good.'

'If that be a threat,' I said, 'let me warn you, for your own good, not to threaten me. I have some very good friends who may make it exceedingly uncomfortable for you.'

He knew that I referred to the Governors to whom I had letters, and to those unknown, but doubtless powerful friends who had caused me to be received at a moment's notice.

'I can't stay jawing here,' he said. 'I've got my duty to do.'

I, too, had my duty to do. I had to examine every member of the crew for marks of fever or disease. While I was doing this (and there were four in need of treatment), Pegg applied his methods to three whom the mates said were the chiefs. They were not the chiefs; they were the three most easily brought on deck. After this was over (and I saw nothing of it, or I would have protested), it fell to me to make my first examination of the slaves in the shelves. One of the boatswain's mates attended me with a lantern. I may say that after my little tussle with Pegg, I had some fear that he might chain me with the slaves, for sale later. However, I judged that he needed me as a surgeon at present; my turn would come later.

I went with my lantern-bearer along the 'tween-decks

to the little man-hole which led to the tiers. The 'tween decks was as hot as any closed space under a wooden roof in the tropics can be. But when I came to the man-hole to the hold the heat of that lower place was something that one could lean against. It had been shut in all night, save for the slender pipe of one windsail and two little barred holes.

The heat was but a small part of the terror of that darkness.

I had often been told in conversation round the cabin table that all ships stank below the water, even in the colder climates. They said that water would seep in, by one way or another, and accumulate below and swiftly rot into something that stank like skunks, the 'bilge-water' which so many have mentioned. This smell hung about the lower parts of the ship at all times, and mixed with other smells, of dry-rot, and wet-rot, ship's canvas, new tar, not very fresh provisions, cargo, paint, rope and the presence of rats and mice. Now to all these rank and rancid stinks was added the reek of seventy prisoners, chained prone upon the shelves. The boatswain's mate noticed that the smell affected me.

'It come up very ripe this morning, sir,' he said. 'You'll get used to it. Use is second nature. It gets thicker than this in a busy season. This is nothing. I've known men faint, going round with the chow, but that was in the lower tiers, when we were running full.'

'How can men live in air worse than this?' I asked.

'Why,' he said, 'they do live, the most of 'em. The aim of most folk is to live; even though it mayn't be fun, they'd rather live than not live. If you'll let me go first, sir, I'll hand you down; this ladder is very steep. Hold the lantern, will you, Bill?'

Bill held the lantern, and I came down into the space

86

of the hold, in a heat and stench such as made even Newgate seem a Paradise.

I could not at once make out where I was, for the hold
was very dark. Bill's lantern cast a yellowish glow about
the place. I could see gleams upon chains and upon
staunchions. I did not see the slaves at the first look, only
stood, trying not to be sick in the fog of stench in which
I was. The place was full of noises, mostly uncanny, as
a ship's hold always must be. The water went lamenting
past as we slipped along; down below me the water
gurgled and splashed in the bilges; the planks creaked
and whined; little slow, stripping, progressing cracklings
ran along the beams as she rolled now one way, then back;
there was a kind of drumming noise of wind coming
down the windsail flapping the edge which secured it.
Above all these noises, I was aware of the presence of the
misery of many men, who were lying close to me, breathing heavily, moaning now and then, in rage or stupor,
and shifting about, with many clinkings of chain. Gradually I came to see in the darkness a sort of long, low shelf
or slab on which dark figures were packed, heads towards
me. A long line of heads was on each side of my ankles.
The men had been packed there as close as they would
lie.

'We put 'em low down,' Bill explained, 'for if we have
a good buy down Coast, we'll have room for two or three
tiers above these. And we stick them heads nearest so as
they can't kick, and we can drag 'em out easier if they up
and die on us.'

'Let me see the men who are sick,' I said. 'Hold the
lantern so that I can see.'

He held the lantern in turn over three faces; all three
were close to the hatchway. Being the easiest to come at,
they had been chosen for Jouncer. The three men had all

been cut with the cat-of-nine-tails, and all three mouths were bloody from the Jouncer. They were unconscious; they did not respond to voice or touch; their eyes were inverted and their pulses very slight, so slight that I knew that they were in an extreme of weakness. I did not understand it. I asked the men if they had been flogged with great severity. 'No,' they said, 'they only give 'em a dozen or so, more in fun than anything, just to make 'em dance. A seaman would have thought nothing of it; just nothing at all.'

However, these men were not seamen, and did think of it. For all that I could do, all three died before noon, and were flung overboard.

'That's one of their tricks,' Pegg said. 'That's their sullen spite.'

I said, 'I told you that these men would die if you tried your methods on them. They have died. These men have something in them that will beat you every time you pit yourself against them.'

To my astonishment, Tulp spoke up. He was a little drunk, having somehow found some rum. Whenever he was a little drunk, strange knowledge shone from Tulp; it shone now. 'The Doctor's right, sir,' he said. 'These leeward warrior tribes can all will themselves dead. They're taught the trick young, in case they're caught in battle. Old Captain Quoin told me he'd seen a hundred will themselves dead at once, "all to be dead by daybreak," and they were. They just settle down and die. You'll have all these Matas dead the same way if you try.'

'I'll give 'em something to die for,' Pegg said savagely.

'Wait a moment, Captain,' I said, 'let me try speaking a little to these Matas. Since force won't work with them, let me try persuasion.'

'Try it and be damned,' he said, 'and you'll soon see where you get.'

I lost no time in trying it. I slipped down into that hell upon sea, the lower hold, and spent all the afternoon there talking to Deray and the others. I was worn out at the end of my time there, but came away knowing that I had given them hope. I tried not to give too much hope, knowing how frightful the disappointment might be. I told them that we were going to Sixteen Peaks, and should be there for some days. It was that that gave the Matas hope. I did not see things very clearly in that sweltering, smelly dungeon. I only knew from what Deray and the others said, that the orders, to refuse all food and drink, which had gone abroad among them, were now withdrawn. I knew that every man among them had shed human blood in battle; they were man-killers to a man. Yet as I went about among them, I felt a kind of power of gratitude all about me, for my talk and the little cup of water which I could give to each. I knew, then, why the clergyman in Newgate had refused prefer-ment, so that he might stay with the lost, the despairing and the mad in the condemned holds.

I went on deck, nearly dead from the heat and want of air, to tell Pegg that the men would take their food and drink thenceforth. Pegg stared at me. I was white and sick.

'They'll die if you don't rig another windsail,' I said. 'The man, Bill, fainted twice there.'

He did not answer, but seemed to think, that if Bill fainted the air might be coming up rather ripe. At any rate, as I sat on a hatch and gulped the air, he gave word for a second windsail to be rigged. As one was on deck all ready, it was soon set; air and coolness in some measure did go down to that lower hell.

We loitered on towards our port, in light airs, in sweltering heat, with the leaks gaining. By now, we were in the leeward seas, in the deadest of the land of Dead Ned, farther to leeward than the crew liked, in a part where slavers seldom came. We were going into the almost unknown, from which few indeed came out, whoever went in. Indeed, the crew talked as though it were the Coast of Death himself. 'A many ships have gone down to the leeward,' they said, 'and never returned.' I asked Tulp about it; he always knew the truth of these things.

He said, 'Yes; I believe it is so. All down the Coast to leeward the natives are savages and cannibals; they've taken a lot of ships, first and last, and ate the crews. And then, in many ports there is fever; ships have gone in for water and lost all their hands, and just stayed and rotted there.'

At that moment a man who was aloft working on the rigging high up, gave the hail of 'Land—Ooooo.' He pointed to the north-eastward away on our port bow, where the heat-haze was moving away like the smoke of an autumn bonfire.

'That'll be the Sixteen Peaks,' Tulp said. 'I'll fetch my glass.'

On the instant, it seemed to me that the heat sensibly lessened, something of a freshness seemed to come into the air. I remembered how the Admiral had said that it was always cool at the Peaks. Now here was proof; the dream was proving to be true. I gazed and gazed, seeing only the heat-haze slowly shifting. Mr Tulp came down from aloft with his glass, and said, 'If you go up into the top you'll see the tops of the Peaks quite clearly.' I was sailor enough for that by this time; I borrowed his glass; went up into the mizen-top, and there, holding on tightly and steadying the glass on the rigging, I took my first look at that shore.

At first, I saw only high rolls of forest with the smoke or haze upon them. Then, rather to the eastward from these, I saw what I had so often seen in my mind, a bunch or cluster of spires bright at their spiky summits with the last of the light. Some were red, some grey; they were the Peaks of Quichet's drawing. Old Admiral Cringle, then Captain, had looked at them from the *Hannibal* in just that way from perhaps that very point, and had stood on to his fate from where I then was. It thrilled me to the bone to see them thus. Then, quite suddenly, the light passed off the Peaks, and a smoke of haze drifted over the sea between me and them.

Early the next morning, when I came on deck, I saw all the Sixteen Peaks shining in the morning sun a few short miles away. I gazed at them intently, as though they were old friends given back from the grave. I decided for myself which red one held Edmond Quichet's cave. We were standing-in to the shore. I could see, from the changed colours in the water, that a great river emptied there by various channels; this river had formed islets at its mouths; all were overgrown with jungle. There was no sign of man there; no settlement, no smoke; no crowds of natives leaping into canoes to race out to us for dolly. Billy Crackers had been wrong about the M'gai with their hundreds of cheap slaves. Well, here we were, away to leeward at Sixteen Peaks, and in that harbour, if we could get into it, we should have to find our leak or leave our bones there. Pegg was cursing because he had counted on a multitude of slaves here, and native divers to help him careen; now there were neither slaves nor so much as a pilot to bring him into the river.

'This is another of these sepulchres,' he was saying.

'Fever under every tree and not another soul in sight. Which the devil is the channel?'

He ordered a gun to be fired, hoping that the natives would answer the signal; there was no answer of any kind.

We stood into the river-mouth; the boats went ahead and bore out lines to the trees ashore; by means of these we were presently drawn into a turbid, reddish river, with forest on one side and wooded islands on the other. Then, presently, we were out of sight and sound of the sea, in a great lagoon or bay, several miles long. This I knew was the anchorage where Edmond Quichet had had his settlement. There was no sign of any settlement now. All seemed savage forest, with a few birds and a few animals, who paid no heed to our coming. Men seemed to be strangers there.

We were now heaving with song and fiddle to the berth which Tulp had chosen. We passed out of the lagoon proper into a bay or bend on its western side. I knew, directly the hawsers tautened to drag us into it, that it was the very place which the *Hannibal* had moored in years before.

The years had not altered its main features, as the Admiral had described them to me. There was a patch of sandy and stony beach, much strewn with dead branches all barkless and white as bone. Beyond the beach was the character-mark, 'a bank or little cliff, perhaps twenty feet high, over which a stream fell into a rocky basin.' It seemed a very heaven on earth, with the brook, the many flowers, the fruits and berries on the trees, and bright birds pecking at them. Soon, when Pegg judged fitting, our anchor was let go; we moored there. When we were moored, I looked to the westward across the lagoon. From where we lay, I could see only six of the Sixteen Peaks; I know not which. Four of them were grey, two

red. Their strangeness made my heart beat fast. Were they
not alive? Had they not somehow wanted me and called
me thither? Now they had me there; I was arrived.

I stared at those peaks, till my duty wrenched me away.
I went below to look at the slaves in the lower tier.

When you have been in Newgate, you will know very
acutely the acuteness of the senses of prisoners. I knew
that I was in the presence of a terrible excitement among
those shut-up men. It shocked me with pity for them.
They would be landed while we mended the leak. They
would see that old haunt of theirs (where they had moved
as hunters), for the last time, as shackled slaves, and then
would see Africa no more. I tried to tell them not to
mind it too cruelly, that fate had dealt them a cruel turn,
but that they were still alive. That was the comfort (my
only one) that I used to give myself. I did not get much
comfort from it, nor did they get much from my halting
version of it. I came up from that awful den, shaken with
the state of mind that I had found there. I remember leaning on the rail to gulp the clean, fresh air and thinking,
'Poor fellows, poor wretched fellows, it can only make
their misery the greater; for they have no chance; none;
and when last they were here, they were free warriors at
home.'

Already the beach was busy with our crew. Most of the
hands were ashore, under the carpenters, cutting uprights
in the grove of spearwood near the water. Our plan was
to build huts ashore, to land everyone and much of the
gear, lay the *Albicore* upon her side, find the leaks and
mend them. Some men were already setting up stakes for
the tents.

When you have many hands, you can get a great deal
done in a short time. This work of securing poles and
stretching canvas was that which the seamen had had much

practice in. They were working well and cheerfully. They were ashore, which was a change to them. It was cool, which was another change. They were to sleep out of the ship, which was another change, and they had been told that if they worked well, one watch at a time might go fishing later, in the lagoon. Besides all this, they had all the water they could drink, and as much ripe fruit as they cared to pick. Bushes full of samberry, as they called it, grew just up the bank. The crew had not been so cheerful since they joined the ship at Liverpool.

As I could do little more on board, I went ashore and worked with the others at laying out the huts and tents.

We did not finish it that night, but were ashore at it before daybreak. We fenced the outer line of it with stakes and heaped driftwood. At the angles and in the centre we mounted the ship's guns. The space about the slaves' hut was ditched, fenced and entangled. Above these checks we built two raised sentry-boxes, in which men with muskets kept a look-out.

The slaves were brought ashore, two by two, heavily chained and watched by armed guards. Whatever hope of escape they may have had was taken from them by our precaution. Pegg was often rash, but in this matter he took every care. He left nothing to chance. Any slave making even a gesture of trying to escape would have been killed on the instant. They were watched till they were shackled to the spare spars on which their platforms rested. Even when they were shackled, the chains were searched every half-hour. Yet, hopeless as their case seemed, I noticed and reported a great change in the slaves. There was no trace of the sullens among them now. They had lost the hopeless look which had so wrung my heart on board the *Albicore*. There was a gleam in their eyes, which came from an inner fire. I put the change

94

down to their coming into the light and the clean air, and to the fact that they were given abundant fresh water and even some allowances of samberry. 'It'll keep 'em from getting scurvy,' Pegg had said. 'It's a bastard when slaves get scurvy.'

He was uneasy when I told him that the slaves were the better, even after four hours ashore. He said, 'I'm sorry to hear it. I don't want these black dogs to be too uppish. I don't like having 'em ashore at all. I'll have a rowser stretched along 'em, in case they try to come it fresh.'

He ordered a rowser, which is a cruelty I disdain to describe. I knew that if stretched it would be impossible for anyone even to try to escape. It made me sick, that I had reported their looking better. Even with the rowser he was not satisfied. He told off another two men to do slave-guard inside the slavehouse.

I mentioned the raised stands on which our sentries stood to watch the forest. The whole lagoon was so savage, so lonely, so without trace of man, that fear of attack had not entered my head. No men had frequented that place for years, so far as I could see. It was too far to leeward for slavers. As I was passing under these raised sentries, I heard one of them say to the other:

'It's not much good our being here. We can't see over that bank in front of us. If there were blacks there, they could be on us before we could fire a shot.'

The other said, 'It's the Old Man's perk to order some damned silly thing.'

Now almost as he spoke, there came some sudden outcry from the men inside the slave-hut; a cry like 'Stop him; quick; look out; he's free. Look out.'

It was a sudden alarm; when most of the hands were in siesta. I heard someone running away from the farther end of the slave-hut. I could not see who it was since the hut was between us, but instantly the sentries fired; and with yells and curses all the camp sprang to life. I darted into the slave-shed, where I found three men, all much scared, telling the slaves not to try that again. I saw that Deray was gone.

'Has a man escaped?' I asked.

I got no answer, for the camp was now running to arms, finding a gun here, but no powder; or a horn there and no gun. However, a dozen shots were fired. Then, with a shattering bang, some bright spirit fired a cannon, point-blank, into a tree. I now caught sight of Deray. He was in the lagoon. He had plunged in, had swum under water, and was now up for a breath; he was swimming strongly and well, whatever chain he wore. He dived again, as the men got ready to shoot; and now Pegg came running, swearing, having woken from his nap.

'What are you playing at?' he screamed. 'Get to the boats after him. Get the boats out. He's there. Don't shoot him. I won't have him shot. I'll teach him and the rest a lesson. Get to the boats.'

He struck, kicked, swore and stamped. The men dropped their guns and ran to the boats; but here they were stopped by Staggers.

'Keep all fast with the boats,' Staggers said. 'No, Captain Pegg. No boats, please, till we've had a look at the irons here. We may have the whole seventy running, if we don't mind.'

He set the tide flowing back to the slave-hut, where after much testing of irons, the frightened guards were told to tell their story. They were too scared to tell much, even if they knew much. Somehow, as they were loosing Deray a half instant, to get the rowser fixed, he struck them, right and left and was away. They had yelled; the sentries had fired; but he had dived and swum under

96

water, then gulped a breath and dived again. As far as men could tell, he had come ashore on the mainland among some bushes and was gone.

Pegg stamped and swore; he said he had a good mind to flog the guards for letting the man get away.

'It was nothing but your carelessness; nothing but your tomfool, pig-headed imbecility and damslam carelessness. What d'ye mean by letting him go?'

However, at this point Staggers came to say that no other would get away in a hurry.

'Don't talk to me,' Pegg cried. 'But for you stopping the hands at the boats, we'd have got that man and taught them all a lesson.' This was no doubt true, but did not mend the matter.

I had finished my work for the afternoon, and greatly longed for a walk, to see something of Africa and to stretch my legs. I was much too scared of being lost in the bush to venture far; still, a short walk would not lose me. I could keep beside the water all the way. I longed to get away from the company for a while and to be free from the tyranny of office.

I took a stick, as a guard against snakes, and went to the main gate, below the raised sentry-stand. I said to the sentries, 'I am going out for a walk. I shall be back from this same direction, so don't shoot me as I come in.'

'Never fear, sir,' they said, 'you go out; we'll watch out for you.'

I went out; and on going forth noticed at once that the comment of the sentries some hours before had been just. It was easily possible for enemies to creep up to within thirty yards of the fence utterly out of sight of even the sentries on the stands. I walked up the slope in front of the fence to make sure. It was only too sure. Men could creep through the forest to the top of the slope and there (themselves unseen) observe all the camp and what was happening in it. And, if the creepers-up were marksmen, they would be able to pick off any man in sight.

I pushed into the bush for a short way. I had heard how easy it is for white men to be lost in bush. I saw, then, why. Every yard of that mysterious wilderness was like every other yard of it. It was something endlessly repeated, a dark, thorny thing, a soft frondy thing, a green shiny thing, then another, then another, thorny, shiny or frondy, all a little taller than man, each a little confusing; all together baffling and fatal. I rattled with my stick among the bushes a good deal, from fear of snakes. I was now in the bush quite out of sight of the camp. Presently, I returned to the top of the slope and went back to the gate. I hailed the sentries to ask, had they heard me rattling the scrub?

They said no, they had heard nothing.

This troubled me, for if our sentries could not hear a noise wilfully made, they would certainly not hear stealthy enemies. I met Tulp near the officers' quarters, and told him that the camp was badly placed.

He said, 'I wouldn't worry. There's no one here. The beasts and the birds are just about as tame as if they'd never seen men. Besides, we shall be gone tomorrow, with any luck. Even if we were attacked, we've got the cohorns mounted. No savage will face cohorns.'

It was true that the murdering pieces and swivel guns had now been mounted all along our fence at intervals. They were loaded and primed. They contained scattering charges of pebbles, broken glass, old gun-flints, etc., etc. These and the bigger guns made a very strong defence. Still, I was uneasy. When I saw Pegg, I asked him if he felt anxious about the Matas. We were in their country; their hunting-parties might well be near by, and would perhaps have heard or seen us. He said that he had heard no sound and seen no sight of any Matas; that all the stories went, that the Matas were gone from those parts of the Coast, from dread of the M'gai; and that the next day he was going to explore the eastern side of the harbour for the M'gai. They would be coming from that quarter with their slaves, and could not be long delayed.

He was always rashly confident; his confidence now did not reassure me. Still, the older seamen, who had been many times on the Coast, did not seem to dread any attack.

Our men were now back from their fishing and were gathering to supper. They had built big fires to the seaward of each hut, so that the sea-wind, now setting in, might blow the smoke through the huts and keep away the mosquitoes; though indeed the night was striking in too cold for mosquitoes.

We supped in our tent to the seaward, with a sentry pacing outside. There was a novelty about it, which had a charm for me. We had a dinner of fresh fish and stewed samberries; a rare feast, in fact, however rudely served. After supper, our crew started singing their old country ballads and tales of pirates. They were fond of singing and sang well. We went out to listen to them.

I know not how long we listened; the time passed so sweetly, with song after song, usually full of feeling. One song there was about a great storm and the unhappy crew of the *Elizabeth*; it was very long, and had a chorus. It meant very much to our seamen. They sang it at the beginning and half an hour later sang it again. It made a great impression on me. I remember it to this day, it had such a strange, melancholy tune.

It was dark all about us, with intensely bright stars in heaven. The noise of the distant surf had deepened with the darkness; its melancholy roar filled the seaward side of the night. Inland strange owls were crying; and some unknown creature, bird or beast, made a chacking, shrill noise. In the trees a kind of cricket was trilling. In the forest quite near us, twigs fell, with the sound of footsteps; creatures rustled, and sometimes cried. Our sentries paced to and fro, with occasional hails:

'Port watch hut . . . Guard awake . . . Matches burning. All's well.' 'Slave-house guard awake . . . Matches burning. All's well,' etc.

Presently, the singers took up for the third time their song of the *Elizabeth*, and sang it through to the end. Then they broke up from their song. We saw their dark figures passing away to throw more wood on the fires and wrap their blankets round them. And now that the camp was silent save for the sentries, I heard a sad, low song, hummed rather than sung, among the slaves. I had heard this song before from them, for they crooned it in the hold sometimes. Now they took it up together at first very gently, then in a pitch so strange that it seemed to fill the night. I could not help but listen. It was so sad, so plaintive, so uncanny. I stood listening to it for some time. Presently, I found that Tulp was beside me. He had been stealing round to see if the sentries were on their feet.

'What is that song?' I asked. 'I've often heard them sing it. What does it mean?'

'It's only a silly native song,' he said. 'It is only:

"'No more, never any more, never again,
   No more fish in the river.'"

Pegg came out from his berth and walked across to the slave-shed. 'Stop him dam noise,' he called.

They stopped, then, for a little while, but they soon

began again. Quite suddenly they stopped on the words 'no more fish,' or the words which Tulp said meant 'no more fish.' It was just as though all the strings of the instrument had snapped; they broke off, and there was silence. As I was made uneasy about this, I went to the slave-shed, which was lit by two candle-lanterns and by the fitful firelight. I saw that all the slaves were awake and in a state of great excitement. A long row of eyes gleamed at me. I asked one of my friends if anything were wrong; if I could perhaps do anything for them? He said no, unless I could tell him how long they would be there. I said I did not know; it depended on the sailors. I asked the guards if anything had disturbed the slaves. He said he judged they were all upset at being on the shore again and having their friend get away. 'But *they* can't get away,' he said. 'I've been over their shackles twice. What with them and the rowser they'll lie where they're put. Children act the same way sometimes, when they get excited. I wish I'd half their chance to sleep. But these lads, doing nothing all day, haven't the same wish to sleep as we have.'

'Neither the wish, nor perhaps the power,' I said. 'They aren't on a bed of ease.' I knew from Newgate how hard it is for a prisoner to sleep at any time.

I, too, was a prisoner there, with little hope of release. I was reasonably free from fear of arrest until we made the Indies; say, two months or a little more. But when we made the Indies the whole dreadful fear would have to be faced again. Well, it was two months away. I might die long before that time came.

And yet, much as I dreaded the future, I did not want to die. I lay down in my hammock in my tent with a lively fear upon me of being killed quite soon where I was. I was lying down to sleep in Africa, and did not feel at all safe. I had heard of lions which would steal in to eat men in their beds; of bats which sucked the blood of men, of crocodiles which left the rivers at night and prowled ashore, of hyaenas which bit away the faces of sleeping men, and of terrible snakes which crushed or bit. All these were in Africa. Besides these were the savages, the Matas, who ate white men, the M'gai who killed Matas.

I felt again intensely how easy it would be for the savages to creep up close to our camp unheard and un-suspected. Perhaps even now a troop of blacks armed with great spears might be within forty yards of me. Then the thought came to me, had the slaves learned some-how by some savage signal unperceived by us, that their friends were at hand? Had Deray got to their friends and sent in a message somehow? I was uneasy. It was foolish to hate life as I did and yet to dread death. Man is foolish in that way very often. I could not sleep for my anxieties and fears. Just when they were beginning to exhaust me into sleep, I began to feel the cold, which struck from underneath me into my back, so that I shivered and ached no matter how I crouched. At last I turned out and went to the tent door.

In the stillness of the night, the noises of the river and the surf, the wash, gurgles and ripple, the great lapsing roar, were very near and plain. The old moon was aloft now, very bright. Owls were cruising near us. I had heard that natives imitate the cries of owls, and signal to their fellows with owls' cries. Were these owls birds or natives? Fish leaped and splashed in the lagoon. All the bush was alive with little patterings and scutterings; there were brayings, trumpetings and coughing lowings as beasts came to drink or called their fellows. Wherever I looked, there were fireflies gleaming and fading; up above were great stars and what was left of the moon. I was comforted by the peace of the night and went back to my bed.

This next day was a hard day for the crew. They had the task of clearing all the weights in the *Albicore* to the side, so as to heave the injury out of water. When the work had been done, it proved to be useless; the carpenters could not reach the leak. When this was known, more weights were landed. The ship's berth was changed and preparations made for heaving her right down upon her side. There was a very good place for this, close to where she lay. The preparations used nearly everybody all day long. When the hands came ashore for the night, it was already dark; they had been at it since before dawn, and were nearly worn out. There was no singing that second night. Indeed, it came on to blow and rain, so that we were all wet and wretched, as well as weary. The one good thing about the night was the storm. I had heard on board that savages never attack during a storm. I felt a kind of security from the statement, though I know now that it was false.

The next morning broke brightly and warmly, to bring us cheer. Tulp contrived to persuade Staggers to persuade Pegg to give all hands a two-hour siesta that day, for indeed the hands needed it. Pegg needed it himself, and, therefore, granted it. I thought that I would walk down the river towards the sea, find a good fishing-place and do a little fishing. I could not possibly lose myself in that direction. The Sailmaker lent me a frame and line with some hooks; I cut some salt beef for bait, and set out.

After about ten minutes' walking, going leisurely, I saw the sea blazing in front of me, with no sail in sight nor any trace of man. After a minute or two more, I came to a deep little gully or water-course running directly across my path between myself and the sea. It was a place

of great enchantment, covered with flowers over which
bees were busy. In the bottom were many big tumbled
rocks, past which a little river ran. I went down and found
on the mud of the river-brim a little black dug-out canoe
upside down at my feet. She was plainly not new. I poked
her over with a branch; she was half-full of red mud. I
tipped her out and scraped her, then lifted her to the
water and washed her clean. Here indeed was a treasure;
here was a boat in which I could explore where I wished.
She had been skilfully hewn and then neatly burned from
a trunk of light hard wood. She had a little low thwart
and had been smeared within and without with a black
gum which had hardened like cement. This was scratched
and cracked in places, but in good order. Better still, her
paddle was tightly lashed to her seat with a thong of hide.

Perhaps nothing in my life had given me greater
pleasure than this finding of the canoe. It made me in
some sort a king over my destiny. With her I could, if I
wished, go off into the lagoon, up the rivers, or among
the islands, and finish with the *Albicore* for ever. I could
set up somewhere as a hermit, living alone on fish and
fruits, perhaps more happily than I had been able to live
with men. I had but to thrust into the reeds among the
islands to be hidden from sight; they could never find me.
If I were to be sold as a slave or taken as a felon directly I
reached the Indies, might it not be wise to escape now?
I might hide in Edmond Quichet's cave; presently I
might perhaps meet the M'gai or the Matas. One white
man with some little skill as a doctor might be received
into the tribe. I might live as a savage thenceforth and
marry a savage; go native like Billy and have a tusk
through my nose. I dallied with the thought awhile; and
decided that I had pledged myself to be the doctor to the
Albicore; it might be that I might save many lives by stay-

ing with the slaves. I could make their lot a very little lighter by staying; I ought to stay. None the less, I picked up the boat and hid her carefully in a hole among the rocks. I meant to go exploring in her.

After that I went fishing near the beach and did well. When a man is fishing with success, he pays little attention to the passing of time. I fished for a long time, much longer than I thought. I returned to find my friend the Sailmaker, who was looking very grave about something.

'I beg you pardon, Doctor,' he said, 'but may I ask if the Captain said anything to you about the warning?'

'I've been out of camp, fishing,' I said. 'What warning?'

He looked at me very closely. Three or four hands had gathered, each with an anxious face.

'Why, sir,' he said, 'after the knock-off time, this afternoon, some of us went for fresh water to the spring; that would be about three o'clock or so. When we got there, we found what we didn't like.'

'What was that?'

He handed to me something that I did not at first recognize. On taking it and shaking it clear, I saw that it was a much-used native sling. The pouch of it was of soft leather, the strings, as I judged, of gut. It had been kept soft with oil.

'That's one of their slings, sir. I picked it up here. Look, sir; if you will but step with me, I will show you the place.'

It was but a step. I went with him. He showed me a place just above the spring where a dead, fallen tree-top lay. In among the grass, flowers and decayed wood was a sort of form, where a man had lain for some little time.

'That's the place, sir,' the Sailmaker said. 'That's where the sling lay. If you will sniff the ground, sir, you'll sniff it was a native. The palm-oil's as strong as a badger, still. A savage was here, sir, looking right into the camp.'

'Didn't the sentries in the boxes see him?'

The men looked uncomfortable and angry, as they always did, when they had cause to complain yet lacked the courage to do it. The Sailmaker fidgeted and then said, 'Captain Pegg had the sentries at work, sir, most of the knock-off time. They weren't in the boxes, or they might have seen the man.'

'What were they doing, then?' I asked.

'They were tidying up the Captain's tent, sir.'

'Did you take it to the Captain?'

'Mr Tulp did, sir.'

'Do you know what the Captain said?'

'He said one of the hands had been trying to be funny.'

With some misgiving, lest this explanation should prove to be the right one, I asked Pegg what he thought about it.

'Think about it?' he said. 'I think one of the hands slept there in the knock-off time, so as to have the fire-smoke over him, to keep away the flies. He had the sling all ready, in case he was caught. He was going to say, he'd seen a savage there, and took his sling away. He knows I've given strict orders, about not sleeping out of camp. That's all it was. He was nearly caught, so he left the sling and ran for it. Now, of course, he daren't own up. I know this coast, and I know seamen. Everyone must know by this time that this lagoon is deserted; not a M'gai nor a Mata within a hundred miles.'

That night we were in the last of the moon. When I woke, the moon was pretty bright, which told me that it was near morning. I felt uneasy somehow and scared. I thought at once of the warning, and wished that I had not heard of it. I sat there, listening for I knew not what, but repeating the French phrase, '*Soyez en garde.*' Now it may have been a prompting, it may have been my half-mad, nervous touchiness, but I felt too uneasy to stay where I was. I felt that something was wrong. So I crept out into the camp and listened.

The fires were smouldering and gave out some warmth still. I could hear the slow steps of the night-guards up and down, the distant noise of the surf, the nearer gurgle and whimper of the river; the cry of the owls and the occasional splash as a fish leaped. The forest wavered, sighed and creaked a little, twigs fell and creatures scuttled, the fireflies shone out and disappeared. I heard snores and heavy breathings from the sleeping watch. Some of the slaves cried out a little and clinked their irons as they shifted. I moved out a little towards the slave-shed, and ran into Tulp, who was half-asleep leaning against a post.

He said, 'It's a cold morning. It might be January, at home.'

I asked, if the slaves were all right. He said, 'They were, when I came on deck,' and lapsed into his huddled position again.

At the entrance to the slave-shed, I found one of the guards fast asleep; the other was toasting himself a ship's biscuit on which a piece of fat salt pork was melting.

He said, 'They're all right, Doctor. They're all awake. I've just been in.'

I said, 'I suppose it's the cold that wakes them?'

He said, 'It is cold. But these black fellows always wake at this time. It's their danger time.'

I could not think of going back to bed. I was too well awake. I went round the camp and spoke to some of the sentries. On the eastern side of the camp, I saw that the sky above the Peaks was beginning to shew colour; it would very soon be morning. I waited till it was rather lighter; then I thought that I would go down the river to my fishing-place, to catch fish for breakfast. So I took the fishing frame and bait, and told the sentries to let me out and not to shoot me on my return. They said they would not shoot if I would bring them some fish: I said I would certainly share what I caught with them. One of them said, 'It's a lovely morning for a bit of fishing': it was. As I left camp, I heard the cook and cook's mates roused to prepare what our men called 'Soup-o,' a sort of hot drink given before they turned-to. There was no sight nor sound anywhere that might have threatened or suggested danger: none. It was one of the most peaceful, lovely mornings I have seen.

I had some little anxiety, I admit, as the first part of the way was dark with bush. However, I soon came into sight of the sea, with lines of breakers away on my right and the Peaks against coloured sky on my left. Out to the west a long roller caught the light so that a kind of slow arrow of fire ran right along it; that was very beautiful. At this moment, the ghost-birds, as our men called them, a kind of big white owl, began floating past me to their roosts. I think that they had been getting shell-fish or something of the kind on the rocks by the sea.

As an idle man will, I turned to watch one of these birds as it floated past me. It was making for the forest near the camp. As I watched, it seemed to me that something gleamed in the scrub in that direction. It was not a swarm of fireflies, nor a blink of our camp-fire. It was too far to the left to come from the camp. It looked to me not quite like the flash of a lantern, but more like a mirror throwing back a ray. Bright metal might have done it. It startled me but did not seem to startle the ghost-birds; they kept their course and dived into the wood. 'It was some shiny leaf,' I told myself, and went on to find and launch my canoe.

I set forth in her, going cautiously, for I had not been in a boat at all like her. Soon, I was in the big river, standing across to one of the big wooded islands. Waterways stretched among these islands into romantic distances. The great trees rose up, with their tops in colour and often flaming with flowers. I was enchanted with what I saw.

All the last half-hour had been noisy with the birds and monkeys, who scream for joy of the morning with shrill, harsh, exhilarating cries. Suddenly from the direction of the camp there came quite clearly across the water the yell of savages, and shot after shot. The yell swelled up at once into a rage and storm of battle, in the midst of which there came shots, the loud bangs of cohorns and many a scattered volley of muskets and small arms. 'My good Lord,' I cried, 'the slaves have risen, or the Matas have come. I must get back.'

But getting back was not so easy. I had come easily to where I was, being helped by the set of the current and guided by the breaking of the sea. But on trying to get back I found a network of waterways, each exactly alike, with the same red flood-wrack, the same mixture of giant trees, soft brush, flaming flowers and tangled creepers on its shores, nothing to shew me which was mine, and each one with a current not easy to stem. I took two which had little current, and soon found that each led nowhere. All the time, as I paddled, I heard shouts, yells and shots, now loud, now shut from me by jungle. I had hoped to hear the roar of the ship's guns; I did not hear them. I did not hear the cohorns banging again; I could not hear any ordered cheer such as white men use. As I went, the shots became fewer; such yells as came to me were those of savages.

Sometimes in a dream I have tried to hurry and found my feet tangled or glued or hobbled. In my paddling to the battle I found my way checked. I had not got into the way of paddling against a stream; the boat needed a rigid paddler, and I had not that habit of rigidity. Often I took a turn which took me from my way.

Still, I went on, and at last heard no more shots; only yells; then a sudden sharp volley and a fearful yelling and screeching; and now the smell of burnt powder came down the wind to me; and I could smell the wafts of camp-fire smoke and the slave-house. Then, suddenly, I heard a crackle of fire.

I was now, as I judged, near the camp, but shut from it by a part of an island and the breadth of the river. I drew my canoe ashore, and made my way through the tangle across the island to find out what was happening. The tangle was all criss-crossed with lianas, and I dreaded to make much noise. All the time, the smell of burnt powder drifted down upon me; presently, I saw driving smoke and wafts of burning stuff blowing with it. There was no more shooting, but the noise of rejoicing in the camp was devilish. I had no doubt now, that the camp had been surprised and taken. What of the whites? Where were they?

I must say, that I had not much liked the *Albicores*, but they were my comrades, the only ones I had; my lot was their lot; I was in this adventure with them. My heart was sick for them.

There were some thorny bright bushes, very thick, with yellow flowers on them, very fragrant. They made a sort of wall to my island at one point, with a few little gaps through which I could peer. I was at one of these gaps, when I saw savages moving on the opposite shore, down the river from the camp. A great many men were in the party; many had guns, spears and shields; but many were our naked slaves, some of them not yet wholly freed from wrist and ankle-irons. All were in a state of savage glee; they yelled and hopped; some of them had the heads of white men in their hands; they played at catch with them and danced. I could recognize the heads; oh, horror and terror. And for all their glee, they were intent on blood; they were searching and sometimes sniffing the ground for tracks; they knew that they had not killed all the whites and were looking for more. Then I saw that one of them saw a trail and pointed it to the rest. It was my trail, no doubt; I had gone to my canoe on just that line. Half-a-dozen of them gave tongue, like dogs, and leaped into a run along the tracks, straight to the rocks where I took the canoe. 'Ah,' I thought, 'they'll know that I'm in a boat, and will search the islands for me. But they cannot have killed all the hands. They had only half a dozen heads. The rest will be in the ship.'

The party went on towards the sea, out of sight from where I was. After half an hour, they returned, going back to the camp. They were still dancing and shouting. One of them had two white heads, which he clashed together as cymbals while he danced. In the camp itself, the fire had smouldered down. I judged that it had been one of the sails over the huts. Plenty of people were yelling in the camp, but no gun was fired from the ship. I feared that all the whites had been killed.

I lay where I was for some time, till I could stand the suspense no more. I crept from my cover back to my boat, in which I softly paddled away. After a while, I landed again, and crept under cover to a point from which I could see both the ship and the site of the camp. The ship lay on her side still; no men were on her; the camp was full of dark figures moving about; the huts had had their roofs burnt off; the smoke was still blowing about. Further up the shore, some more savages moved. What shocked me most was the fact that the *Albicore*'s big boats were still on the beach, just where they had lain the night before. No man of them could have escaped by water. I could only conclude that a great might of Matablancos or M'gai had charged the camp while all hands were at 'soup-o,' and killed everybody before they could get to weapons or to the boats. I could see no white man anywhere. All that I could distinguish across the lagoon were savages.

I had had fine thoughts, as I have said, of joining the savages and becoming one of them. The memory of that warrior dancing to the clashing skulls put this kind of plan right out of my head. I was sick with terror, shocked with horror and blank with despair. Still, after a time, I said, 'I must get away. I must down into the midst of these islands and hide.' So I crept into my boat and put forth again away from those scenes. I paddled down strange channels, among the forest and the creepers, taking any turn which seemed to lead away from the savages, till at last I felt that I could do no more, but must lie-up and think.

When I came to a stony place, where I could land, as I supposed, without leaving many traces, I crept ashore and carried my boat to a space under a tree. There I lay and quaked, a lot too scared even to think of fishing for my dinner. You will ask why Dead Ned's paltry half-hung life should be so precious to his silly soul? Often, in the past few weeks, I had longed and longed to die, and so be out of it. Now that I had an excellent chance of dying I shrank from it. Well, when a man 'longs to die,' he hopes to do it gently, without pain, from some quiet failure of the heart; he shrinks from being slowly cooked at a fire, with little bastings of palm-oil, and would rather not be eaten afterwards.

I told myself that I was a lot too near the camp still, and had better find a covert further from it, and this at once, before the savages came fishing in the boats. So I put forth in my boat, and crept from waterway to waterway, till I found a place that seemed quiet enough. I put out my line and fished and caught some good fish. Then just as I was at point to eat one of these raw, a big bird flew up from her nest close to me with a cry that must have told any savage within half a mile that a white man was somewhere there. I was sick with the scare, and put forth away at once, by these alleys in the forest, so dripping and dark. Often the awful flowers seemed faces leaning out to bite me; often what I took to be a dangling creeper turned out to be a waiting snake. Now that I was away from the nest, I told myself that I had been a fool not to take the bird's eggs. Then I came to a dark place in the gully of a backwater.

It was the best place that I had seen hitherto, and I took it, because I was too tired and scared and sick to go further. I pulled my boat ashore, and pushed her under cover. Then I hid myself as well as I could and ate some of my raw fish. It was not a dainty dish, but I was hungry and felt much better for the food.

After that, I fell asleep and slept like a dead log of a tree. It was coming to be dark when I woke. I heard a distant shot or two from where I judged the camp would be, but no other noise of men. Soon the gloom of the forest deepened, and with a roar and a whirr the birds began to come back to the tree-tops high above me. For half-an-hour the flights gathered among the islands, and then their myriads settled and sparred, screamed, pecked, arranged themselves and then shook the whole colony out of arrangement, and at last fell silent. I muffled myself up in my coat as well as I could, and settled down to sleep. I had expected to be eaten by the mosquitoes; but with the sunset, it struck too cold for them to bite and for me to sleep. I had to sit up and chafe my limbs and fingers, all the time quaking at the noises round me, all the forest so stealthy, all the waters so full of threat. There were strange things, owls or jackals, screaming in the night not very far from me. Sometimes, the note of the screech made me wonder if they were not some of the *Albicore*'s crew gone mad from terror, and wandering there. It was bad enough when it was dark; but the last of the moon rose in her appointed time, with a white light which made the darkness uncertain; and terrifying. That night seemed to me to last a year; however, all things end; that ended; the treacherous beasts padded home, the birds woke, yelled, wrangled, flapped, and at last, with roar after roar of wings, went away into the light. Warmth came, to take the aches from my bones. I caught a fish and ate it raw; the world did not seem so full of evil.

I found that I was about two miles from the camp, and able to see right across the lagoon to it from where I was. The *Albicore* lay on her side, hove down. A little wisp of smoke rose up from her side. It thrilled me to see it. It looked as though her men were burning the barnacles from her, which, of course, would shew that they were back at work on her. After long watching, longing for a glass, I judged that it was nothing of the kind. Someone had set fire to her and the fire was not doing well. I tried in vain to see if anyone were in camp; it was too distant, and the bush made too dark a background.

Nearly all that day, I lay in cover watching the site of the camp, seeing no sign of life there, and no boat plying.

The smoke, whatever it was, ceased to go up from the hull; the fire was out. Late in the day, some great flights of black-and-white birds, of the kind the Portuguese call Dominicans, flew past me straight towards the camp. The light was very good and strong. It seemed to me that the birds went straight to the camp, alighted there, and after a time rose thence; but it was too far away; I could not be sure. What if the savages had gone? I knew that the Matas were a race of warriors and hunters, not likely to stay long in one place. But would they not be staying here now? Might they not be mustering near the lagoon in order to fall on these M'gai, who were going to take their hunting-grounds?

Far as the eye could see, it was their country. Their settlements might be within half a mile of me, for all that I could tell. The place was vast and blind; anything might be round the corner. When I had left camp to go fishing, a war-party, certainly two hundred strong, must have been lying almost within touch or scent of us, unsuspected by anyone. Not unsuspected by the slaves, perhaps: no; somehow the slaves knew; certainly they knew; why, they were all awake. Who could doubt that word had come to them that their friends were near? I had no doubt of it. The Admiral always said that savages had some way of speech which the whites have not. 'They cry like birds, or like bats, and understand what is meant; they send out whispers across the jungle, and the whispers carry.' And at that moment, as I thought these things, I was scared, because close to me as I lay I heard a voice whispering; someone was saying, 'Hush, hush. Listen, listen, never answer. Hush, hush, hush.' It was quite close to me, to my left. For an instant I was sure, that one of the crew had escaped and lay near me, and the joy of the thought was terrible. I crept towards the noise: it was a big turtle covering a clutch of eggs with her flippers in the hot lagoon sand.

When the light died, I crept out and took some of the eggs and ate them; I then burrowed myself a shelter in the hot sand, and found comfort in it. I slept better than I had slept since I left the ship.

When I woke, I looked towards the camp. It was now black midnight, with starlight dancing in the lagoon. In the camp there was a little red spark of fire, a one-man fire. Might it be, that one man had crept back, and now lived there? I remembered how Dr Copshrews had said, 'The healthiest place is where an epidemic has just ended.' Possibly the safest place here was where the murder had ended. Possibly more than one man was there; half the crew, perhaps. I watched that tiny light with longing. It grew no bigger; now and again it seemed to go out, as though someone had put more wood upon it. What if it were some poor wounded or sick man, sorely needing help? I was a physician, pledged to help the sufferer, and that the man yonder by the fire might be wounded or have a broken bone. In the end, I could not bear that thought; the darkness gave me a boldness that I lacked. I took my boat and drove forth in her. I meant to see what poor wretch it was that kept vigil there among the ruins.

The moon rose before I started; she gave some light to me. You may be sure, that I watched with all my eyes as I began to loiter down with the current. I saw now that the fire was not a camp-fire, no, but something like a pile of logs, that had been fired and left to burn itself out. One corner of it, or rather one big log of it, was now an ember, which glowed, and faded, smoked, and then sparkled with little flames.

I could see and hear jackals or wild dogs all about the

camp; they were yapping and scratching; certainly no man was there. I passed very close to the *Albicore*; she, too, was deserted, lying on her side. I drifted past her, quite close, with a pang in my heart.

After I had fallen well below the camp, I struck off to the nearest island and drew ashore. I ate some eggs, and took some sleep. When it was light, I found a place from where I could see into the camp. The dogs or jackals had gone, now, and the birds were feeding there without fear.

The boldest course is often the best; I paddled to the camp at once, and landed there. As I feared, the killing there had been complete, though already, the dogs, the vultures and the ants had removed the traces of death. The relics of the battle lay about; certain places had been much trodden. I judged that the camp had been taken by surprise and lost in a few minutes; and that then the survivors had fallen back on the boat, and had been killed there, in trying to launch her or defend her. The place was littered with rags, bits of clothing, and the loose grass slippers which the seamen plaited for themselves. I came upon a broken musket with a burst barrel; it had been loaded with repeated charges, full to the muzzle, by some crazy man. The crammed barrel, with many unexploded charges in it, had been blown from the stock. Part of a black-and-white shield lay near it. It looked as though it had been blown off at a gun-muzzle. Further up the beach I found a spearhead bent double by a bullet. However, Europe knows the wreck and mess of war too well for me to describe it further. With the wreck and the mess remained the haunting, that possessed the place, that terrible things had been done there, and human life torn from its strength too soon.

In the fighting, the long-boat had been shot through and through in twenty places; she had caught fire, from a linstock which was still in her; and someone had staved her with an axe. She was useless to me. The second boat or cutter had had a fire lighted in her; she was burned through, beyond any repair that I could make. The little skiff was gone.

I said, to myself, 'Now I will go on board the ship. It is just possible that someone is aboard her and still alive.'

The *Albicore* lay partly hove down upon her side. I had thought that I had seen her on fire; certainly, I had seen smoke coming from her. When I drew near her, I found that this fire had probably been accidental. She had had a mass of reed laid on her exposed side, ready for the burning off of her barnacles. When the camp huts burned in the battle, some burning flakes from them blew over her, lodged in the reeds and set fire to them. Some of them had burned, but the rest, being damp, had presently smouldered themselves out. A plank or two had been charred a little; nothing to hurt. It had rained that morning, and after so much heavy rain, the ship had not been dry enough to catch.

I clambered up to her deck with some difficulty, after tying my canoe. You will not guess with what anguish I went to the hatchways, and called 'Is anyone below there?' and waited for the reply which did not come. She was deserted, save for her rats, and silent, save for the gurgle of the water in her and the noise of creaking and moaning which no ship can ever be without.

I asked myself, 'Why have not the Matas burned the ship?' Even if they have not burned her, why have they not pillaged her? She has about her the only wealth they understand, much copper and abundant iron; and, of course, a great store of powder. Why have they left her unsacked? There must be some overwhelming reason; what was it?

Plainly, the warriors had been in a hurry to leave; WHY? Might it not be, that the enemies of the Matas, those M'gai of whom the tales had gone, were already at their borders? Billy had said that the M'gai, those terrible men, were coming to the Peaks. How would the M'gai treat Dead Ned, when they came upon him? Would they welcome a doctor with a letter to the Governor of the Carolinas, or would they fatten him on yam for a week, and then cook him in a pot with pepper-pods?

I crept cautiously to a port, from which I could look out for the enemy. I was reassured by what I saw. The blue, still lagoon bore no sign of man upon it. The birds seemed feeding everywhere, among the beaches and the trees, undisturbed; no men were about there. My eyes went everywhere, and then rested on something white, among the bushes of the nearest island. The white was the bow portion of the *Albicore*'s skiff. It was poking out of the thicket of water-brush, as though the rest of her had sunk. I could not understand how she could have got into that position. There she lay, seemingly tipped on her end, and held down by a weight in her stern, in quite shallow water. My heart leaped at the sight, for if I could salve the skiff, then I could, like Robinson Crusoe, take what I willed from the ship, and get away.

I went off to her in my canoe. She lay in the outermost of the fringe of scrub which grew in the water near the island. In my unstable canoe, I could not shake her clear. I could see, that she was held down by two or more bodies that lay across her stern-sheets, and that the weight of these had so pressed her down, that she had caught as she drifted underneath a bough of a snag, which now held her. I thought that if I had an axe and some seamen's tackles, I might free her. After some search in the ship, I found these, a small boarding axe, a block or two and a coil of light rope. With these I returned to the island. I landed, drew my canoe ashore, and began my task.

A seaman had told me, that if ever I were trying to save anything from the sea I ought to begin by getting a line to it, 'for then,' he said, 'it won't get away from you.' I remembered this, and began by making fast my line to the exposed part of the boat. Then, drawing the axe from the rope about my waist, I turned to set her free. I cut the boughs that held her down; and saw, as I did so, the crew she carried; and having seen, had to come ashore, sit down and weep. There were three dead bodies lying across her. One was Tulp; I know not who the others had been.

They had been shot or speared in the water, while trying to get into the floating skiff, had fallen across her, and had drifted down in her into the brush. I had liked Tulp; and was sick with grief for these men. You will say that half the grief was for myself; grief often is; but it is none the less grief, and more than one can bear.

I hove the boat free, and saw her grisly crew slide from her. I had then to wade out to her to tip her over and float her, and drag her ashore. I was a glad and a very weary man when I had her safe. I determined to lose no time, but to pillage the ship at once. So, towing my canoe, I set forth and came alongside the *Albicore*.

My wants were all simple: food, shelter, warmth, the means of making fire, some drugs, weapons, powder, tools, lines for fishing, a few pots, pans, a spar or two, a small cask or two for storing water and provisions, a small boat-sail, a little tar, light rope and so forth. I told myself that this was my last chance of getting anything. After this I should be like the savage, who has to make what he needs for himself. But I had a terror of the blacks. At any moment, as I knew, they might come swarming down on me. At last, I clambered into my loaded boat, and shoved away, with my loaded canoe in tow. All the five miles of lagoon, all the forest, all the islands, and the great Peaks above them, seemed to be full of eyes staring at me, to see which way I was going. My way was to a channel where I should no longer be seen. It was not far to that point; and certainly, as far as I could see, I was alone; utterly alone.

I had not rowed with my tow more than a hundred yards, when there came a loud snapping noise from the *Albicore*. I looked up at her, and saw the ends of her heaving-down ropes flying upwards into the air. An instant later, she righted herself in a violent roll. She rolled violently half-a-dozen times, then steadied to an even keel. 'Now she will soon sink,' I said to myself. 'The plank has been partly stripped; I shall get nothing more from her at all.'

Just before I pulled into the gloom of the channel which was to hide me, I noticed the Peaks away to the east of me. I thought, 'Why not go to Edmond Quichet's cave? Why not make that my home? There is shelter and water there, so the Admiral always said.'

With fishing-lines and hooks, I knew that I should never lack food in that place. Fruit of sorts grew wild there in most of the year. I could maintain myself surely, alone.

I asked myself, was it not better to be alone, than to be with men? What had I found among the whites, except monstrous injustice and cruelty? What should or could I expect from the blacks except the same? If I lived alone in the wilderness, it might not be much fun; nay, I knew now that it would be terrible; but better than anything that I could expect from men.

When I had reached a seclusion in the heart of a cluster

of islands, I drew ashore, unloaded and also beached my boats, then ate, drank, wrapped myself up and slept heavily.

I awoke refreshed and, determined to go on to the cave, if indeed, it existed, or ever had existed. First I had to patch the boat with rope-yarns and tar. And when I did start, I had to keep in the network of channels among the islands, going now north, now south, and only getting to the east at lucky times. Still, I dared not go openly by the lagoon. Even in my fear, the beauty of those water-channels touched me to the heart. It was strange to me that so marvellous a place was not inhabited, save by the fishing-birds and the fish and the snakes. Theirs were the only eyes that watched me, so far as I could tell. I rowed slowly on, with pads in my rowlocks to keep them from grunting to the stroke, and the westering sun sometimes glimpsed in the tree-tops to guide me.

A great many people write that suffering is good for people, that it strengthens their moral fibres, and so forth. I never find that the writers of this rubbish seek out suffering for their own good, or relish it when it comes to them. It had not been good for me; I was ill. As I rowed along the channels, edging my way through them towards the east, I was sure that a lot of people were on both shores of the stream, talking behind my back. They were all talking in a mutter about me, saying, 'Here comes Dead Ned. This is the man who was hanged. Here he comes; he will soon be taken by the M'gai, who will skin him and rub lime-juice on him and eat him. But what matter? It is only Dead Ned.'

I tell you that I was sure of these voices. Often, I turned round to see who was there; but I would only see the channel, with the trailers drooping; here and there a splash of light; here and there butterflies; sometimes dragon-flies or gaudy birds; and sometimes a fallen tree, which forced me to go back to find a new way. As my eyes grew more used to the forest tangle, I began to think that I saw figures in the half-darkness flitting away whenever I turned my head. When I became sure of these, I thought they were M'gai. Of course, they were only birds; the mutter of their speech was the flutter of their wings; they were rising up and going twenty yards forward whenever I drew near; little flocks of them on both sides. As they went, incredible multitudes of little caterpillars dropped to the earth or water to avoid them; and the fish rising at these made a kind of whisper. At times I scared away strange beasts, which looked at me and then seemed to fade into the jungle.

Then, quite suddenly, my channel ended in a forest of reeds. They were ten or twelve feet tall, these reeds, and grew in water not less than another ten feet deep, a crystal-clear water, quite other than that river to the west. The stems of the reeds were pale yellow, and built, as it were, in joints of about a foot long. They threw out long spear-headed leaves of a pale blue, a pale green, a bright silver-grey, or all these at once. The leaves were all in movement like the leaves of an aspen; they fluttered like myriads of butterflies. Little birds ran about and flicked among them. The birds were as exquisite as the leaves; for they were pale blue and green and silver-grey, and had tiny scarlet top-knots. There were hundreds of them, and in the peace of the reeds they twittered with tiny sweet cries. They had no fear of me, but I had some fear that I might scare them away in a flock and betray my coming.

The reeds rustled, shivered, bent and closed in upon me, so that their beauty made the entire world. I could not row, and the water was too deep to pole. I laid in my oars and very quietly and cautiously pulled the boat forward by the reeds. We slid thus slowly along, till presently I was aware that I was out of my channel between islands, in a more open space, where the reeds were even taller and thicker in the bright sunlight. I was shut in by them, but knew that on my right hand I was under the Peaks. After a time, I saw through the reed-stems a greater brightness beyond me. Very quietly I drew the boat towards it till I could see into a still, clear pond in which some exquisite white cranes were wading. Just across the pond the red Peak arose. It was the very Peak of the picture in the Admiral's room. There, just as the Admiral had said, was a tiny natural boat-harbour of rocks. This was the place. The Admiral had come to this spot; now here was I, his heir, succeeding to his inheritance.

In all that space of lagoon and islands I could see no mark of men. I drew out one oar, and using it as a paddle slowly moved into the harbour. Once the Admiral had landed there; now I landed. I drew the boat to the rocks and tied her fast. 'Now,' I said to myself, 'now I will see Edmond Quichet's cave.'

It was drawing towards the last hour of the daylight when I set forth up the scree. If you ask what my feelings were, I should say a kind of mixture of stunned terror and stupid wonder. It was all something of a nightmare, that yet might become something of a dream.

In a little while, having climbed to a point of vantage, I stopped and looked behind me, over the lagoon, spread out like a mat. The *Albicore* was out of sight, behind an island. I could see the sea, now, clearly away to my left, beyond all the network of islands and channels. The birds were beginning to come in from the sea. In the west, the sky was reddening and the sun drooping down into the red. Away to the west and north, the forest spread in great rolls, with never any sight of man.

It was not wise to linger, for I felt that if I could see all this expanse, a clear-sighted savage anywhere in that field might see me. I went on, therefore, and soon stepped out of the fragrant bush into a gully where the very grass was scanty and no bush grew.

Up above me, very near me on my left, the Peak rose up, much as a vast red spire might rise from a tower. A hawk was cruising about the top. Something in the movement of the bird and the angle at which I had to hold my head, to look at it, made the Peak seem toppling and toppling to the point of toppling over on to me. And when I looked from it to my right, there up above me were three other Peaks, each like a great alligator standing on its tail and looking at me with a smile. I tell you, they all seemed alive. Remember, that I was not too sane, after my last few days.

The gully suddenly deepened, so that I walked, as it were, in a trench, shut in by a great rampart, made of that red shale or clay (I know not what to call it), which glistened with wet and seemed to have the power to keep off any plant. It was liker a nearly dry red paint than anything else. Trickles of water made shiny tracks all over it.

Well, this gully went up, curving out towards the south; then in its curve it swept round towards the east. I followed along it, with my eyes alert for any snakes or tracks, and my ears keen for any noise of men. All the time, I had my stupid wonder, that I was here, where the Admiral had been. It was not a long climb, though the slope was steep. For an instant I thought I heard voices. I stopped, drew a pistol and cocked it. The noise was not speech, but running water just round the bend ahead. 'I'm near,' I said. 'That's the brook the Admiral mentioned. It runs through the cave.' I was very thirsty and longed for a drink of it.

Quite suddenly, the gully fell away. I was there. I was on a little level grassy court. On the right was a low earth bank, three or four feet high, with an amazing view over the sea and the Coast, and far-away islands. On my left was the Peak, towering up towards a blaze of little clouds in mid-heaven. The grassy court was full of flowers. A brook of abundant water flowed across it and through a gap in the bank down a sheer cliff to the lagoon. The brook ran from a cave, which made a tall triangular doorway into the red cliff of the Peak. I had no doubt that I was outside Edmond Quichet's cave. I stood still and called, 'Is anyone there?'

On the instant, three white men, each carrying a spear, appeared at the cave door and looked at me with wonder. The biggest and most stalwart of them, an old, erect, very noble-looking man, with long hair not yet much touched with grey, was Edmond Quichet; the others were young fellows. I would have known Quichet anywhere from that little portrait and the Admiral's description, 'He was unlike anybody else.'

All three were excited at my coming. Edmond Quichet called, '*C'est toi, donc, Raoul.*' The others said, '*Mais non. Ce n'est pas Raoul.*' One of them called, '*Qui êtes vous?*'

The other ran to the bank, looked at the sea and the lagoon, and said, '*Non. Pas de vaisseau.*'

'*Dites,*' said Edmond Quichet. '*Vous êtes de France?*'

'*Non,*' I said. '*Pas de tout.*'

I dropped my pistol to the ground. Also, I held up both my hands to show that I meant no ill, and stood so for an instant, while the three looked at me. Then Edmond Quichet held out his hand to me, for me to shake. There never was anyone like him, surely, for swift decision. Not many men could have decided at so swift a glance that I was harmless. I was unwashed, unshaved, and had a look of having been in the jungle for some nights, and of having been a felon for months. I went straight up to him, shook his hand and said, '*M. Quichet, n'est ce pas?*'

'Yes,' he said, speaking good English, and looking at me with a searching gaze and much bewilderment. 'You are not from France?'

'No', I said, 'from England.'

With some amazement, and, as I thought, disappointment, he asked, 'Where is your ship? What are you? Are you in a slaver?'

'Yes,' I said. 'I am a doctor. The rest are all killed by the Matas.'

'Are you hurt, then?' he asked.

I said, 'No. But I saw them dancing with the heads.'

I began to weep at that, in a silly way. He was very gentle to me.

Presently, he asked, 'How do you know me?'

'I come from Admiral Cringle,' I said.

He looked at me with more bewilderment, and said, 'But come in, then.' He took me by the arm to lead me into the cave. As we entered, a big snake, with a kind of knob upon his head, slid out of the door beside me. 'Never fear,' Quichet said. 'He is harmless. That is Hannibal. We call him from Cringle's ship. He is invaluable here; he keeps down our mice, which would otherwise plague us.'

I entered the cave with that same stupid wonder; here I was, at that very cave from which the Admiral had brought the painting. I had the feeling that I had been there before, and that I knew it all from of old.

It was just as I had imagined; big, cool, light (from gashes in the rock), dry, too, in spite of the brook. A fire upon a hearth burned clearly, sending up into the cave a little very fragrant smoke. There were beds for four, slung, native fashion, from frames and posts driven into the ground. There was an arm-rack, with spears in it.

'If you can talk,' he said, 'please answer me these things: they are very important. When did you sail? What was the news from France when you sailed?'

I told him that we had had a very slow passage and could give him no recent news; but that all my latest news of France had been of great upheaval and disorder.

'When you left England,' he said, 'what was the opinion about the French trouble? That it would end?'

'No. That it would grow worse. The report went at Monos Grandes that no French ships are on the Coast this season.'

'I fear it,' he said.

He walked swiftly to the door of the cave and rapidly told the young men all that I had said, that no ship would be likely to come from France. He returned to me and asked my pardon for leaving me. He seemed much distressed by what I had said. He brooded over it for a minute, while I looked about me and marvelled.

'Here I am in the cave. This is Edmond Quichet himself. I am here talking with him. Whatever it is that troubles him, it is something overwhelming.'

However, he was one who rapidly judged of situations and of what could be done in them. He turned suddenly to me, with an infinite gentleness.

'Forgive me,' he said. 'I am not asking about you. You seem in sad distress. You say that all your crew have been killed by the Matas? When was this?'

'I can't think,' I said miserably. 'It was yesterday or the day before, or the day before that.'

'Where? Here in the lagoon?'

'Yes; far over there to the west.'

'What Matas killed your men?'

'Hundreds of them attacked us. We had some sixty Matas slaves. One of them got away and I suppose brought the others. I was out fishing at the time and so escaped. I've been hiding ever since.'

'I do not understand,' he said, 'what brought you to look for slaves at the Seize Pics?'

'We were told that the M'gai were bringing slaves here in numbers, and would be camped here with the slaves.'

'Who told you that?'

'A white man, a trader, William Crackers. He said that they would certainly be here with slaves, because they wanted powder for one of their wars.'

He pondered this; it was plainly important news to him.

'Did this trader, Crackers, say that the M'gai were short of powder?'

'He said, "They want all the powder they can get."'

He thought for a little while; then put his troubles from him to consider mine. He looked at me with the bewilderment that had been upon his face when he first saw me.

'Tell me,' he said, 'you say you come from Admiral Cringle. He was Captain when I knew him. How is the Admiral?'

'He is dead,' I said.

Again he seemed bewildered. 'You will forgive all my rude questions,' he said. 'You say you come from the Admiral Cringle, who is dead. Yet you come as a doctor in a slave-ship. That is strange to me. But, perhaps you come as a student? Many young men seek to see the World; are not you very young?'

'Yes,' I said. 'I am.'

Plainly, I was a suspicious character. If I seemed so in

Africa, surely my chance in the Indies would be slight. It is better to take the bull by the horns. The Admiral had said that Quichet had the two faculties of being able to persuade and to command. Now that I saw that face of goodness and gravity, I knew how truth will draw truth wherever it exists. I said, 'I would like to tell you the truth about myself: however dangerous it is.'

'The truth about one so young and so charming cannot be very terrible,' he said.

'It is terrible and always will be terrible and dangerous.'

'You are neither,' he said gravely. 'But continue.'

The sun was going down now, and had a great glow throughout the cave.

'I am a doctor, the son of a doctor,' I said. 'I was to have been Admiral Cringle's heir. He told me of you, and showed me your paintings. He was murdered in October by somebody. By unlucky chance there was much to connect me with the crime. All sorts of things were against me. I was tried and condemned and then hanged for the murder; but my friends brought me to life. But I was still under sentence, and people got to know that I had been saved. My friends got me a post as surgeon in the slaver there, the *Albicore*. My name in the ship was Edward Torrance. My real name is Edward Mansell. I did not kill the Admiral. I do not know who did. It was a man. And I even saw him leaving the garden and did not know it. If I am taken anywhere in the King's dominions, or anywhere else, I shall be hanged again, even if they have found the real murderer.'

Remember, that I was in a weak state of nerves, and had no great amount of control left; when once I had begun, I had to tell everything.

'Come,' Edmond Quichet said. 'It is well known in my country that the English, with all their very great and remarkable qualities, are without common sense. But I had not imagined that they would be so entirely without it as to think you a murderer, which you so visibly are not. This is absurd. But come, we will talk tomorrow. You have been flying for your life. You must wash and feed and rest. So your name is Edward? Come in there, my grandsons, to meet Dr Edward. These two are my grandsons, Charles Pierre and Edmond the Young. They do not know English so well as I, but know a little.'

The two came in and shook hands with me. They made me welcome there, and brought me hot water to wash with, clean linen clothes, and then prepared a supper of broth and meal-bread.

I was so very weary that I nearly fell asleep at supper. They got me to bed in one of the cots. I know that I said, 'I must keep a fair watch with you; if you will call me when it is my turn.' Quichet said that they would keep no watch; no enemies were near. I was too tired to question this, or any other matter. I rolled over in the blankets and fell asleep at once.

In the morning, I woke refreshed, and took more note of the three men.

'Will you tell me,' I asked, 'if you are Kranois?'

'I am French,' Quichet said. 'These two are Kranois.'

'I know a little Kranois,' I said, and spoke a few sentences, learned from Mr Kamansh.

'You have more gift for tongues than most English,' Quichet said. 'If it be not a rude question, may I ask if you learned your Kranois from a man with odd black specks in his left eye?'

'Yes,' I said, with some surprise. 'Do you know the man?'

'No; not now,' he said, speaking with some distaste. 'I did. Did he speak of wishing to return?'

'No,' I said.

We went out into the flowery court to see the great sea and all the shining lagoon.

'Sir,' I said, 'I can't thank you enough for believing that I did not kill the Admiral.'

He looked at me with his strangely beautiful grey eyes, which had a look of great gravity and great sweetness mingled. 'I have not yet been much mistaken in a face,' he said. 'Besides, who would kill Cringle, except for greed? You have no greed and no murder in your face. Forget it; begin again.'

'I wish I could,' I said.

'Do it, then,' he said. 'Let me help. Look at me, now: do I look like a pirate? You know, I was very nearly hanged as a pirate. Cringle could have had me hanged; would have if he had done his duty. We are both under a cloud among your dear countrymen and ought to be friends. Would you care to come with us to our city when I return?'

'Indeed, indeed, I should,' I said. 'But what can I do there? I bring you nothing. I am a doctor, of sorts, it is true. I have a certificate here. Could you employ me as a doctor?'

'A doctor is one of the many things man always needs,' he said. 'But we are in sore need of many things at present; that is what brings us here; and I fear we are not going to get them.'

'You, in sore need?' I said. 'You have no enemies, you said. You have cities, so Mr Kamansh told me; and all the natives think well of you.'

'They have been friendly,' he said, 'but as your Cringle may have told you, even they sometimes turn against us. They drove us out of here long ago. The slavers bribed or tricked them into doing that. But as a rule we are very good friends with the Matas. It is the M'gai whom we dread. This land sometimes throws up a warrior king, who breeds a race of fighters. The M'gai are such. I've been afraid of them for a long time, and have sent three times to France for weapons and powder. We have been expecting a ship daily for three or four months. But we are so far from France, and no letters come to us; we know not what is happening. I know not well what to do.'

'Could you not buy guns and powder from the English at Cabo?' I asked.

'No,' he said. 'They would not sell to us. Your people know very well that the Kranois are against the entire slave-trade. Besides, you are too shrewd. You send weapons for sale on the Coast here, but what weapons? Things that explode and kill the shooter at the first shot. I want real weapons, not what your clever men call trade.'

I asked him if he could tell me what the Kranois were, whether they came from Greece?

'I do not know what they are,' he said. 'Some Mediterranean race. They were more numerous once; "seven cities"; now only two, twenty miles apart. I am in the smaller.'

I asked how he came among them?

'I was sent by my rulers,' he said, 'to explore the land, and to discover, if we might not plant the country and so end the depopulating by the slavers. I was the first white man to see the Kranois. I liked them and got on well with them. We thought that we could make all the land a great French state, with a port at Seize Pics here, and a French Governor among the Kranois. The slavers saw that that would ruin them. They charged me with piracy, and stirred up the Matas to attack me. After that, the Kranois were not so friendly to me. There was no more talk of a French Governor. I stayed there, of course. It is my home. I had married a Kranish lady, you must understand. Then two years ago, a war-party of the M'gai raided and destroyed the last of the little cities and carried away many cattle. That was only a warning. It was then that I came again into favour. I was sent for and asked if I could obtain weapons from France, to prevent any other raid. You say, better late than never. It was late in the day, but I contrived to send messages, one after the other. Now it seems that no weapons will come.'

'Will the M'gai come?'

'I fear it. In my bones, I know they will.'

'Sir,' I said, 'how did it happen that you did not see our ship when she came in, or hear our guns? Could you not hear the guns of the battle?'

'We have been inland, up the river, for some days, getting news of our people,' he said. 'We only returned yesterday.'

'I hope, sir, that you heard good news.'

'There is no war yet,' he said. 'That is always good news. It is a pity that we did not see you. We might have bought some weapons and powder from you. But if we had tried to buy, perhaps you would have seized us and sold us as slaves. Such things happen on this Coast of Dead Ned.'

'But, sir,' I cried, 'why not take what weapons and powder there were in the ship?'

'But you said the ship was destroyed?'

'No, sir. We were camped ashore while the ship was repaired. The crew is destroyed.'

'See how poor a guide reason may be, when we consider the English,' he said. 'It never entered my head that slavers would come with sixty Mata slaves into this hunting-ground of the Matas, and then sleep on the shore.

It is so incredible. Then you have a ship still, with powder and guns on board her?'

'Alas, no,' I said. 'I fear she may have sunk by this. She was laid on her side to be patched. She had broken her bonds and come upright. That means that her leak is under water again; by this time she may have filled.'

'Come,' he said. 'Where is she? In the west channel, you say? Quick. Tell me. What guns had your ship? What powder? What trading-powder?'

'No trading-powder,' I said. 'About one ton of ordinary powder, all stowed aft.'

'How does the doctor know that?'

'I was friendly with the gunner. Of course, some of the arms were landed for use in the camp. The powder that was landed is gone. But the guns and the cohorns are lying in the camp still; all that we took ashore. The Matas left them.'

I then named the *Albicore*'s armament, which I knew with exactness. It was a heavy armament for a small ship: she was equipped as a privateer.

'Come,' he said. 'That is magnificent. And possibly half a ton of powder?'

'A full ton,' I said.

'But surely the Matas have plundered the ship?' he said.

'They had not yesterday. I was on board yesterday, plundering her myself.'

'The men who attacked you must have been a war-party,' he said. 'They must have gone on to some foray or they would have plundered. We must get to your ship at once. Come down this way to the boats.'

He called his grandsons, and rapidly explained what might be done. He then urged us out to the flowery court, and along a track as yet untrodden by me to the unseen side of the Peak. We passed between the northern Peaks, and down a slope, to an unsuspected, beautiful lake a mile long. On the shingly shore of this were some huts or shelters, thatched with palmetto, and beside these, drawn up and thatched from the sun, were some large, neat, beautiful boats, all black, having been carefully pitched or painted with a very hard thin black gum, which had a glaze on it like the black glaze sometimes set upon ancient pottery.

There were at least a dozen Kranois there; most of them youngish men. I will not describe them now, except to say that they wore a good deal of silver, studded with amethysts, and that they all came to greet me with a ready charm and simple friendliness. I tried my Kranish on them, with tolerable success, as we ran the boats out and set forth to the *Albicore*.

We found her very low in the water, as I had expected, but luckily not lost, nor had she been ransacked. We stripped her hurriedly, but well. We had loaded all our boats with gear and had set off towards the cave, meaning to start at dawn up-river towards the city, when I looked back and saw the last of the *Albicore*. She looked like a hulk condemned. Just over her, however, I saw the sickle of the young moon bright in the green sky above the forest.

As we drew near to our landing-place, we were met by our camp-keepers, with two canoe-men from the upper river. Word had come down to us that the M'gai would certainly attack the Kranois at full moon, if not before. They had already held their war-feast, the messenger said; they were as the trees of the forest in number and threatened to come like the forest-fire.

'Right,' Quichet said. 'We must start at once, now. We may just get there before them.'

He made some necessary changes in the equipment of the boats so that their loads might sort better with their crews. This did not take more than half an hour, during which some gear was brought down from the cave, and a cup of broth given to all. After that, we took our places in the boats and set forth into the night, on and on, up the sometimes sluggish, sometimes whimpering river, under forest that sometimes hid the stars, then anon stealing out into lakes where we could set sail, under stars so bright that they were terrible. We saw no lights of men; all the vast land seemed uninhabited, or given over to water, endless water, with forest and fireflies and reflections of stars.

At two in the morning, we pulled-in to a shore and made fast for a while. The rowers ceased their clockwork; we all came ashore, wrapped ourselves in sheepskin, in what seemed to me atrocious cold, and slept upon a spread cloth painted with a native tar which kept away insects and snakes, so they said; also sleep, for me, at least, that first night, for it had an acrid stink that sickened me. I lay flat and rested my back, and relaxed utterly, so that I might not feel the strain of the cramped boat any more than these Kranois. Lying there, looking at the stars, I thought that perhaps Ned was now dead for ever; I should be beginning again now. I was re-born into life. What sort of life was it to be?

We went up the great river for a long time, till it narrowed and grew swifter. For one day we went, as it were, in the naves of endless, dark, green cathedrals, whose clerestories flamed in the light and were glad with birds. In places the forest was gone; it lay heaped and tossed and tangled, as the tornado had left it; or blackened and piked from some fire which had burned out the size of a county.

At times, great beasts would rise in the river near us. Once we saw a serpent twenty feet long swimming with an erect head and open mouth across the river in front of us. He hissed at us; we were only too glad to let him go. The inside of his mouth was grey; this was very shocking to me. At times we came to reaches where there were abundant fish. Here there would be flights of exquisite ospreys and other fish-eating birds, plunging and taking, quarrelling over the catch and preening after eating. Then, in another reach, the trees would be hung with shrouds and streamers of many sorts, all covered with flowers of a beauty not to be told, and smelling of honey, so that all the reach was humming with the bees, the wasps, the humming-birds and the butterflies. The river was all starred with dropped blossoms, and with insects stupefied with the honey, slowly struggling to death. Sometimes these reaches were so bright with the sun and so exquisite with colour that the Kranois seeing them would break into song. Then a darker reach would follow, with no sound at all, all still save for the deep note of the river.

From time to time, often as though our passing in those still reaches had disturbed the balance of centuries, if not of thousands of years, there would come a sudden alteration in the peace and the stagnation, something would happen. A moment of suspense would change to a stripping and a ripping, and then a tree would totter and collapse, generally just behind us. The little wind or draught of our passing had disturbed it, so that the life, already held by a hair, could no longer endure. We would turn to see its fall, which sent up always a sort of smoke of insects and little birds.

After some days of rowing up the stream, I felt that the river was a part of our days and of our lives. Its song was something to which we tuned our efforts and by which

we lived. For the rest we fished as we passed, we tied up
to banks when it seemed safe from snakes, we sometimes
cooked and feasted; and sometimes even slept peacefully
in the smoke of fires lit to drive away the flies. Then we
would re-embark and press on, up that mysterious stream,
up that dim, dripping, dark nave towards the promised
sanctuary.

Then came the grim day when we met a canoe with a
message that, 'The M'gai were moving.' The only counter
to their moving was to move faster ourselves. We divided
the men into three watches and gave up all rest beside the
banks save in the heats of noon. We came out of the
forest into a more open land, of what men call savannah,
with rolls of grass and the trees in clumps and copses.
Foliage there was of another colour from the dark, hard,
metallic green of the forest, it had no blaze from flowers;
all was of a dusty, faded green, with much yellow in it,
yet the yellow toned down as though it were tired.

As we went on, we were presently hailed by another
messenger, who called to us from the bank and asked to
be taken on board. He said that no doubt the M'gai meant
to attack the city, but had not yet appeared before it. All
their army was afoot, so the reports said. He thought that
we might just reach the city before they came. We should
meet a horse-train with carts and wagons at Five Men
Bend. We could load our stuff into the carts.

'You have the arms, I see,' he said.

Quichet told him that they were not the arms he had
hoped for, still they were arms.

We stood on, in line, with Quichet's boat leading.
Presently I saw that the bank ahead was low, and that the
main stream swerved off away to the westward; this was
the bend. I saw then that the Five Men were knobs or
butts of stone, too big to have been raised by man, not

far from the bend itself. Now we heard the whinny of horses ahead, and saw figures moving on the river-bank. Quichet hailed them in French and Kranish; and was answered in French. So far all was well. We drove in, to a beach of shingle, ran the boats up, and met there the men of the convoy, who backed their carts down, so that they might be loaded. All there were in a good and lively dread of the M'gai, who were spreading terror and death. If they were not there, they were thereabout, and had killed some out-lying herders. They had sworn to level the city of the Kranois with the plain.

The sky in the east was now silvery with morning; it was acutely cold. Gleams of silver were on harness and armour, as the men backed down the carts. The horses were little, hard, active ponies, all kicking with the cold and catching something, no doubt, of the anxiety of their masters. Quichet and I took four of the light carts for the cohorns. Each of the four carts was armed with two co-horns, and had in it a breaker of powder and box of bullet. I took charge of the match for two of the carts; Quichet took the match for the other two. He led the convoy now. I brought up the rear.

After some hours of marching, the clumps and copses became scarcer; we emerged suddenly upon a great open expanse of grass. It seemed to stretch on for ever in the deep, clear light. In the distance, possibly thirty miles from where we were, great masses of mountain rose up and shone with snows. Between us and the mountains, and away also upon our right, were pickets of horse driving cattle. All these trains and droves were converging, as we were, upon the common centre, now plainly to be seen. There ahead of us was our goal, the long-looked-for, long-hoped-for home, the City of the Kranois.

It stood upon a gentle rising of the plain; you could not call it a hill; and yet when you were at a distance, and when you were near it or in it, the city dominated the plain; there was the queen, enthroned.

The walls were a full eighteen or twenty feet high, ramped and battered back for two-thirds of their height and perpendicular at the top. Who had built such walls? Who were these Kranois? The walls were of well-laid, hewn stones of hard, white-grey. There was a gate in the wall in the side of the city nearest to us; we were on a track which led to it.

There were some biggish buildings within the walls; some of the lesser buildings had been lime-washed white; and the walls and the seven tall watch-towers were crowded with people, among whom weapons flashed in the light. I saw shutters open at the upper windows; banners were thrust forth to welcome us; all of them were white and blue for the Kranish colours; we were seen.

Quichet came back to me from the front of the column and said, 'Those are the outland herders bringing in the droves; they have left it long; for see: out there are the M'gai.'

'Come on, then,' I said at once. 'Let us bring the co-horns out to that side; a shot or two may keep them off.'

'You are right,' he said.

He called to his grandsons. We drew out our armed carts to the east from the column, so as to protect the droves making for the city. I had spoken and acted instinctively. It seemed to leap into my mind that that was the thing to do. I blew on my match to make it glow, and kept my eyes on what Quichet said were the M'gai. He was right; there they were; a group of a dozen men on ponies and a party of about twenty braves on foot. They were on a swell of the plain about half a mile from us. I judged that they were debating if they could stampede the droves before they reached the walls. It was plain to me that they could not; for if they tried it we should have a fair shot at them; we took up position, and waited, while the slow, mooing, loitering, stupid cattle moved on to the gates. Meanwhile, the M'gai men rode nearer on their ponies; not very much nearer; because, as they advanced, some horsemen rode out from the city towards us and soon joined us. The M'gai were joined by their foot soldiers; and then both parties stared at each other, five hundred yards apart, and made no sign of attack; while the cattle slowly dragged on to the gates.

I know that my heart beat when I saw those great walls, and the helmed and cuirassed guards inside the gate. We went in, last of all, after the carts had gone, and saw the guards heave the gate to, and lift up, and ship the three great balks which served as bolts. I was shut into the City of the Kranois.

The cattle had been driven into the space below and just within the walls. They were lowing there, and nosing to some stalks which had been flung there. The carts had gone up the lane round a bend between walls out of sight into the city. I was standing with Quichet looking about me, when someone came running and thrusting (a good many people were there, some citizens and men of our convoy), and called Quichet by name, asking him to come.

Quichet smiled and said, 'I'm here; I'll come.' He turned to me and said in English, 'I shall only be a few minutes. Wait here for me. I'll show you to a shelter.'

He went off hurriedly with the messenger, and left me to look about. His grandsons had gone somewhere; I could see nobody from the boats; all my friends had scattered. I felt very much alone. The drovers moved here and there, trying to keep the cattle from bunching and blocking the passage-ways; the men near me moved up on to the walls to look about. I did not like to leave the place, lest I should miss Quichet when he came for me.

I stayed there a long time, waiting for him, and wishing that he would come. I wanted to get the guns mounted, at least, and to be up, on the walls, so that I might see what was happening. Half the citizens were up there on the walls, and were made dumb by what they saw. When I had loitered for more than an hour, I went up to the walls, and up the stone stairs to the fighting platform. When I looked over the parapet, I was stricken fairly dumb myself.

We of the convoy had entered the city in front of some forty savages. Now, the M'gai army was in sight; they had taken position on the rising in the plain where we had seen them, and were settling into camp there. I stared at this force, and tried to judge its strength; certainly some thousands were there.

In their order, their certainty and quiet power, they gave me the sickened feeling that was in the hearts about me. I had been staring at the camp to the south-east. I now looked to the south, along the track by which we had come. On that side, on the farther side of the little river which we had crossed, an army was slowly marching in a column two abreast. They stretched in a narrow ribbon along the southern side of the stream, almost to where it joined the bigger river. These men were not five hundred yards from us. They halted, suddenly, and sat in rank, while two men upon ponies rode along the line and surveyed the city.

Nothing happened after that for a long time. I suppose

that I waited on that wall, weary, anxious, hungry and not a little scared, until noon, when to my joy I saw Quichet coming down the lane for me. I called to him; he saw me and signed to me to stay on the wall, as he would join me there.

'It is hard to do one thing,' he said, 'when others want you to do ten. I could not get away, as I had planned. These are the M'gai. We are shut in to the north just as we are here; they are coming now to a parley.'

Indeed, a movement among them had begun some minutes before; the army of the M'gai had formed and were advancing on us in line. I counted eight main divisions of them, and reckoned that each contained seven hundred men. The regiments or tribes were each readily distinguished; one wore tall plumes of birds, one the skins of spotted monkeys, one leopards' skins, and so forth. They marched silently and with speed, and halted about a hundred yards from the walls. As they halted, they grounded their spears and long narrow shields. Each man began very gently to tap his white hide shield with his spear hand, till a gentle drumming noise filled the plain. It grew louder and louder, till it rang and roared and echoed. Each drumming man, under his head-dress, seemed not less than seven feet tall; each grinned as he drummed, so that the rows of teeth made a white streak down their line. The broad blades of their stabbing spears shone in the sun, and each man glistened with oil. They had a ripple in their walk, a sort of ease and insolence in their bearing. Perhaps few of them had ever seen a city before, and knew not quite what sort of puzzle it might be. But it was plain, that they judged, that their spears would soon solve the puzzle. Their chieftains stood in advance of the line; and now, presently, the leaders rode up, dismounted, left their ponies with young bucks who wore scarlet birds as loin-cloths, and advanced to the parley.

They moved with insolent ease and mastery, as though all the land belonged to them. While they advanced, and after they had halted, the M'gai beat their shields and hissed. I know no more frightful sound than the one they made thus. We were joined at this point by a Kranois, who had been in the M'gai lands, and spoke their tongue.

A young chief called something thrice in a questioning tone, and at Quichet's bidding this Kranois replied to ask what was the reason of this coming of the M'gai into the land of the Kranois?

I give the answers and the questions as they were afterwards translated to me. They follow the ritual in use among the savages of Europe and elsewhere thus:

The M'gai. Lo, how, you reject our King's friendship. He cannot understand why you citizens have retired within your walls, instead of greeting so great a King with feasts and the giving of wives. The King asks only friendship and a refreshment of cattle for his young men. Let you, therefore, open all doors, bring forth fat cattle and let us feast together. It is only by feasting and the interchanging of wives that friendship between nations can be maintained. This, many great nations have asked of us with tears and prayers.

The Kranois. We cannot understand such talk. This for centuries of moons has been the land of the Kranois and of their cattle. You, the M'gai, have come hither uninvited and have killed our cattle and herdsmen, and this without provocation of any kind. We will not offer feast to such visitors. Rather, we say, that we have sent for our friends, who are even now upon their way, to demand payment of the men killed and cow for cow.

Let your King, therefore, depart, and take with him his
army.

'See, men of the M'gai,' their King cried, 'they reject
our friendship. These Kranois are men of blood and war-
mongers; they ever were. They scorn our offer of peace.
What, then, shall we offer them, Men of the Broad Spear-
Heads?'

The Men of the Broad Spear-Heads at this suddenly
flung us shields and spears and shouted, 'War.'

'So be it,' the King cried to us. 'We will give you
War.'

No act of war followed at that instant; he turned,
mounted his pony and rode off. His regiments saluted his
passing with lifted spears. When he was half-way to his
camp, the regiments turned, moved from the city, reached
their old positions and sat down.

I remembered reading in some history-book of Louis
Quatorze how 'the King's army sat down before a town.'
Here was another King's army sitting down before a
town; and I was inside the town, and could see how
ominous it was. We were shut in; how could we drive
them away? And if we didn't drive them away, how long
could we live shut in?

Well, we watched them sit down before us and set
their guards, then Quichet said, 'But come, now; we are
both tired out, and they expect you. Come along the wall;
it is quicker, so.'

He led me along the southern wall-top, right to the
western end of the city, where there was a citadel of no
great height, but very big. He lived in the southern end
of the citadel. He led me across a paved court and into his
house, which was lime-washed white, within and without,
and smelt of that brisk djriza gum that, when burned

will keep all flies away. Coming out of the sunlight, it was dark and confusing at first, for the windows were small, and shuttered against any sling-shot from the enemy.

After some darkness of passage and corridor we came to an unshuttered room which faced west; I could see through the open window away over the plain. There was a cot bed in it, and a big coarse basin of blue and white pottery, full of hot water.

'This will be your room,' Quichet said. 'You might like a wash. Food is ready for us, through the door there, in that second room.'

I swilled some of the mud of the river from myself and went to the second room. It was small and faced west like the other. A girl was standing there, waiting by the spread table. She was dressed in a white linen and wore a little fillet of white in her hair. As I appeared, she moved swiftly over to welcome me; she shook my hand and said, in French, 'Be welcome. You are tired and hungry. I am M. Quichet's grand-daughter, Yvonne.' She had dark eyes and very beautiful brown hair; the face was pale; it had a darling look of life and charm on it.

I said, 'How do you do, Mademoiselle Yvonne?'

'We do not say Mademoiselle among the Kranois,' she said.

'Yvonne, then,' I said.

Quichet came in; we three sat to food, which two of us sorely needed.

'You will need rest, both of you,' Yvonne said. 'You have had no rest since you left the Coast.'

Something in Yvonne made rest quite the last thing that I longed for. I had been sad and sick at heart till I had come into that room; now I was alive again. I was once more one of a home, a member of a community; these were friends; and there arose in me a welling-up of feeling that this business of the war was one that I could do.

'No rest for me, thanks,' I said. 'I must get to those guns. I am a gunner, of a kind; we must get the guns mounted.'

'Grandfather tells me that but for you we should have nothing,' she said.

'I hope that your grandfather will tell you everything about me,' I said.

I was sick at heart to think that when he did tell her everything perhaps she would not speak to me again; still, I was not going to pose as anything.

'What chance have we of ever driving off the M'gai?' she asked.

Now, I had read that savages do not undertake sieges. Yet here were savages who plainly did and could. I, therefore, could not say that they would be gone in a day or two; they would not. I knew from my talks on the way that the other city of the Kranois twenty miles away might send help, of spearmen and bowmen, but that the force might not be strong enough to reach us. I could see that our city was not strong enough to sally out and fight the enemy; and that no other help was to be had.

I looked at Yvonne and said, 'We have walls, which they cannot scale, and certainly cannot breach. We have some guns, which will cause them some damage. And we have ourselves, who are utterly unbeatable.'

She smiled.

Quichet said, 'That is the spirit.'

'Come on, now,' I said. 'We must get the guns mounted. We will beat these M'gai back into the wilderness.'

We had risen from our seats, to set about it, when something rushed over my shoulder and cracked a piece of plaster out of the wall. Another followed it, and took something out of the ceiling. 'Sling-shot,' I said. I leaped to the wooden shutter and jammed it to. A third stone struck it as I closed it. I had a glimpse of the western field before it closed. There, dancing with joy, and hurling with exquisite grace, were some fifty M'gai slingers.

'We must get the guns to these gentry,' I said.

*Kicking Ned, or the Skysail, or
Perhaps, After All, The
Trust-to-God*

I sometimes call this part of my tale THE SKY-SAIL or, perhaps, after all, THE TRUST-TO-GOD.

Once, in the Albicore, *as we ran in the Trade, and I admired the tower of sail upon the mainmast, a seaman said to me, 'Ah, sir, but we ought to set a skysail, above the royal, there.'*

'But a little sail, so far up, cannot do much good,' I said.

'No, sir,' he answered, 'but nothing sets a ship off, like a skysail. It finishes her off.'

'Do sailors ever set anything even above a sky-sail?' I asked.

'Some set a Trust-to-God,' he said. 'Not many have one; but it's a very fine thing, a Trust-to-God. It finishes a ship off, even better.'

W E went out from the house, and presently reached the steps which led to the platform of the south wall. Here Quichet and his grandsons were stopped by some men who were coming along in search of them. I thought that the men were sergeants or minor officers of some sort; they had blue and white Kranish tassels on their chests. I was disposed to like all the Kranois, but I did not much like the looks of these two. They said 'that the Quichets, grandfather and grandsons, were awaited at headquarters for their report.'

'Right,' Edmond Quichet said, 'we will go there at once. You, Ned, will you go up to the wall there and wait for us?'.

'Yes,' I said. 'How long will you be?'

'Twenty minutes, or half an hour.'

'Very good. I will see where we can mount the guns.'

'Don't go far, or get yourself lost,' Quichet said in French. 'Besides, this is war, and you might unwittingly rouse suspicion. They are touchy about foreigners.'

'I'll be careful,' I said.

We waved to each other; they went off with the sergeants, and I, after seeing them away, went up to the wall.

Even in that short space of time the slingers had done their task; they had caused all the dwellers near the walls to close their shutters. The slingers had now withdrawn

into their lines. I could lean upon the parapet and take
stock of this new phase of my dream.

One of the worst points of being shut up is, that you
take the shut-up point of view, you lose your individual
soul and become a part of a herd in a pen whose shut-up
soul is half a soul. I stared at the positions of the M'gai;
they were making themselves snug in camp, with huts
and fires; they were penning the taken cattle, or whetting
their spears. They were settling-in, till their task was done
and the City taken. They looked like conquerors. When
I looked from them, so sure of their might, to the faces
of the Kranois, I felt that I might be in Newgate again,
in a Hold big enough to contain thousands, all of them
'going out on Monday'; they were awful faces. They had
the real Newgate look, of horror and terror, with wandering eyes, a sort of weak smile ever giving way to a savagery, and then the horror and terror again, with the eyes
unable to settle, and the mind ever on Monday and eight
o'clock. To look at them was to know that no man there
had any hope; despair was everywhere. Now that is the
most catching of all complaints. I took it. I heard what
they said, and took the sickness from them. They had
been asleep, while the M'gai had been active; they had
been fools (to put it mildly); they had neglected warnings.
Now, suddenly, the M'gai were there. Very quickly, as a
stranger will in an intense time, I began to understand
the folly of the Kranois. They had great estates away to
the east, where the Plainsmen, or country-dwelling
Kranois, bred cattle. These Plainsmen had warned them
repeatedly, that the M'gai meant to attack. But there was,
as I now found, an intense antagonism between the city
and the country-dwellers. These two parties of the
Kranois had been jealous of each other, and had thwarted
each other in all possible ways. And now the Plainsmen

were proven right. The city men, or Old Party, had disbelieved and were unprepared. Now war was on them,
the spears were at their throats, and nothing was ready. I
could see a lot of helpless people in the square, staring at
some guarded doors, over which pennons fluttered.
Within those doors the City Fathers sat, and I hope felt
sorry for their follies. But what were the City Fathers
doing? Why were they not doing something? What good
was talk, at this stage? Why had they not sent men with
Quichet to get my guns mounted and put into action? I
could be training guns' crews, and putting long-shots
into the M'gai headquarters.

As Crackers had told me that a good gunner should, I
made careful estimates of the distances of the M'gai positions. I told myself that with certain charges of powder,
we could reach them and give the M'gai some surprises.
I watched carefully for some sign that the M'gai had guns.
As far as I could discover, they had perhaps half a dozen
trade-guns, as the trade called them, that is, cheap iron
tubes upon stocks, which were meant not to fire. Certainly, as yet, they had no powder, for they fired no shot
at us. I could see nothing like even the smallest cannon
among them. I was cheered by this fact, and needed cheer,
for there were a great many of these M'gai, and their
insolence of bearing was much unlike the woe of the
citizens.

From time to time, savages would stroll out singly towards the walls. Always, these strollers were big, leading
men, over six feet in height, magnificent in bearing and
in build, with great plumes over their brows, and an
array of bright bangles on their arms. They were almost
naked. Most of them had long narrow shields, black and
white; nearly all of them had two short spears with long,
rather broad heads. These boasters would impudently

stroll towards us, threaten us with their spears and shout insults. It was shocking to me, that the Kranois made no attempt to shoot at them, not an arrow, not a sling-stone was sent from the walls at them; and this in a city said to have many good bowmen. Well, it was galling to me and hard to bear; but what was harder to bear than this tacit surrender was the look upon the faces. When I looked at those faces, I raged. Where was the commander? What was he thinking of, to let the citizens get into this state?

The time dragged on, and nothing happened from within the city. The debate at headquarters continued, and as there was no decision there, the hearts of all the city were as water within them. It was precious time wasted and daylight thrown away.

Meanwhile, these sick and scared citizens shuffled by; looking poison at me, the foreigner, and plainly thinking, as men will in war, that being a foreigner I was no doubt in league with the enemy. At last a young man, whom I had noticed a little while before for his fair hair, which was a rare thing among the dark Kranois, drew near to me. He had a charming, smiling, sun-tanned face, and moved with the swing and distinction of a beautiful body. He wore a twist of soft gold-leaf on his right chest; I judged this to be a mark of distinction of some sort. He came up to me with his smile, and said to me in odd French,

'You came with Quichet, I think?'

I said, 'Yes.'

'I am called King,' he said. 'You are Monsell Ned?'

That was near enough, so I said, 'Yes.'

'I am not a King,' he explained. 'We act old plays of ours after the spring rain; I played The King last year.'

He did not look like a city-dweller. I asked, 'Do you live in the city here?'

'I'm a Plainsman,' he said. 'My home's out there:' he pointed to the east.

Seeing two Kranois at the parapet, leaning to see the view, two M'gai slingers danced out and slung some stones at us. They went either high or low.

'See,' The King said; 'they let these fellows do this. Why aren't they shooting these fellows?'

'That is what I ask,' I said. 'Who is in command?'

'An old soldier.' He gave the man's Kranish nickname, which means Old Sword. 'He went too fast fifty years ago,' The King said. 'He has gone too slowly ever since.'

I said, 'I have guns and powder here. We might be scattering those fellows. I've been waiting for word to mount them ever since I came. Do you know about guns?'

'Not much,' he said. 'Raoul Quichet told me about them. We expected to have them a long time ago. Are they as terrible as he said?'

'Yes,' I said. 'If I could have parties of men to help me, I could put the fear of death into these fellows.'

'They must have decided something soon,' The King said. 'I've been in the council till I could stand it no longer. Presently, they'll send heralds round to the different wards, no doubt, to tell them what to do.'

'What will that be?' I asked; 'to mount our guns and fire at all their positions?'

'You won't get fire from those men,' The King said. 'Cold water is more their mark. But here come the heralds; there they are, sounding in the Square.'

A noise of penetrating, melancholy horns, blowing wavering notes, came from the northern and central parts of the city. At the same time we saw some officers with their heralds coming along the southern wall close to where we stood. Some of them turned east, some west; some advanced upon us. The herald blew his note for silence; when silence had fallen on those gathered to hear, an officer said, 'that the city was besieged, and that it fell to the citizens of each ward to defend the wall of that ward. We, being in the southern ward, would have the wall in front of us with its towers to defend. We should go at once to the officer of the ward in the central square, who would enrol us in our watches, give us weapons and explain our duties. We should know his office by a green flag hung from it.'

The King said, 'I must be off to my own people; this farce will be the death of us.'

As he moved away, the herald officer, who had been wondering at me, asked, 'Who are you?'

I said, 'A foreigner, who came this morning with weapons, with Edmond Quichet.'

'A foreigner, you say; what foreigner?'

'English.'

He had never heard of any such people; he looked at me with suspicion and dislike.

'You belong to this ward?' he asked.

'No. I belong to no ward. I have weapons here.'

He looked at me with greater suspicion.

'If you are here you must belong to this ward,' he said. 'You had better go to the officer of your ward and enrol like the others.'

'But I don't belong to any ward,' I said. 'I have only but now arrived in your city. I have weapons here, to mount on the walls. The terrible weapons, which Quichet wished to bring here.'

'I cannot go into what you have or haven't,' he said. 'You are in this city and must take your share in its defence. This ward is as good as any other. You, there. Show this foreigner the Square and see that he enrols in the south ward.'

'Let me say again,' I said, 'that I am a friend of Edmond Quichet. He will tell you that I have a lot of guns and powder here for the defence of the city. Such things may be vital to your defence.'

'I happen to be responsible for the employment of foreigners here,' he said.

He turned from me; he was already off to spread his tidings elsewhere. It was my first taste of the Kranois city official. Two or three of his underlings shewed me, that I was to go with them.

They led me up the slope of the lane to the high open heart of the city. I had seen from parts of the western wall that there was a big square here. Now I came into it, from the south, and saw the singular beauty and strangeness of it. On my right, there was a biggish temple, built simply of stone, with a fine relievo carved upon it, of involved figures in a kind of dance; this was gaily painted in colours singularly bright. Beside this, on both sides of it, was an outcrop of the dark rock which supported the city's northern wall. From this rock four spouts of stone gushed clear abundant water into stone troughs. I suppose that the water came somehow underground from the distant mountains; anyhow, there it was, a joy to see. Water at least would not fail the city.

I took a swift look at that, then looked about. The Kranish city was bigger than I had thought. The Square was full of life and muddle; all the bigger and more important houses fronted on it; to the one side, there were many women and older boys going for water at the springs, with jars upon their shoulders. In the midst, near me, many pens of cattle had been hurdled in. Many of these were uneasy, for as one could see, they wanted water. No one had yet made water-troughs for them; though some of them had had fodder tossed to them. A few plainsmen Kranois were sitting on the ground beside these cattle. I could already tell the Plainsman by his look of the open air. These few men had a sullen and angry look; they had tried to get something done for their precious cattle and had been told that the commanders had something better to think of. There they sullenly waited, knowing that there in the pens was the food, very likely the only food, that the citizens would have to live upon; and yet these city dwellers said that they had better things to think of.

My guides, or guards, stopped to hear their complaints. A leading Plainsman said that the cattle had been brought in, just before midday. Some official had then promised that the troughs should be made at once, so that the beasts might be watered. In the paralysis of war, this had not been done. The man who had made the promises had disappeared; other officials, when asked, had made similar promises and then also disappeared; meanwhile, the heat grew and the cattle suffered. Those fountains in the Square were sacred; their water was for the temple service and for the citizens. The Plainsmen had respected the holy water for some hours, though with a growing rage; now the matter was coming to a head. At that moment, as I watched, the young man, The King, came out towards us; he looked very handsome, and as I thought most indignant. He went straight to the group of men near us.

'What is it?' he asked. 'What is the trouble?'

'King,' the men answered, 'these hens have brought us no troughs, and the cattle suffer.'

'What nonsense,' The King answered. He looked swiftly at the cattle, and said, 'You mean that they have had no water yet?'

'Not a drop,' they answered.

The King said, 'Form a guard about those troughs. You cattlemen, take the cattle to water, pen by pen.'

The Plainsmen who had been sullenly glowering, at once sprang up and took the cattle from the nearest pens to water. My guards cried out against this outrage; so did the citizens; the women screamed; here was the holy water being defiled by cattle. How they were to live, if the cattle died of thirst, had not entered their heads. However, my own personal guards had their orders; though they were plainly fuming with rage against these Plainsmen, they had to take me to my ward; they motioned to me to come on.

On the western side of the Square some of the bigger houses had banners at their doors, with the blue and white stripes of the Kranish colours. These houses had sentries in front of them, wearing blue and white. I judged that these were the headquarters of Old Sword's offices; and so they were. I wished that Quichet would come out of them, see me, and take me in to the commander. However, he did not. My lot was to go to a much meaner house on the south side of the Square. A green flag hung from its window; a longish line of young men stood outside the door, waiting their turn.

My guards went straight to the door, and knocked in an authoritative manner. It opened at once an inch or two, while the weary line of men called out complaints, that the newcomers ought to take their turn and not come thrusting in thus to the front. There were cries of, 'Thrust them back to the end. We've been here all the afternoon.' A weary sentry inside the door (he had been holding the door in the heat against perhaps fifty assaults) asked who we were. The guard said,

'We've got a foreigner: the Chief says he's to be enrolled at once.'

'Shove him in then,' the sentry said, 'and one of you come with him.'

At that instant, there came a great outcry from the crowd by the fountains. The women and citizens had tried to stop the cattle from licking the holy troughs, and the Plainsmen, in anger, had loosed some pens of cattle among them. I saw some surging cattle and flying women; then I was thrust past some men who were waiting in the passage, and so brought me into an inner room. Three young men sat at a table. One had a parchment before him, a saucer of red wet paint and a hair pencil. He was the keeper of the roll. Next to him was a man with a pile of red and a pile of plain counters. Next to him was a man with a duplicate parchment. Behind these scribes or clerks was the Ward Commander, a big, slow, elderly man with a kind and stupid face. As we entered, we saw the first scribe look up and ask a man's name. The man replied, giving a name, then the scribe looked for it on his parchment, could not find it, and asked the other scribe if he had such a name on his list? The man said, 'No.' The first scribe then asked the recruit, if he belonged to the South Ward, and how it came that he was not on the list. He was then asked, if he understood either the bow or the spear; he said, no, he was a tailor. He was entered upon the lists, the second scribe then gave him a red disc and a plain disc, told him that the red disc would get him a spear at the South Ward arms distribution centre below the temple, while the plain disc must be kept and shewn when the food was brought round. He was then told that he was enrolled and subject to military discipline. He was now to go to get his spear, and then report to the tower captain at the south tower.

The tailor gave a sort of sickly grin and was about to shuffle away, when a new man entered by a door at the back. He was a little, rather dapper man, wearing white clothes. On the right chest of his tunic or upper garment, he wore two of those twists of soft gold leaf, which I had noticed on The King. He was not a young man; his face was colourless and seemed an odd mixture of the faces of sheep and snake, brainless and yet dangerous.

He said, 'Here. Not quite so fast, my friend. Ward Commander, this will not do. We shall never do anything with these fellows if they go about their tasks like this. You, my friend, are now sworn to serve this City.' (This last was to the recruit.) 'You will just bear in mind another time to throw up your right hand to your commanders.'

At this moment he caught sight of me.

'What on earth is this thing?' he asked.

'A foreigner, Master,' my guard said, saluting. 'We were to see him enrolled in the South Ward.'

'A foreigner, eh?' He turned to me. 'One of the Quichet party, I suppose?'

I said, 'I came with Edmond Quichet.'

'With the foreign help that was promised, no doubt?'

I said, 'We brought some excellent weapons, which are not yet unpacked.'

He turned to the Ward Commander and said, 'This Quichet has passed his whole life in trying to bring this country under foreign dominion. This is, no doubt, the spy who will report later how the land may be subdued. Who said that he was to be enrolled here?'

Now my guard had slipped out, to see the fun in the Square; there was none to answer.

The Ward Commander turned to me and said, 'You speak Kranish. Who said that you were to be in the South Ward guard?'

'I do not know,' I answered. 'An officer who said that

he was responsible for the employment of foreigners here. He came round with heralds, and said that I was to join the South Ward guard, since that was as good as any other. But I have these weapons below by the gate and know how to use them. It would be better that I should be using them now against the enemy.'

'It is for us to judge of that,' he said.

He rose slowly from his chair and asked Sheep-Snake to come with him into the other room. When they returned, Sheep-Snake said,

'There must be some mistake in saying that you are to go to the South Ward. The Central Ward is a much better place for you. You will be taken there.'

I said, 'You are keeping me from using the weapons against the city's enemies.'

'Yes,' he said, 'no doubt we suffer . . . still . . .' He gave the word to some men who were in the inner room, who came in, and threw out their hands in the way he seemed to enjoy. 'Take this foreigner to the Central Ward,' he said.

They closed in upon me, one on each arm. 'No need to hold me,' I said. However, it was just as well to keep close together, for we had to thrust all three like sheep at a gap to get past the mob at the door and so into the Square, where by this time, the cattle had drunken, and the Plainsmen had won. They sat by their pens now, calmly exulting over the angry citizens, who stood apart glowering at them.

I could not understand why Quichet had not sent for or come to me. I asked one of my guards where Quichet was; I was sure that everybody in the City would know Quichet. He had not seen Quichet, and did not wish to see him. He said that he thought it odd, to say the least of it, that Quichet had come back to the city with the

M'gai. I tried to explain, that we had just crept in before
the M'gai stopped the entry, and that we had brought
weapons which might blast the M'gai away. I was asking
him, if I might go to make sure that the powder was in
a safe place, when the officer came past with his heralds.
He had been giving orders along the walls, I think. He
stopped, when he saw me.

'I thought I sent you to the South Ward,' he said.
'What brings you here? Why have you not done what I
ordered? You will go at once, now, to the wall where
you belong.'

I said, that I was a stranger to the city and had certain
means of helping her, and that all this bullying and
threatening was silly; it was simply keeping me from
being of use to people. He said, that a Kranois needed no
talk of the kind from a foreigner, and that he, who was
responsible for the employment of foreigners in the city,
meant that I should serve on the south wall, with the
guard. So, with this, I was marched off to the south wall.
He followed me there and handed me over to the old
commander of that section or ward, saying that it would
be best that I were kept from going too near to the gate.

I had thought the commander of the ward a simple,
stupid man. His men called him Old Gah, I do not know
why; they liked him, and so did I.

He said, 'You can take the spear there, then, and go up
on to the wall, till we do our drill. You are not to go
down to the gate, you understand. Have you practised
with a spear?'

I said, 'No. We had given up the use of spears, having
so much better weapons, guns, and so forth.'

'Well,' he said, 'take your spear, there, and go up on
to the wall, with the rest of the guard.'

I did as I was bid. The spear was heavy, with a hardwood handle, and a short steel triangular head. It was very like one of the boarding pikes kept in racks in the *Albicore*. It was odd to be holding a spear on a city wall, watching an enemy below me. Once again, I was struck by the comfort in the M'gai camp. They had settled themselves in. Many little huts had been built; many more were building. I saw little companies of M'gai drilling together. Although it was hot, the smoke from many fires blew about. I could see that these were forges. Many men were making or mending weapons. I saw the smiths strike on their anvils, and the bright iron flash under the hammers. As I looked, a train of perhaps a hundred laden pack donkeys came up to their camp from the northeastward. They had a line of supply there, it seemed. 'Why are they left like this, undisturbed?' I groaned. 'These Kranois have done nothing against them, but let them settle down. Now is the time to drop some round-shot plump into their midst.'

I saw that the men of my ward were watching me curiously. Presently one of them, a very friendly young man, came up and asked what I thought about it.

I said that with my weapons I could shift some of those fellows from where they camped. He did not know about gunpowder, so that this was lost on him. I asked if anything had been done to molest the M'gai during the past twenty-four hours.

He said, 'No, nothing. The M'gai are too strong.'

'But the Kranois are good bowmen, so people say. Have they not shot from the walls? The slingers must often have been within bowshot?'

'Yes, that is true; but we have very few arrows as yet.'

'Are people making them?'

'The heralds this morning said that energetic measures have been taken to ensure a good supply of arrows.'

'How long does it take to make an arrow?'

'Well, we have to straighten the shafts first; they were collecting the shafts yesterday. Then the heads take a good time. Then there is the nocking and the heading and letting the gum dry. Then you have to feather, haven't you, and you can't expect that to be done very quickly or the arrow won't go true.'

'Then we haven't any arrows?'

'Not enough to go shooting them off the walls.'

'Do you think I could find a lighter spear than this?' I asked.

'No,' he said. 'We are rather short of spears at present, but the heralds said that energetic steps were being taken to ensure a supply of good spears.'

'You won't have to feather spears,' I said.

'No,' he said, 'but it takes a good time to make and fit a head.'

'You think they are being made?'

'Yes, if they have the shafts and the steel for the heads; they were seeing what they could muster.'

'Where are the smiths and armourers?'

He pointed towards the east of the city, where work was going on; smoke rose and hammers beat on metal there; there was a clink and clatter.

'Then just at present we cannot do much against the enemy?'

'No, but word has been sent to the Big City, of course, and the scheme is, to get weapons ready here; then, in a day or two, the army of the Big City will come down upon the M'gai, and we shall issue out at the same time and take them as between two jaws. We shall have weapons enough for that, by that time.'

'Yes, but have you food enough in the city for those days before the army comes?'

'Well, that is what we don't know yet,' he said. 'We hope so; but most of our corn is in the granaries out towards the Big City, a good way from here. It was to have been brought in, but there has been so much to see to, in these last few days, nobody seems to know if it has been.'

'Who was responsible for its coming?'

'O, nobody very much.'

'Then perhaps it hasn't come?'

'O, I should think that some of it has come.'

I had begun to see that the long ease had made the Kranois un-forethoughtful. I looked from my perch on the wall over the city. It was a fair sight, so trimly built, and so brightly lime-washed and painted. The Kranois delighted much in wind-vanes, which in so windy a city looked delightful, as they swung and flashed, each one of a new and gay design. Some pigeons were flying about in troops and flights of twenty or thirty, wheeling and flashing in the sun. I heard at various points the shouts of men who were drilling companies of spearmen. Three such companies were at drill in the space just below me; they had no spears, only sticks and tools, the shafts of scythes, three-pronged forks and so on. Some had not even these, and did nothing but change formation and remake it, as though the end of war is to make a sensible being no longer human.

My guns, with all that we had brought from the boats, had lain in the wagons just under the wall when I first had gone up that morning. Now, I looked down and saw that they had gone.

'Hullo,' I said, 'the wagons with the guns are gone. Did you see who took them?'

'An officer from the Chief came with a team of men and wheeled them away.'

'Where to?'

'I don't know; one of the store-houses, probably.'

'They'd better keep them away from fire,' I said.

'They will,' he answered. 'The heralds were giving orders against fire in the city. But in God's name, what is this?'

Even now, I do not know how it was done. There were, opposite the south wall, not less than twenty-five hundred M'gai in camp. At some order or signal, not perceived by us in the city, about fifteen hundred of these darted into order of battle and rushed at the city, each man yelling and screaming in a way that made the blood run cold. I had disbelieved in the 'war-cry'; now I learned its efficacy. They came at a speed which I had not believed to be possible; and though the main body came fast, a vanguard of slingers came faster. They rushed at us, let fly each some half-dozen stones with the speed of lads drawing sticks along a paling, and were at once out of the action, slipping back into intervals left for them in the main body. As they withdrew through these intervals, the main body seemed to surge forward. Then I saw, that the advanced parties carried scaling-ladders. I had an instant of horrid fear, that now the time was come. We were to be carried by assault. All along the wall, whistles were blowing to call the guards, who came running from all directions. The sling-stones came over in a hail. A stone hit a man near me on the side of the jaw and made him yell. I saw a man or two fall. I shouted to some bowmen, 'Shoot. Shoot them,' but as they knew no English and were staring at the sight of the charge, which was so beautiful that it was difficult not to stare, they did not shoot. In any case, they had been told to save their arrows, except in a case of emergency, and no one had yet told them that this was an emergency. Suddenly, the slinging stopped, for the M'gai were now just under us. The ladders came up against the wall, with a clack, and in an instant the M'gai were rushing up them. Just near us, the ladders were too short. I saw terrible, yelling faces under plumes, eyes like the eyes of lions, teeth like the teeth of tigers; a man flung a short spear or javelin at me from just below me. I caught it as it went over me and flung it back at him. It missed, not only him, but everybody else, how, I cannot tell, except that in the fury and confusion, screaming and roar of an attack, man's effort is wild, and destiny decides. In an instant, I saw that the M'gai were aware that they could not scale at our part of the wall. Instantly, by some signal that none of us perceived, the word went or the thought passed, 'This must stop. Get away.' Instantly, the braves were down the ladders, the ladders whisked away into the rear; the slingers were back again, sending stone after stone at us and at the sectors right and left of us. The stones whizzed, clacked and banged; men fell and wailed and died, great shards of old plaster fell.

Now on the wall just to the east of us, there came a rallying-cry. I could see that the M'gai there were up, disputing the parapet. I saw a knot of Kranois heaving and thrusting at them. At that instant, another ladder full of savages came up against the wall between us and them; no Kranois were there to check them. A surge of M'gai came rolling up over the parapet. One of the biggest of them leaped on to the platform, slipped, and recovered. There was no time to be lost. I called, 'At them, quick,' and charged this man before he was well on his feet. Old Gah was beside me; he speared this man at once, just as he knocked my spear out of my hand. I stooped and got his spear from him, and in stooping was knocked down by the men behind me, and knocked down some M'gai who leaped on to me as I tried to get up. Both sides jabbed at me with spears, but war goes by destiny; they just missed me. I know I did not expect to get up again; and yet, in an instant, the fight was over and inaudibly the word had passed, that the M'gai were to retire. The attack was called off. The M'gai were back over the wall; the ladders were all whisked away, and back came the slingers with the sling-stones, whish, crack, splitter-splatter, whach, whish, whish. This time two or three arrows went after them, and missed them.

Well, they went back, and we drew into groups out of sling-shot to talk over the battle. Old Gah said a nice word to me about my charging the ladder. I said that if I had had my guns, I could have broken the rush long before it reached the wall. I asked about the guns and powder, and said, that I could shew what could be done with them, if permitted.

He said, 'You young fellows, you think you know it all. You don't, you know. You are too impulsive, like all you foreigners. You only get us into trouble.'

I said, 'Sir, I seek only to help this city. Will you let me only try one of my weapons, if only once?'

'See, Ned,' he said. 'We have heard of your weapons. Years ago, when Quichet was young, he had some of them. They burst up, and killed a very fine young man, of whom we had the liveliest hope. I was a friend of his; and I've never liked Quichet since. If you go bursting one of those things on this wall, the wall will come down. There is a bad bulge in it already, just a few feet west there. We have our own views of how to fight the M'gai; and remember, that we are not the main fighters of this war; we are doing all things in union with the Big City, with whom we keep in touch. They will march to fight the M'gai; when they come, we shall march out to help

173

them; until then, our task is to make ready to help, first by drilling, then by making weapons.'

'My weapons are already made.'

'So are our plans, Ned,' he said.

He would have said more, but at that moment, Sheep-Snake appeared, with some of his minions.

'You have a foreigner in your ward, of the name of Ned,' he said, to Old Gah. 'Where is the fellow?'

'You mean this man?' Old Gah said. 'He's here.'

'He ought not to be there,' Sheep-Snake said. 'The orders are, foreigners are not to serve on the walls at all, but to be cattle-tenders. His place is with the cattle in the Square. I have sent three times, if not four, to find him, in the Central Ward, and all the time he has been here.'

'I know nothing about that, sir,' Old Gah replied. 'He was sent to me by the staff, and has behaved very well in the fighting.'

'He had better behave well,' Sheep-Snake said. 'Come down from the wall there, you. Put aside that spear. Adopt a military attitude when you are addressed by your superior.'

I fear I did not. I pretended not to know what he was saying. Old Gah said that I did not understand the language very well.

'He had better learn it, if he's to stay in the city of the Kranois,' he answered. 'You are my prisoner, my military prisoner, do you understand? If you mutiny, or try to escape, you will be speared.'

I was marched to the Square by an escort, and handed over to a cattle foreman. He was one with whom I had talked the day before. He was a stern-looking man, burnt to the colour of a brazen image, with a broad face, a little pug nose, a slit for a mouth, and eyes like sparks of fire. His hair was bleached by the sun to a kind of pale dust colour. He was wrapped in a blanket of dirty yellow wool, which he threw off to welcome me. My heart warmed to him, for as soon as the escort had gone, he said, 'You are just to do what you please. Imagine making a man like you a cattle hand.'

When one has been an outcast, a little recognition is like rain upon the desert: the flowers spring up.

'Indeed,' I said, 'I will do what you tell me to do.'

'The less you bother cattle, the better. Give them food, water and sleep and a turn with the opposite sex at times, and they'll be less trouble than city-dwellers, who don't know that war isn't foolery.'

'Did you see anything of the M'gai attack just now?'

'No. I heard it. But I've seen the M'gai. I come from out there away to the east, on the verge of the cattle country. I've been neighbours with them for years. It is only since their present King came that they've been resty. I am one who likes the M'gai very much. They are good straight people; when they say a thing they do a thing. It's only lately that they've got this idea of grab and kill. That isn't the people; it's the brute who rules them, and his little gang of murderers. But they're like children or like sheep; they obey; they do just what they are told to do, and believe every tale as true.'

'They're extraordinarily fine fighters,' I said.

'That was all the old King. He made the army, and it was his eldest son, whom the present King murdered, that made the way of fighting. You haven't seen it yet, the thing they call the lion's jaws. They come on, rushing like a fire on a plain in a high wind. No Kranois could reach that speed. Then, as they run, their wings swing out at both sides and make the jaws round the enemy; and as soon as they are well round, they close, and no enemy yet has ever got out, they say. I've seen them do it with lions on the plain. I haven't seen them do it with Kranois yet. But when the Big City army comes I'll no doubt see it tried.'

'And is there no defence?'

'Of course, there is; but they've not met any tribe yet that has one.'

'What defence is there?'

'Something that will keep the jaws from closing. Arrows will. Get your men into a triangle, with all the pikes pointing out, and let the archers shoot over the pikemen's shoulders. Arrows'll stop any men; a good arrow through the heart.'

At this point, a man came up to him and said, 'I want five men from you, to cut spear-heads.'

'What's the sense in that?' my new friend said. 'I've just this minute received five men, to tend the cattle here; now you want them for spears.'

'I've got to have them for spears,' the newcomer said. 'So hand them over.'

'Well,' my friend said to me, 'you'll have to go; no doubt they'll send you to me again as soon as the light goes. We have to bed these cattle down before dark.'

Four other cattle-tenders, all of them Plainsmen, who disliked the rule of the city men as much as my friend, rose up unwillingly from their blankets and followed to one of the workshops in the east end of the city, below the temple. Here about a hundred men were at work, some preparing spear-shafts, trimming the sticks so that the shafts were clean, and pointing down with small axes. My task was to help at the pointing. I had never had much work with a small axe, and now had no one to shew me what to do. A man said, 'Take a look at the shaft on the wall in front of you. Make a tapering point like that.'

Now, if you think that I was stupid at it, go you, and cut some stout ash-poles and take a small hatchet, not sharp, and with no grindstone handy, taper down the poles till you may use them for, shall we say, hop-poles. You will find it a very pleasant job, but not one that you will do easily. However, I went on at it, and spoiled a pole or two. I longed for a knife, or a chisel, or a spoke-shave; anything but a hatchet. They say that a good workman does not quarrel with his tools. A good workman demands the work that he can do; then he will be known by his tools.

There was a good deal of singing. I enjoyed the job there; we were sheltered from the sun; we had abundant cold, clear running water to drink, for a brook ran by us from the springs. Another delight was the continual singing in the temple where relays of women were singing psalms in intercession or prayers for help. Young unmarried women 'belonged to the temple,' I was told, and always sung thus. They sang sweetly in the gentle Kranish mode. I was cheered to think that among them probably Yvonne was singing, perhaps with thoughts of me.

I had worked at these spear-shafts for some hours, I suppose, when the Sheep-Snake creature came round after me. He had, I think, wanted to see me tending cattle, and had not found me doing it; he now had come after me to annoy me at some other angle.

'So,' he said, 'the foreigner whom I put to tending cattle has come away to an easy task, shaping spear-heads. What do you know of shaping spear-heads? Guards, march him to the defaulters' drill at once. He may learn there something about spears, before he has the pleasant task of cutting them.'

So once again I was taken under guard, this time to a

sad-faced, saturnine, black-haired man, who looked as though his parents had not wished him to be born, and as though he now shared their views. He was known everywhere as Old Crow; for he was liker an old derelict crow than anything. He was wearily taking a party of bad lads and erring citizens in what he called spear-drill. He had a short spear; the others had sticks, or even reeds. He looked at me wearily, told me to take a stick from a heap of wood, and fall in at the rear, and pay attention to all that was said.

'This that I'm teaching you is the spear exercise,' he said. 'I cannot go back to the beginning. We have come now to the exercise known as Exalting Spears, which is an exercise of ceremony number two, following on exercise one, ceremony and salute.'

To one who had learned gunnery under Crackers it was something of a come-down. We were doing this exercise in a clear corner of the Square, not twenty yards from the temple entrance. As we listened to the Old Crow wearily explaining for the tenth time that we were to wait for the order, the complete order, and not to act on the first word of an order, that the word Exalt meant nothing; it was NOT an order; it was a caution. How could we tell, till we were told, what it was that was to be exalted? But that when he said, Exalt Spears, why, then, he wanted to see all the spears go up as one ... while he was droning over all this, and the sad dogs, the defaulters, were nudging each other, and passing low remarks, when there came from the north-eastern angle of the city the appalling noise of a M'gai attack, and the cries, whistles and alarm calls of the garrison on the wall there. I said, 'The M'gai again,' and at once grabbed Old Crow's spear from him and was just half-way up the steps to the platform of the wall, when I saw M'gai in the

Square itself below me. 'They are in, then,' I said to my-self. 'They've got us this time.' However, just above me half a dozen M'gai were clambering over the parapet. I flung myself at these. I saw The King attacked by three braves, and had a great towering warrior overtopping myself. I stabbed at him, and hit him somewhere, and he fell from the parapet into the town. I saw The King swing left and kill one of his braves, and by the very movement miss the spears of the other two. He swung right and killed one of the other two. A rush of Kranois drove me into the M'gai; and then we were at the ladder heaving it over, all crowded with M'gai coming up it; we edged it sideways with a bar, so that it slithered over and fell. All the time, the sling-stones were whacking the walls, women were screaming, the cattle were panicking, and the M'gai were yelling their cry. Then, in another minute, this attack, too, was called off; the M'gai had melted away. Looking down into the city, I saw that three M'gai lay dead in the Square. Still, they had had a time of some success. They had been inside the city; they had rushed the walls, and gotten inside; they had killed a cow, a woman and three men inside the Square, and four other men on the wall; and this with a loss of only six of them-selves. What I could not understand, was how they had taken the wall by surprise. I saw The King speaking to some of the wallguard there. He was asking about that very point.

'Surely,' he said, 'you know that these M'gai have the ears and the noses of dogs. They know which part of a wall is weakly held. You were surprised here, with no-body on guard but two unsupported sentries. You were only saved by the fact that the ladders were too short. If they had judged the height of the walls better, they'd have cut the throats of half the city by this time.'

The Commander knew that this was the truth. He was scared at the narrowness of the escape.

'And even now,' The King said, 'even now, after the lesson of this morning, there's no one ready to hurry them back, after an attack. Not one archer on all the north wall; and three and a child on the south. You have bows; why don't you use them?'

'Sir,' the Commander said, 'we are saving all the arrows for the battle when the army of the Big City comes here.'

'If you're not very careful,' The King said, 'if you don't mend your ways, the Big City will find no city left when it gets here.'

He saw me and came towards me, to greet me in French. 'Well, Ned, I've been looking high and low for you. I traced you to the Central Ward, then to the South Wall; then to one of my cattle-herders. He did not know quite where you had gone after that.'

'First, to make shafts, then to the rogues' squad,' I said.

'God's blue sky,' he said; 'and, of course, you have not had your weapons unloaded from the wagons yet.'

'No.'

'I'm weary of this,' he said. 'I've been talking to the Chief in there till I am tired. This is no way to check the M'gai. Anyhow, I'm not going to stay longer. I'm going out tonight with my men. With two hundred horse, I can make the M'gai very restive; not camped as you see, enjoying themselves.'

I hoped that he would say, 'I want you to come with me'; as he did not, I was a little dashed from asking if he would take me; but, indeed, I was kept from asking by the thought that I ought to stay where Quichet (and Yvonne) were.

The King went on, 'There he comes, our Commander: that old man on the old white pony yonder. I must speak to him, and then I shall be going. But I'll have a word with you first. We shall be having our battle, probably, in about forty hours from now.'

There were cheers from some of the citizens in the Square as the Chief rode up to our corner. He rode an old white pony, which was one of the city pets; he had taken pleasure in fostering the city's interest in the pony, and had found that it repaid him; some of the women called him 'Lillyboy' after the pony. The Chief was an oldish man, with a look of authority and kidney trouble. He gave me the impression that he was at all times acting the part of the father of the city, the citizens' saviour, which indeed he had been some forty-five or fifty years before. He always seemed to be saying, 'You Kranois know me. You know your Old Sword. Lillyboy will not fail you,' and so forth. But his arrival, smiling, on his old pony, in the undress uniform, or old woollen tunic that he affected, in a part of a city undefended by his negligence, and nearly lost through his incompetence, and this a few moments after a surprise attack, which he had not foreseen and had done nothing to counter, all this was bitter to The King, who had fought for his life in that space only a quarter of an hour before.

'Sir,' The King said, going up to him, 'if you do not have one-third of all your spearmen on the wall, and another third just below it with their weapons, all the time, you'll lose this city. The third time they attack the ladders will be long enough. They were in here, as you can see.'

'I see,' he answered, smiling, not at The King, but at the citizens who were smiling at him. 'I see; but they do not seem to have got out again.'

He swept his hand towards the dead M'gai. The citizens laughed and applauded at this. I noticed, now, how curiously bitter the citizens were against the Plainsman; they were going to support Lillyboy against the Plainsman, that was clear.

'Sir,' The King said, 'I am going out from here, as you know. I'll try certain schemes that occur to me, and you shall have word from me at the times arranged. But I do beg you to give attention to this young Englishman, Monsieur Ned, who has brought weapons that may make all the difference to the battle that has to be fought here.'

'I do not know any foreign weapons that the Kranois cannot do without,' the old Chief replied. 'Even he, I see, has given up his weapons for the good Kranois spear; is not that so, sir?' he asked, turning to me.

'Sir,' I said, 'I am using a spear because the city has not let me try my own kind. I assure you, that my own weapons are more effective than spears; more than ten times as effective, for the M'gai do not know them.'

'I had some experience of that kind, when I was young,' he said, 'down by the sea at a place called Sixteen Peaks. We Kranois can do without such, I hope.'

'Yes, indeed; we can do without them,' the people answered.

'In war, you need all the help you can get,' The King said.

'Ah,' the old man answered, 'that is just where we old men differ from you young ones. Remember, we, too, have known war. We were in war before you were born, or your father, for that matter. You are going out at sunset, or a little later. See you don't knock up all your horses before the fight. Send me word as arranged.' He touched his pony with a foot, and moved on with his following towards his quarters not far from us.

'There you have our leader,' The King said. 'Well, I hoped I might get you leave to use your guns. I must get my men and go, now. After the battle, we may have a more sensible city to welcome you to. Good-bye, Ned; we'll meet after the battle, I hope.'

'I hope so, King.'

We shook hands again; he moved across the Square to his two stolid-looking trumpeters, who were waiting for orders. I saw The King speak to his men; they blew their calls, which were not like the soldiers' calls of Europe, but much more the calls used on the great ranges, in blowing the cattle to salt or to milking. At the sound of it, I saw the horsemen mustering to their horses. Then, as I was hoping to see the cavalry move off, the light went off the houses, and the glow ceased in the sky. The night had begun to move in. A sudden sharp voice, which I had come to loathe; it was a thin dry voice, without any oil in it, with no life in it; suddenly broke in upon me:

'I thought I sent you to tend cattle; what are you doing in the Square away from your cattle?'

'O, so it's you again?' I said. 'I've been fighting the M'gai.'

'You were drafted to the defaulters' squad. What are you doing away from it?'

'Fighting the M'gai,' I said.

But my Plainsman cattle-herd appeared suddenly. He was no respecter of city men or soldiers.

'Come on here, Ned,' he said. 'I want you, now, with the cattle. Let this fellow stay and talk to himself.'

I went off with the cow-herd, while Sheep-Snake stamped with fury, and then stormed off to tell someone or find someone.

'That man is no good,' the herd said to me. 'However, I'll put you down with some mountain bulls; he'll never

find you there. It'll be dark before he gets his escort to
ram you into prison.'

He led the way slowly down a lane which led to the
south-east tower. I heard the horsemen in the Square
moving off. I longed for The King to appear, saying,
'Ned, you come with me; here's a horse for you,' but
had no such luck. I was hurt at the time, that he had not
asked me. He told me later that he just had heard, that
some in the City Council were for using my guns, and
that if this were so I had better be there to use them. My
Plainsman stopped at a rather dark penthouse under the
south-eastern wall. Here, strong pens kept the best of the
bulls which had been saved. They stood in a row, un-
easily shifting, all trying to get their heads from out of
the beams which kept them penned; their horns kept
rattling on the wood.

'These are our bulls,' my man said. Together, we fed
and watered them. 'Don't heed that city-fellow,' my man
went on. 'I heard a fellow of his saying that if ever they
got into battle together, he should get a crack sooner than
any M'gai. Don't heed him.'

'I have to heed him,' I said, 'he has much authority
here. I'm only a foreigner.'

'Authority, that fellow?' he repeated. 'This is a war. A
man like that keeps no authority in a war. Nor is a useful
man a foreigner. What are you at home? A soldier?'

I said, 'No, a doctor, but I have had lessons in the use
of guns.'

'I'd rather use these guns,' he said, 'than doctor people.
I'd like to know doctoring, too; for it comes useful,
doctoring, with cattle, out on a range; the cattle may
suddenly sicken, or your man is hurt, or bitten by a snake.'

We talked of a good many things; presently he said,
'We'll go the rounds now of the Square, and then turn

in.' So we went out, and found the cattle bedded down for the night, while the night-tenders walked slowly round the pens, singing to them. 'Cattle like being sung to,' my man said. I think that it is true. Certainly, these cattle were used to it, and took it as a part of the routine of rest. The city was quiet enough, but for the drone of the song. I heard the slow steps of sentries on the walls and below. Now and then, a sentry hailed, or answered the hail of his officer. The horses were gone from the horse-lines; a man told us that they had gone out, oh, about an hour after sunset, and had not been attacked; they had ridden clear, 'and now let the M'gai look out.'

We went up to the northern parapet, and looked over the plain. The M'gai camps were quiet; very few figures moved in the light of the fires. I said to my friend, 'It doesn't look as if they meant any trouble tonight.'

'What is the likely thing?' he asked, 'for them to wait till the Big City sends an army, or for them to attack before the army comes?'

'For them to attack,' I said.

'And you are a doctor, not a soldier,' he said.

His words gave me a thrill through the marrow. I envied him his courage. To him, it seemed part of life, that there might be death before morning. He had lived on those terms all his days, out on the ranges, where the snake, the lion, the crazy steer, or the slipping pony might end the liveliest at any moment. I must say, that I could not face it thus.

'So you expect the M'gai over the wall?' I said.

'I always expect savages to do the sensible thing,' he said. 'It's what I do myself.'

'What will you do tonight, then?' I asked. 'What is the sensible thing to do tonight?'

'Sleep soundly,' he said, 'and before sleeping have everything handy, and two things in especial.'

'What are they?'

'A bottle full of water, and a piece of hard bread; be sure of those; and be sure, never to use more than half of either, till you KNOW you'll have more. It is not so easy to know, in war. But I'll see you fixed with those. We'll turn in now and forget it.'

He had rigged himself a den or lair underneath the northern city wall. In this place he found for me a blanket, a string-covered bottle with a wooden stopper and a bag to store my biscuit in.

'Now,' he said, 'you get down to the bull-pen, and sleep while you can. But first make sure that your bottle is filled at the spring.'

I bade him good-night, and moved to the fountains near the temple. I bent and drank, then filled my bottle, and stood a moment, listening to the singing of some women within the temple. As I stood, wondering at the sweetness of the song, and the strangeness of my fate, that I was in a kind of Troy, in the heart of Africa, shut up, and to be killed, perhaps, before daylight, I heard a sound of people moving towards me, and made out that a party of women drew near. They were a relieving-party, coming to take their turn of service. I moved aside as they went in. Presently the party who had been singing came down the steps. They went to the spring, lifted the running water in their hands and let it fall, speaking each some prayer aloud after the water had fallen. The last to speak was the one nearest to me. She was Yvonne.

After they had prayed, each knelt a while on the stone lip sprinkled by the water. One by one they slipped away into the night. Yvonne prayed after the others had gone. Even then, she seemed loth to go, but at last with a little sob she turned to go. I said, very softly, 'Yvonne, is that you?'

'Ah,' she said. 'I have not known where I could find you. Someone said that you had been hurt in the fight just after that.'

'No, I wasn't hurt,' I said, 'but I was in the fight.'

'Do you know, that you are in deadly danger?' she asked.

'I?' I said. 'Why, of course, I know that the whole city is.'

'It is not the enemy outside,' she said, 'but the City Council. In these last hours, our friends have been seized; the Council now is wholly of the Old Party. They are debating killing my grandfather and my brothers.'

'But, Yvonne,' I said, 'whatever for?'

'For? To hide their own shortcomings. They themselves have brought the war, by their folly. They have taken no warning, and now seek a scapegoat. Anything to shew the citizens that these foreigners have betrayed them.'

'But, good heaven,' I said, 'this is craziness.'

'It may be. In war, everybody is somewhat crazy. And when people want to hurt somebody, and can't get at the enemy to hurt him, they will invent an enemy whom they can hurt. They loathe grandfather, because he opposed some of the old abuses here. They used to hold cattle-ranges, which they let to others and never visited. The sub-tenants made the Plainsmen almost their slaves; there was so much abuse of power. Grandfather caused it to be made unlawful, not to manage the ranges in person. The Plainsmen love him for that; the Old Party have never forgiven him and never will. Now, with everybody scared, they say that the invasion is a plot, to bring the Plainsmen into the city and presently with the help of the

M'gai to make the city and the Big City, too, subject to the Plainsmen and the blacks. And now that the Plainsmen's horse have gone out of the city, now is their chance. They mean to assert their power by making an example, as they call it.'

We were now walking slowly backwards and forwards in the Square, in the open space just to the north of the cattle-lines. We had the city to ourselves pretty much. The cattle-herds were still quietly singing to their herds. We saw the sentries slowly pacing under the lamps at the City Council's doors. It was a clear night, very dark and starry.

'They have shut up grandfather and the others in there,' she said, nodding towards the citadel above these doors.

'Could we possibly get at your grandfather and brothers? Could we help them to escape?'

'Not possibly,' she said. 'They are in the citadel there, which is the quarter of the Old Party. I do not even know whereabouts their prisons are; somewhere in that great black mass. All the bodyguards are quartered there; no one could pass in without a special seal, or somebody to vouch for him. And where could we escape to?'

'The King will help,' I said. 'He will be back in little more than a day now. He and his Plainsmen will defend you.'

'I do not think he will be allowed back,' she said. 'We Quichets are in the nets. But I am so glad to warn you. You are in danger; you should hide, and can hide. The cattlemen will hide you.'

A man on the northern tower now blew a melancholy horn.

'That is for the changing of the watch,' she said. 'People will be thronging here. I must go; so must you.'

'Yvonne,' I said, 'will you be at the temple tomorrow

night as you were this night? If you are, can we meet
again, like this? I'll meet you at the spring then, if I am
not a prisoner. Will you do that?'

'Yes,' she said. 'I will if . . . But hide; get the Plainsmen to hide you all tomorrow. I must go.'

She was gone from me into the darkness; men came
stumbling up to relieve the guards. As I did not want to
be recognized, I slipped away to my corner near the bull-
pens, and took my blanket for bed.

Every primitive sleeper, that is, every sleeper who is in
the open or away from security, wakes before dawn,
partly from cold, partly from fear. Then was the danger-
time when man was young; the lessons then learned are
born into all of us. I woke up with a start, knowing that
something was about to happen. I sat up, and found the
morning nearly on us. There was a cold and brisk breeze
blowing about the town. My first thought was, 'What
are the M'gai doing?' The question was usually settled
by their war-cries and the rattle and clack of their sling-
stones, neither of which came to my ears at the moment.
My neighbour, the farrier, was asleep still. I got to my
feet and rubbed my hands. It was horridly cold. Almost
at once, the sentries on the north-east towers blew the
alarm horns, and roused the guards to the alert, and at the
same instant beautiful birds of fire sailed swiftly over the
parapets and swooped and settled down, to burn brightly
where they fell. 'What on earth?' I said. But others and
others came. I knew then that it was the M'gai attacking
by firearrows, or wads of burning tow tied to reeds. The
alarm brought the watches up to the platform, and as they
reached it, the sling-stones began, that noise that one
despised yet dreaded, whish, whish, rattle, crack,
dribble, dribble, plop. The plaster began to fall and cries
came to shew that men were hurt, too. Then some of the

fire wads lodged in a reed-thatch not far from me. The
reeds were bone dry, the wind blew the fire; in an instant
the roof was blazing, and at the glare of the blaze the
M'gai war-cry rose, and not near us, no, at the north-
western tower. The attack was to be there, then. But as I
turned towards the north-west, there rose the devil's own
racket at the south-west end. Above all the noises, I
heard an intermittent thud, which was unlike any noise I
had ever heard. 'I know what that is,' I said aloud;
'they've got battering-rams where the wall's weak.' At
that, I made up my mind that I would get my guns on to
them, if I had to do it all myself. I saw a spear. I ran with
it, along the wall, till I could see what was being done.
The sling-stones were coming over in dozens, from a
couple of hundred blithe young men who were enjoying
themselves. In amongst the stones some fire wads came.
I no longer thought them beautiful.

They had ten rams, and were delivering quite five
blows a minute at the bulged wall. Nor was this all that
they did. At the end of two minutes or so, after every
tenth ram-strike, they paused. Nimble M'gai then darted
forward, and with levers of hard wood hove away the
stones which had been dislodged, so that the rams might
continue. They had already made an impression; they
had started a slither of stone which might become dangerous. By the time I reached the wall above the breach,
the Kranois had woken to the danger. They were flinging
stones at the ramming-parties. I called out to them to
bring up bowmen. 'Bring bowmen and shoot them,' I
shouted. One man said, 'We're not to use arrows on any
account;' another said, 'They've gone for the pitch-pots.'
I should have said that the Kranois use a black bitumen
on the woodwork of their houses, as a safeguard against
the ants. This stuff when heated in pots and flung in a

liquid state from metal ladles makes a wicked weapon. But as the Kranois had not prepared any, there was what the seamen called 'hell to pay and no pitch hot.' Two of them brought up a cold cauldron full of the solid stuff, and then prepared to light a fire under it. I joined the others at the wall, flinging stones. However, the M'gai slingers were much more skilled than we. The stones came at us from right and left, while the rammers dealt their blows below us. 'Fetch bowmen,' I cried. 'A few arrows will stop these fellows.' They repeated that no arrows were to be used on any account until the battle.

Where were my guns, all this time? One cohorn only, nay, one musket full of slugs or blunderbuss full of gravel, would have stopped all this battering at once.

I flung stones, I say, till there came a great rush of smoke and a crackle and blaze of flame away to the east. 'Well,' I said to myself, 'I must find out where the wagons are before the fire gets to them. This city may be blown sky-high otherwise.' I ran off, peering right and left for the wagons. I could see no wagons. A man came down the lane towards me; I said, 'Where are the wagons that were here yesterday?'

'Wagons?' he said. 'What wagons? You don't want wagons when the city's on fire.'

He was wrong. When a city is on fire, it is very important to find any wagon full of gunpowder. However, I could not find this wagon. I came instead to a house blazing fire, while men were running aimlessly, although the water conduit was rushing brim full just beside them. There were buckets there, too. Well, in a wild emergency, it is better to be doing something than uselessly trying to do something that can't be done. I snatched a bucket; they were the light canvas buckets just stiffened with cane, which all the men of the plain take with them. I dipped it into the conduit and flung its contents swoosh into the blaze. It is astonishing what an effect water has in an emergency. Put it over the head of the most dangerous politician, and it may save a state. Dash it on to a swooning man, and he will stand up and continue his task. Fling it with a fair aim on to a blaze, and you will see an astonishing change; but when a strong breeze is blowing and the fire has taken a hold, the change is for an instant only. I repeated it. I called to others, to seize buckets and put the fire out. As it happened, they were a good lot of young men, only wanting a lead; they did as I bid, so that we put out the fire.

We were hot and black when we had finished; so was the house; we only saved the shell. We were rinsing ourselves in the conduit, when we heard the devil's own uproar from the north-western tower, and almost on the instant a roaring blaze broke out near the south gate. I told you that some men had brought pots of bitumen and had set them to boil there. They forgot all about them, in the excitement of the day; the pots all caught fire and set fire to the houses near by; a glorious blaze they made. All worn as we were from our fight, we had to run there to quench the burning. We had to make a chain of bucket-passers, then a double chain, then a triple chain, before we could get it under. I do not know if anyone from headquarters looked for Ned the foreigner that day. I judge that headquarters had enough to do that day. But I remember thinking that headquarters had been divinely led to shift the powder wagon. Had they left it where we had left it, the south gate of the city would have been blown then right clear of the walls and the southern wall would have fallen.

After the fire was out, we fire-fighters were told to go up to the north wall, 'to relieve the poor devils there.'

We set out, wondering why they should be poor devils to be relieved: what were we? However, we found, soon, that the north wall had had a fiercer struggle than ourselves, and had let the M'gai get in. As we marched across the Square we found dead M'gai there among dead cattle. They had been right in. What had stopped them was partly their fear of ambush, partly our Old Sword, brave as a lion, cool as ice, smiling and cheerful, on his old white pony. Old Sword had restored the battle there. When it came to a body-to-body tussle, Old Sword was pretty good. Well, the battle was over.

Presently the sun went down, food was served out, and we were able to prepare for the morrow.

Now word had gone about for the past twenty-four hours that the army of the Big City, a drilled and disciplined body of spearmen, more than fifteen hundred strong, was on its way to us. Shut up as we were, we were in touch with this army. In the day-time, signals were flashed to and from it. Besides these, carrier-pigeons flew into the citadel, and at night, the adroit scouts of the plain, or friendly natives, came through the M'gai lines to the foot of certain walls, where they were looked for and helped in. After dark that evening, three or four such messengers came in at odd times, to tell us that the army was making good progress. It was coming along behind a screen of horsemen, quite unsuspected as yet by the M'gai, who, indeed, had been pretty busy with us all day long. Soon after the coming-in of the last of these messengers, officers came round quietly to each ward, to say that everything was going according to plan; that the army would come in from the Big City just before dawn. It would attack the M'gai upon an arranged signal. The horse would hamper one wing of the M'gai from helping the other, and the whole strength of our own city would sally out, with spear and bows, to join the Big City army and end the war. Any confident talk of victory will cheer the heart. I know that I felt the difference made by these officers; the temper of the city rose with a bound; men became confident and began to long for the morning. After the food, all citizens received their orders; and men were busy with preparation, sharpening spears, drawing rations of hard bread, cheese, and raisins, filling water-bottles, and then going to appointed positions. I had heard no word from any citizen of the foreigners in prison in the citadel; and from the silence judged that they were still alive. No man had come to arrest me. Yet when, after the food, I went to tend the cattle, two guards from headquarters came up, to say that the foreigner, Ned, was wanted at headquarters.

'This is the man,' they said.

I asked, 'What am I wanted for?'

They said, I should be told there; they only had to bring me.

I went with them, feeling that, indeed, they meant me no good, and wondering if this were to be the end. You will say, that I might have run or fought, or done something. If you will go to a foreign city and be arrested by the police, tell me, later, will you, if you ran or fought, or did something? I went, and was taken to a lamp-lit room where two men were copying lists at a table. They looked at me, and then went on with their work, repeating the names on the lists and commenting on them. I gathered from what I caught of their talk that they were making lists of foreigners and Plainsmen not liked by the Old Party. They went through about a dozen names, with comment about some of them, who were not considered to be safe. The names were unknown to me, but I was struck by the knowledge they shewed of the characters and positions of the suspects. Then one of them mentioned the name Eevono, which made me listen with all my ears.

The other said, 'She's a singing woman.'

The first said, 'No foreigner is to be that after midnight tonight. She will go with the rest.'

The other said, 'She's pretty, too.'

The first said, 'That will not count for much when the safety of the city's at stake.'

After that, I listened with all my ears for a hint of what was being planned. I gathered that these foreigners or suspects would be arrested; but what did 'go with the rest' mean? Were they to be put outside the city to the M'gai or put to death within the walls? I could not learn this. I had no doubt that Eevono was Yvonne.

Presently, I became conscious that a noise, which was going on intermittently not far away, was the noise of digging. Men were digging somewhere quite close to me. I wondered what in the world they could be digging. I heard the unmistakable noise of spades on stones, and the falling of earth tossed aside. It went on for a long time; then Sheep-Snake and two others came in; took seats, and asked me a lot of questions: who was I; how long I had known the M'gai; what my position with the M'gai King was; what I meant by coming to the city; had I planned to blow down the south gate with my foreign weapons; was I to receive a grant of slaves for this, when the city had been taken? They were crazy questions, you will say; they made me understand something of my danger.

Presently, when all had asked me questions to the weariness of the soul, I was told I might go into the yard, while they deliberated. One of the men opened a door for me. I went out into a yard fairly well lit by the fire. In the yard half a dozen depressed prisoners were wearily digging a trench of an odd shape. It was about five yards long by two broad, and about three feet deep. They had been at it a long time and were tired; a couple of spearmen watched them.

Now when I saw this trench, I knew that it was a grave, and that it was meant for the suspects on the lists which the men were preparing. It was almost deep enough, so that it would soon be ready; if it were soon ready, doubtless it would soon be used. As I came out into the yard there, the guards and the prisoners looked at me, not as one looks at a foreigner, but as one looks at a doomed man. Believe me, I know that look; it differs from all other looks. Their looks said, 'He's one that will lie here. This earth will go on that face. After rain, this is where his toes'll come through.' One of the prisoners who was digging began to whistle a little tune, and another sang a line of song to it: 'A flower for my lady's garden.' There was no need to tell me that they were only prisoners; and that I was condemned.

I suppose that I had been twenty seconds in the yard, thinking these thoughts, when the alarm trumpets blew from the tower just above us. These trumpets were followed by the violent ringing of a bell. When the bell ceased, everybody in that quarter of the city waited for the shouted orders which were quite certain to follow. They followed at once. There was a general warning that there was to be no rushing, no confusion, but that all citizens were to repair at once to their battle stations. 'Go quietly' (the orders went), 'and await further orders when you reach your stations.'

The prisoners near me ceased to dig, and looked at their guards. Their guards looked at each other. One said, 'Well, we must go to our ward.' They said to the prisoners, 'You keep on with this grave, or you'll likely lie in it,' and then, shouldering their spears, they set off to their stations. All the city was full of people moving hither and thither. As soon as the guards had gone, the prisoners put down their spades, looked to see if the coast were clear and went too. I had seen a door on the other side of the bonfire; I slipped to that, unbolted it, and got away into a lane, just as someone came into the yard for me. I did not wait, but ran for it, and got into the Square. There was a fine confusion there, of men going to stations, not knowing if it were a real alarm or a prelude to the morrow's battle. It was a cloudy night and, except for a few lanterns, some glowing ruins and a bonfire or two, there was little light to go by. The cattle were up and inclined to panic. I kept thinking, 'These people will stop Yvonne, probably, on her way to the temple tonight, before midnight. All the party of us will be in that grave before dawn.'

As the cattle were all in a stir, I knew that my friend, the cattle-chief, would be with them. I came upon him, as he strengthened a pen by beating in the hurdles.

Even before I spoke, he said, 'Come on down the line a pace, till we see these pens secure. There's been blood shed here, and the cattle are all crazy tonight because of it. Now, son, what's the trouble?'

I said, I thought we were all to be killed, including Yvonne.

'My mind misgave me you might not be too safe,' he said. 'You can't stay here. This is the first place they'll search for you. That crazy farrier has told them you slept at the bull-pens; you can't go there. And you can hear, wherever you turn, that they're mustering and learning where everybody is. Still, it's dark; I'll find you some place.'

'I want a place for Yvonne. She'll be at the temple at twelve.'

'You mean, she's a singing-woman?' he said.

'Yes; but they're going to take her.'

'In that case, come, now,' he said. He plucked me by the arm and hurried me off towards the western end of the Square, and down a road unknown to me, to a lesser square. 'It's the Quichet girl, Edmond's grandchild; isn't that the one?'

'Yes,' I said; 'she's the one.'

'I know the girl you mean. She's been out at The King's half a dozen times. I'll find a way to warn her, if warning's any good. For yourself, I've a place here.'

My friend opened a door for me and pushed me into a house, where a lot of the Plainswomen were sheltering.

'See here,' he said, to one of them, 'this lad has had a knock on the head from a stone. Take him up to the roof and let no one come to him till I come myself. Let him lie on the roof with the gear. Don't let anyone trouble him; and don't let him talk. I'll come for him later.'

The woman was his sister. They helped me up the steps to the roof, which, being almost flat, had been used as a store. They had rigged sheers, and had hoisted up some thirty trusses of the sweet-smelling fodder. They told me to lie down till they could contrive something; and then left me.

I lay down to rest among the fodder-bales, thinking of Yvonne, and my friends. The city was at first noisy with men passing to stations or singing in companies; presently these became quiet. I was weary from the day: I slept heavily, in spite of my danger. It seemed, in my sleep, that I heard horses galloping: but I did not wake till my friend roused me in the cold of the intense dark, to come up to the northern wall, where some of the cattlemen were doing a turn of guard. He said, 'Don't ask about your friend: she'll do.' He had a helmet for me of an old type to cover my eyes: this made a fine disguise for me. It had been a quiet night, my comrades told me: no attack. They said that riders had come to the western gates from the Big Army. This had been the galloping that I had heard. Indeed, as I took my place on the wall, a rider galloped up not very far from me, and called something which I could not catch. He waited there for an answer. Leaning at an embrasure, I could see him, drawn up, close under the wall. However, on his repeating his call, some answer was given to him, and he rode off, with what seemed expostulation, slowly at first, then at a gallop.

I asked, how they could ride up through the M'gai sentries.

A Plainsman said, 'The M'gai are afraid of horsemen. Besides, they seldom attack one man; they think he may be a herald, a wizard or a god. They would never attack one of those.'

There was no light at the moment; all the M'gai camp-fires were out. A cock of the long-legged skinny kind that inhabits there, crowed a reedy crow and lapsed again to his dreams. It was pitch dark and cruelly cold. As sleep was impossible, and as no M'gai were near the walls, we thought that we might be doing a good turn if we went from the walls and set about the work of the cattle, so that the other watch might have less to do when roused. Beating our hands to warm them, we went down the steps and so forth to the Square to the cattle-pens. Here I found that a watchman was already at work bringing in forks-ful of fodder from the piles. Some cattle were already munching. I thought again that this clover-grass smelt like bean-blossom. It reminded me of a field near Chols-

ington, where I had walked with my father, on our way
to the river. Now here I was in the heart of Africa, probably to be killed that day. I had always thought that I
should be terrified before a battle: now I found that I had
no terror, only a certainty that I should be killed, and that
this was a melancholy but not a bad thing.

Our Chief told us, that we were to be the rear-guard
when the army moved. 'Well might they make us the
rear-guard,' he said. 'They know we'll not let them run.'

Men were moving about in the darkness of the Square:
they were the callers of the companies, rousing the
sleepers. All the Square was full of sleepers, who were
lying there in their ranks, under arms. At the calls, they
were waking wearily, stretching, then remembering that
now was to come the battle, and so coming to their feet,
and moving to fall in. I heard the wakers saying, 'Quietly,
now. No noise: keep quiet.' I suppose that all thought
that they were being quiet, but what with the calls, the
oaths of the wakened men, the clink of weapons, and the
frequent clang as a spear or helmet fell on the stones, the
M'gai sentries must have known that large numbers of
armed men were moving within the walls. As I came in
among the throng, I found that food was being brought
round; we cattlemen put ours aside, till the cattle were
fed. As in all wars, there was a great deal of confusion.
Several companies, having roughly mustered, set off
from the Square towards their appointed gates. They got
into each other's way, blocked the roads and had to halt
to let one or other get by. The darkness excused it, of
course, but it was a part of the confusion which I had
come to expect from the Old Party.

As we went to and fro with our clover we passed the
same ranks standing in the same place, waiting for an
order. They stood there on their spears, and chaffed or

cursed us; while we asked them, when they were going to fight the M'gai, or had they thought better of it? They were waiting for the signal, they said. It was of no great matter to us while they stood in their ranks, but presently, after they had stood an hour in the intense cold and darkness, they took to sitting or lying down in rank, and this without order, or in despite of order. Men were growling and angry, asking why they were not marching, and why they had been roused all these hours too soon. Some of them started singing, so that presently there was real uproar. The headquarters heralds had to blow their bugles for silence, and shout from the walls that the ranks were to keep silence. There was a moment's silence after that, and in the silence, which may have lasted for twenty-five seconds, we all distinctly heard a distant noise away to the north of the city. It was a confused noise of shouting and screaming; it came down the wind to us. Quite certainly, the noise was partly the war-crying of the M'gai.

My old Plainsman called to an officer, 'They're fighting there; why don't you move?'

He answered good-naturedly that the headquarters men had gone up to the walls to watch for the signal; all was waiting for that. It could not now be long.

My leader said, 'If you ask me, it has gone long ago; the Big Army is fighting now; any fool could tell that. Get on out and set forward.'

Indeed, a good many felt that that was so; the bugles blew again from the walls and the heralds shouted, that all were to fall-in and stand to arms. This was a very good order; but the effort to obey it made the chaos worse for a while; however, the men did, in the main, fall-in and wait. We cattle-men mocked them again; but it was too serious for mockery. Rumours floated down to us from the walls, that messengers had come to delay the marching; then rumours came from the gates, that they would be open in a few minutes. Probably all the rumours were false; one rumour was that a messenger had just come on horseback to say that the M'gai were in full retreat. This was believed and cheered; it was backed by a story which spread, I cannot think how, save as rumour does spread in war, that the Big Army had routed the M'gai already.

Though it was still dark, a streak of light rather high up in the east, which always lightened before sunrise, was aloft like a sign there. As it lightened, the armourers got to their forges; women came to their doors and children slipped up and down the lanes to see the spearmen. Some headquarters officers came thrusting down from the walls and called, that they had not had any signal yet, but expected one at any minute.

'Get the men fallen-in, sergeants,' they cried. 'It can't be more than a minute or two now.'

The sergeants called to the companies, and passed up and down and looked important. The ranks closed up, and stood again, waiting for an order, which still did not come. After about twenty minutes, there was a clamour of vexation from them. They knew well, or had been busily told, that the M'gai were easily routed if attacked before daylight; now the chances of a dawn surprise were gone, and that fine courage which had been in each one of them was gone, too. The oaths flew fast. 'Why aren't we out? What is keeping us here? Why doesn't the old man move us?'

Then officers would call, 'Silence, there. We're waiting for the north-west party to be out. They'll be on our flank. They have to be out before we can move.'

Then one said, 'Well, if that's so, why aren't they out? They haven't stirred. What's keeping them? I suppose they're waiting for us.'

Then a sergeant would shout, 'Less noise in the ranks, there. Less free with your jaws there. We're waiting for the signal. It'll be here any minute now. Keep your breath for fighting. You'll need all the breath you can get then, be very sure.'

By this time, we cattle-hands had done our feeding and watering. We had filled our bottles and taken our spears (for some had come now). Our chief said that as soon as possible we should move back to the platform of the north wall. I was one of the first in the group to move. I half saw, as I turned to go, the figure of a man in armour who seemed to step into our company. Someone near the eastern gate began to play upon a flute in what was called the ancient Kranish mode; a few, who knew the tune, sang to it; other flutes began. In that darkness at that tense time it was overwhelmingly beautiful. My heart beat quickly to the music. My chief said, 'If they'd use their breath to fight, it might be more to the point. Not a man of them's outside the gates yet. Think of it.' It did not bear thinking of. When we reached the platform on the wall, we all craned over the parapet, hoping to see the long black lines of the Kranois moving out from both the eastern and the western gates, and merging to go on as one. We saw nothing of that kind; my chief was right; they were not yet out of the gate. The night's darkness still held, but in such a way that all objects stood out against it with sharp edges, intensely black. The sky had begun to shew the faintest tints of primrose colour. I could see on my left, the gonfalon of the Commander-in-Chief upon the wall; its white swallow-tail shewed clear in the brisk, cold wind. My chief said, 'Old Sword is up there, somewhere.' Indeed, a moment later we saw him with his staff, not on the wall, but issuing from his quarters, and coming cheerily up the steps to the platform, laughing and joking. They passed along the platform, away from us. We could not hear what they said, only saw them taking post on the wall, and looking over the parapet.

'Well,' my chief said, 'it's broad day, now. What's the old fool thinking of, to be joking there?' He looked with bitterness towards the staff; then said, 'He must know they're engaged. What's he waiting for?'

Then we heard the galloping of hoofs in the plain. Several horses were galloping to the foot of the wall. They had come over the western end of Fair Hillocks (the rise to our north) and were coming straight to where we stood. It was now fast growing light. I could see colour, a darkish blue-green, in a little thorny shrub which had grown into the wall close to me. The horsemen came at speed, straight to the point below the Chief's gonfalon. I could see that the leading horseman was The King. He was signalling with an active hand to the Chief, to come out.

'Come out,' he shouted. 'Bring out your men and fall on. What in Fate are you waiting for?' He reined up a lathering horse just below us. He was white with excitement and fury. 'Why aren't you engaged?'

'Engaged?' Old Sword replied. 'Engaged? We have had no signal. We have seen no signal. We are waiting for the prearranged sign.'

'Sign and signal?' The King answered. 'We have sent to you and sent to you. Why in the name of God have you not marched? I've sent six gallopers to you. They've told you this. Yet here you are still in the walls.'

'Listen, young man,' Old Sword said, when the murmuring of his staff died down. 'The plans for this battle were, that our movement is to depend upon a certain signal. I am not young enough to alter plans because an excited horseman tells me to. Keep your gallopers where you can use them. Don't send them with orders to me. I command here. And being commander, I wait for the signal.'

The King replied quietly, in his clear penetrating Plainsman's voice. 'In that case you'll wait till the moon's purple. I've sent six times to tell you, as I now tell all of you, that we cannot reach the signalling point. We're engaged with the whole M'gai army, on the other side of Fair Hillocks, where you can't see. I've told you this six times by messenger. Now I've come to you myself. You have wasted the chance of ten thousand. Come out at least now and take them in the rear, before we're all killed.'

His voice rang over the city. In spite of the wind most of the men on the north wall heard him. What they heard passed at once down to the men in the ranks below. I suppose that Old Sword was stupefied at being so spoken to; perhaps his mind moved too slowly always to have a ready reply. The staff, stung to silence, looked at each other and at Old Sword: nothing was said.

The King, waiting for an answer and getting nothing, cried, 'Move, man; for very shame's sake, move.'

The Old Sword moved slowly to the parapet, and turned to his left. 'You there,' he said to one of his officers, 'tell them to open the west gate.' As the officer moved, Old Sword spoke to The King. 'I've told them to open the west gate below there. Come you in by it, and make your report in a fitting manner.'

'I've made my report,' The King answered. 'You act on it. My place now is with the fighters, where I can be of use. If you won't fight, at least shew yourselves, so that we may know you're there to fight for.'

With that, he and his riders rode slowly off, nursing

their horses, towards the Fair Hillocks. They did not look back at the city. Their eyes were roving along and across for M'gai lying in the grass to spear them as they went. Now that their backs were turned, I bit my nails with vexation that I had not seized one of the spy ropes secured to the parapet, gone down the wall and joined The King.

The staff officer, said 'Sir, we will have that man before a soldier's court.'

Old Sword, who was ever one to bide his time, said, 'Where is that Tali-Mali who killed the lion that time?'

The staff leapt at once into activity; the word was passed for Kleza, or M'Kleza, who was down in the headquarters somewhere. He was on the wall with us in twenty seconds; a big middle-aged savage.

'Kleza,' Old Sword said, 'what happens yonder?' He pointed to our north-north-east, in the direction of Fair Hillocks.

Now the wind was blowing, making much noise about us. This savage looked, bent an ear, took a deep smell of the wind and at once kindled all over. 'Men fight,' he said. 'Many men fight.'

'That will do, Kleza,' Old Sword said. 'That will do for us, gentlemen. Send word at once. Prepare to march. Open east and west gates. Archers to cover the wings. Set forward.'

There was now an almost full daylight; the men who had been waiting in the ranks for hours gave a cheer at the word to move. I heard the gates open; and almost instantly, I saw some archers scatter out to cover the wings and stop any attack on the columns as they came out. All the troops were at once moving. The staff followed Old Sword from the wall. By this time The King and his troopers had reached the top of the Fair Hillocks and turned over the crest out of sight. Some of the people in the Square cheered Old Sword as he went down to his old white pony, but it was not much of a cheer. As I turned to see him start, I found that man in armour, whom I had half-seen in the Square standing at my side. Something about the figure made me catch my breath. The figure put out a hand and nudged me back to the parapet. All the others of our squad were at the stair-tops, watching the army moving out of the city.

'Don't you recognize Yvonne?' the figure said. 'I was given this to wear. I'm hoping to reach the other camp. Are we to be shut here all day?'

'I hope not,' I said. 'Have you had any food?'

'Yes, and rest. And I've heard that our people aren't killed yet. You and I are both being looked for, but they won't search much till after this. What do you think is happening over there?'

'The M'gai have attacked the Big Army on its march. Our old fool ought to have foreseen that and prevented it by attacking in time.'

'How do you think it is going?'

'I cannot tell. I only heard the noise of it once or twice in lulls of the wind or when the city was quiet. It was not further off when I heard it last, so I suppose there is no retreat yet. On the other hand, The King seemed anxious.'

At this point, my old Plainsman called, 'Come on, boys, we're to leave this now; we of the gallant rear-guard. Come on to the east gate with you. See all your water-bottles full at the spring. War may be glorious or it may be damned, but it's always thirsty and usually full of lice.'

We halted at the gate for some twenty minutes, while other odds and ends of armed men were gathered from different parts of the wall to make us somewhat stronger.

The city was tense and scared. A few women, with very

white faces, came to the doors for news, or to the springs
for water. Some little boys who had formed themselves
into companies came to the Square to drill with sticks;
all the little girls seemed to have become women over-
night. We being halted in the space below the walls could
see nothing of what was happening outside; and hear
little save some distant shouting, mostly orders of some
sort. We could see old men on the walls, peering at what
was happening outside. We all called to them from time to
time, to ask how things were going. They could see very
little except that the men were moving out; then that they
had reached the Hillocks; that the M'gai were not to be
seen; and that presently our army was over the rise and
out of sight. We waited as we were for a long time; then
an officer, an old man, with a singularly merry face, came
up to us and said, 'We must move now. We have to cover
the right rear.'

The gate was opened to us, the archers spread out in a
fan formation in front of us, and so we passed out of the
city. I had not loved my time within her; but still she was
a city. Outside her walls, I had to reflect, that only a few
old bowmen stood between me and the M'gai. I assure
you I longed for my guns. Yvonne at my side said, 'There
is the first step past: we are out of the city, at least.' Our
captain led us in a somewhat loose order away to the east,
straight towards the M'gai lines, now seemingly empty.
As we went, I passed one or two hollows in the grass,
like the forms of great hares, where M'gai sentries had
passed the night. No M'gai were there now. However,
the Plainsman told me, that no doubt half a dozen were
watching us unseen. Our captain halted us, closed us upon
our centre, and drew in the bowman a little. We stood
there, waiting and looking about for a few minutes. Then
a small party of M'gai, with black and white plumes,

appeared on the eastern end of the Fair Hillocks to north of us. They stood there for a time, looking at us; perhaps they were twenty strong. As they received no supports, and seemed uneasy at our presence, our captain said that he meant to clear them out of that. The bowmen were told to go forward, in open order, twenty yards ahead of us; we followed in wedge formation, ready to receive the bowmen amongst us at an instant's notice. The M'gai watched our coming, without trying to attack. As we came to a point that was almost within bowshot of them, they slipped quietly back behind the skyline out of sight. Our captain cheered, and said, 'They're running. Come on, boys, we'll hunt them.'

My cattleman said, 'Go slowly. That is only a trap. They're falling back to draw you on. It is a rule with us, never go over a skyline after M'gai.'

Our captain disliked being checked, but said, 'Perhaps you're right.' He called to the bowmen to come in within our wedge; then we advanced again, up to the top of Fair Hillocks, so that we could see the city behind and below us on the one side, and the unknown world on the other. It was no pleasant sight that we beheld. Coming up the slope towards us, about three hundred yards away, was the whole of our city's army in hollow wedge formation, beset by a couple of hundred active young M'gai, who were slinging it with stones. Men in the wedge were being hit and were falling. Those near them picked them up and made shift to carry them; they were carrying some sixty already, at a rough guess. The body looked unwieldy, baffled and beaten; it staggered along at the pace of the men who bore the dead and hurt. Now and then some archers in the wedge drew bows and loosed arrows. Someone said, then, that Old Sword had refused to take many archers, saying that the battle would be decided by spearmen. A few arrows were shot. The slingers danced about, and sometimes stood still to draw the arrows, which they parried with great skill with their scratch-sticks. They mocked the unwieldy wedge. Shocked as we all were at its appearance, we felt inclined to mock, too. Why was an army letting itself be pelted thus? Old Sword rode within the wedge on his white pony. He was cer-tainly as brave as a man can be; but this was no way to fight M'gai. The thought came on to our hearts like a sledge-hammer, 'What has come to the army of the Big City? Has it been destroyed?'

We could not tell where the M'gai were. Parallel with the Fair Hillocks, about a mile in front of us, were other low rolling fair hillocks. I did not doubt that somewhere behind those the army of the Big City was in the lion's jaws of the whole M'gai army. What on earth was the Old Sword doing, to retreat before a couple of hundred slingers? The old merry captain who commanded us asked this. He at once told our bowmen to go on in open order and shoot the M'gai slingers. Now our archers were elderly men and good bowmen. I saw our first arrow bring down a young M'gai who had rashly paused to mock; then another and another fell. I saw then that the young M'gai at any rate were not disciplined to bear losses. They fell away from our side of the wedge, and left their dead, which the M'gai ever shrink from doing. By this time the wedge was pretty near to us. I could see the faces of the spearmen, all scared, humiliated, angry, white and sullen. Some of our men called, 'Where's the Big Army?' But by this time I saw that a vast body of the M'gai were beginning to blacken the distant hillocks of which I have just spoken. Whatever had happened to the Big Army, the whole M'gai army was there between us and it. The question we asked was, whether the M'gai had destroyed it. Anyhow, it was plain that our men had not joined it, but had been driven off.

Glancing back at the city, I saw the battlements of the north wall packed with watchers, all deadly still. I thought of Troy watching for the heroes returning from the field.

Like the wedge, we were all falling back thither. However, at this point we were all upon the ridge of the Fair Hillocks, and about to go down thence out of sight of the M'gai. It was at this point, that my friend the cattleman took command.

He said to our captain, 'Keep all the bowmen out on to this ridge. No M'gai will rush over a skyline. You can hold them up there with twenty good archers.'

My captain was a clever fellow, always ready to take a suggestion. As we dipped down the slope towards the city, he called out the bowmen and told them that they were to cover the retreat from that point. Something of the same thought came to the Old Sword, for he, too, put out archers. Now we were over the ridge, and going back to the town. Almost at once a volley of sling-stones came over, and an elderly bowman with a grizzled beard was killed close beside me. I saw that he was dead. I jabbed my spear into the ground and took his bow and quiver. I sent an arrow at one of the young M'gai who had darted up to sling. All this time we were outside the army, watching its uncouth clumsy body heaving down towards the town, and beginning to go dangerously quickly. Someone who thought that the formation might break, began to sing some slow-timed song, to steady the retreat. I have little doubt that this was the Old Sword himself, who knew how near to a panic his flounderers were. I sent another arrow at another M'gai. Yvonne at my side, handed me arrows.

Then, almost before I knew what was happening, there came a scream like the end of the world and the M'gai were over the Fair Hillocks, and were between us and the city, attacking the wedge. It was the Black Regiment that was attacking. They did not pay any attention to us archers. They went straight at the wedge with an incredible raging, yelling, screaming fury. I shot arrows at them, so did the archers with me. I don't think I hit anybody, but I saw several men go charging on with two or three arrows sticking in them. Then they got in upon the edge of the wedge, and flowed round it and closed in. However, the wedge stood. I could see Old Sword upon his pony; he was the one happy man in the wedge, I judge; this was like his youth. This needed no brain, only cool courage in which he was supreme. Our position was not good, out there on the slope, with mad M'gai between us and the wedge, and possibly three thousand more M'gai about to leap over the skyline at us.

I saw nothing of the wedge. It was all hidden from me by dark bodies and lifted dark arms. I shot and shot at this heaving mass, till I found no arrows handy. Yvonne snatched arrows from the ground; some of them had had their points snapped off, but I shot them. I saw that the wedge was moved, as it were, sideways by the weight of the M'gai against it, and said to myself that it would break; must break. Perhaps it would have broken. But then there came a roar and a thundering. I said, 'Here comes the M'gai army.' It was nothing of the sort. It was The King, with some three hundred horse, charging the M'gai from the west.

I suppose no battle has been more suddenly changed. What was so amazing was the change in the M'gai. They had been mad devils; then in one instant they were screaming runaways, throwing away their weapons and running like hares. However, it was not part of The King's plan to chase one scattered regiment over Africa, while four or five undefeated regiments might be just over the hillocks; besides, the horses had had a hard morning, and had the day still before them. I heard a whistle blow, and saw the squadrons rally to it. A loose horse stopped to graze just beside me; I caught it and mounted Yvonne upon it. We stood together there staring at the marvellous sight. The wedge of the Kranish army was floundering back to the city. I could see the Old Sword trying to stop it and turn it, but he was not regarded; all those men were for getting back within the walls. All the wall was strung with a kind of bead-work of faces staring. I could see no bodies, only lines of faces. This gave me a strange and haunting impression that saw only souls, all anxious. The M'gai being for the moment gone, we of the rear-guard began collecting arrows and spears with which the ground was stuck thick. An officer of the horse rode up to us, and called, 'Come, all of you. Leave the gear on the field. We want the M'gai cattle and asses.' He mustered us together, and set forth with us towards the M'gai camp, and through this to the old Kranish cattle-pens, in which they had sorted their booty of plundered cattle, and their supply-train of asses. Some old women were tending the beasts in the pens. They fled up-hill from us as we approached and gathered together to curse and spit at us. The officer who had summoned us to this work called out to get all the rope we could to halter the asses together. I had the chance of an instant of speech with him, and said, 'I am not a Kranois. I am a doctor and newly come to the city. When we drive these beasts to the town, may I come with you to The King, instead of going back into the city with them; my friend, too?'

'These aren't going into the city,' he said. 'These are the pedigree stock of the big plain-breeders. These are coming with us to safety. Can you ride? Any of you men who can ride, mount each his ass. So you're the man The King was talking of. He must be somewhere. Did you ever see a pretty chance worse spoiled?'

To be brief, we gathered the plunder, and then set forward to drive it to the camp of the Big Army. We of the city were wondering what had happened. This Plainsman told us everything. There had been a bitter fight from before dawn, some miles from where we were. The M'gai had attacked the Big Army on its march, and had had many losses and not much success; they had then been unexpectedly charged by the horse, of which they were much scared, and had had a severe set-back. If the city forces had but marched out on the alarm, they might have been annihilated; instead of that, they had marched out when the Big Army, despairing of their moving at all, had returned to camp. Seeing them returning the M'gai, had plucked up courage and had followed them. The M'gai regiment left behind to guard the rear had attacked the city army when it appeared, the city army had floundered about, and seeing no other Kranish army about had retreated, and had only been saved from destruction by The King's timely charge.

Now, as I rode on the wide plain (on a donkey, it is true, but with my love beside me), my heart again beat high. I had found no friends in the city; I had found them at once among the Plainsmen; and with the feeling that I was out of the city, came the knowledge that I might save Quichet, and help to beat back the M'gai.

We came in time to the camp of the Big Army, as I have called it. This was on a low hill above a little river. A clump of trees was on the hilltop; a ridge from each end of the hill stretched out and fenced a grassy level where the cattle could both be grazed and guarded. It was a beautiful place, impossible to surprise, having this open rolling land on all sides of it. When I saw it, I knew that the war had changed for the better; here were people who knew what to do.

Long before we entered the camp, I saw that this was not under the command of men like Old Sword and his friends. Here all was order, forethought and design. Here there was knowledge to support the native stubbornness. Vedettes were out, a watch-tower had been built and manned; all approaches were either trenched or fenced or both.

My officer friend, who had taken me under his wing, said that as I had this woman with me, I had better go straight to the headquarters as very likely I would find The King there, if he had come in from the field. Headquarters was a level space on a hill-top, partly fenced with rolls of blanket, which would presently be the general's bedding. A spear with a scarlet bannerole was stuck near it as a guide. Food was about to be served; and the staff officers were coming in for their meal, which was being cooked for them at two little native stoves near by. Three of the main officers lay on their faces on the ground having their knees kneaded and pounded in the Kranish manner after their long hours in the saddle. I saw at once that one of these men was The King, so I called out to him:

'King, I am Ned, whom you met in the city. Can you do something for Quichet and his grandsons? They have got them all shut up and may put them to death.'

He rolled over at once on hearing what I said;

'Is not that just the thing these people would do?' he said. 'They cannot govern; they cannot foresee, or meet the unforeseen, yet they unite to destroy the men who can do both. You must see the Chief. He will be here in a moment; he has only gone to speak to the galloper. In fact, here he comes. Chief, here is the young Englishman, the doctor, of whom I told you.'

I had had some experience now of Kranish soldiers, and thought that I knew what to expect. I was not prepared for the man who entered. To begin with, he was a very young man, not more than twenty-five; I had not expected youth in a leader, nor beauty and grace in a soldier, since Alexanders are rare. I knew at once that this man was of the stamp of Alexander and of those other young commanders who carry all before them, and at once my heart leapt within me, to think that now we might beat back the M'gai. This was the saviour of the Kranois.

He greeted me and welcomed me to the Kranish camp.

'He has bad news about Quichet,' The King said.

'Sir,' I said, 'the leaders in the city yonder are going to kill the Quichets. What can you do to help?'

The young Commander, whom all called 'Golden,' asked, 'What, do you think, can be done?'

'The only means,' I said, 'is to supplant the Old Party. If you leave them in power there, for only a few hours more, they may have killed these men.'

'They may have done that already,' The King said.

'We think not: but granted that they have,' I answered, 'they have not beaten the M'gai; and you can supplant them on the plea, that they are ruining the Kranish cause.'

Golden smiled and said, 'They were not very helpful this morning. I'm surprised at Old Sword. So you think we ought to supplant the Old Party?'

'It will be said,' The King said, 'that the Plainsmen made a war to lose their cattle and then made a revolution to save them; we shall be less loved than ever.'

'You will,' I said. 'But if you beat the M'gai, the city will see that you have saved her, and at present she knows pretty well that Old Sword and his friends have brought her to the brink. What help do you expect tomorrow or next week or next year for that matter from such a set?'

'The King has told me about some weapons you brought. Would you pledge your faith that these weapons of yours are sure to help to beat the M'gai?' Golden asked me this question in a way which made me feel that he was on my side.

'I know that they will,' I said. 'But give me a fair chance, and a few careful men, and I pledge you my faith and my head, that I will shock the M'gai. No savage race has withstood fire-arms yet. They kill at great distances, and with loud noises; they are terrifying.'

'You told me something of the sort,' Golden said to The King. He turned, then, to Yvonne, and said, 'These camps are no place for you women. We will try to find a shelter for you here. Could you guide us about in the recesses of the citadel, if we came to the city tonight?'

'No,' she said. 'I have never been in the citadel. But I know that the temple on the west wall has a door leading to it.'

'I hoped that perhaps you had been allowed to visit your people in prison, and knew whereabouts they are shut.'

'I know nothing whatever,' she said.

'Well, we must find out,' he said. 'Now here is food; after that, we will find shelter for Yvona, and then set to plans.'

After food, that is what we did. When Yvonne had

gone from us, Golden said, 'As leader here, I can supersede Old Sword, which will break his old heart, I suppose.'

'He'll break the hearts of his city if he's left there long,'
I said.

'That is true,' Golden said, 'but I could find it in my
heart to spare him all I can; there's something fine about
him.'

'I know that,' I said. 'War is the test. He is superb
when fighting. But his party is less fine; his party did not
come into the fighting. It was deep down at dirty work,
down in the citadel.'

'And you, King, what do you think?'

'I'm not much loved at his headquarters,' The King
said. 'I'm a Plainsman, and I have spoken my mind very
freely to him. The trouble is, that I must be something
like what he was when he was my age. I think you can
only save these lives by superseding him; that is, of
course, assuming that the lives can be saved.'

'Would this be possible?' I asked. 'Could you, as
Leader, send for him, to confer with you; then, when he
has come, keep him here, while a party enters the city to
save the prisoners?'

'He would never leave the city,' Golden said. 'He is as
vain and as ticklish on the points of procedure as man
can be. He would say, that he was placed in charge of the
city, and could not leave it save with the city's army, and
then only if he thought the situation asked it.'

'Then, could you, as Commander, enter his city, for a
conference?'

'Only if invited,' he said. 'He is the ruler there. It will
soon be too late to send a pigeon into the city, I will send
one now. I shall say, that I am coming to confer with him
at three tomorrow morning, and that it is most important
that he should overlook the irregularity; and at the same

time keep the meeting secret, even from his staff. I shall ask him to flash an answer back to our outposts as soon as it is dark enough and to repeat the assurance that he understands, and that I may come.'

He went off at that.

'What will he do, if Old Sword refuses to see him?' I asked.

'I think he will go to see the Old Sword,' The King said.

We went together to the entry to the headquarters, just in time to see two pigeons loosed from the pigeon-tent. They whirled up and round and away on a wild wing. Golden came back to us.

'The message had gone,' he said. 'You, King, warn the fourth and fifth companies that we shall be starting one hour after midnight. It's a pity to take the fresh horses, but you see, Mr Ned, I am believing in these guns of yours.'

The sun, which had been sinking fast, now dipped to the jagged trees on the skyline and went out. As we could not now expect a pigeon from the city, we went to the watch-tower and climbed to the platform. They had signallers there, watching for the flash-messages. Up there, in the cold, under the stars, I could see the twinkling lights in the city towers; presently, among them, a brighter light began to flash at intervals.

'There it is,' The King said. 'That is the Attention. Now we shall have the answer.'

The signallers spelled it out: 'The Commander in the City sees no need for a conference. His mind has been made quite clear. He will march his men out before daybreak next morning on receiving the signal arranged for this morning. Is he to expect that signal, yes or no? He waited in vain for a signal this morning. He will not fatigue his troops again unless certain that others will keep to plans carefully laid. Will you give that signal to-morrow morning? Reply?'

The King sent out a reply: 'Please expect and admit trusted officers at three.'

After about an hour, when this had been repeated twice, an answer came: 'Will neither expect nor admit.' After this, the messages stopped. Our signallers tried two or three times more to make Old Sword give an inter-view, but now no answer came, nor sign that the message had been seen.

I said, 'They are about to do some iniquity, and dare not let you in. They are going to kill their foreigners at dawn.'

'How do you know that?' Golden asked.

'Why else would they refuse you entrance? He knows that you would support the foreigners. He is going to put them out of the way before you see him. He'll do it to-morrow at dawn, with some word to the citizens later that he had surprised a plot against the city itself.'

'Old Sword wouldn't do a thing like that,' Golden said.

'He would let his party do it,' The King said. 'Ned has a very clear eye.'

We were now back at headquarters with Yvonne. 'Yvonne,' I said, 'we aren't to be allowed into the city.'

'That means that they are going to kill the foreigners,' she said at once.

'That's exactly what I fear it does mean,' I said. 'We can't get in to help.'

'Yes, we can,' she said. 'Some of us can get in, two or three. There's a secret way in to the inner shrine of the goddess, from right outside the walls. I am not supposed to know it; but I do know it. I heard the priestess tell it to one of the priests of your city; he was her lover. They would have killed me if they had found me listening. I was there and heard. It's a hidden entrance among the rocks near the north wall. It looks like old ruin, but some of the stones move. I heard how. Then you crawl along on hands and knees, till you come to the cave where the water runs. It is all a holy path, where the goddess walks. It comes out in the shrine . . .'

'Where they'll be singing,' The King said.

'Yes, but I can take you to a side door. The singers need not see.'

'That is good enough,' I said. 'If two or three of us can get in, we can get the cattlemen to help and open a gate to the horse. When the horse are in, we will seize Old Sword and his staff and have the Quichet party out of danger.'

'What then?' Golden asked.

'You shall supersede these rulers and get to the task of the war. Give me a day or two with the young men; I will then have my guns for you; then we can fight our battle and break these M'gai.'

'We will try it,' Golden said.

It was agreed that we should set forth, so as to be at the rocks at half-past two or so; and that Yvonne, The King and I should try the passage. If we got in, we were to call the cattlemen in the Square and proceed to the least well-guarded gate, which by all accounts seemed to be the south gate. This The King would order to be opened, to admit the horse, who would be outside it, we hoped, waiting to enter. After that, if the horse were once inside, we should proceed at once to headquarters and seize the leaders of the Old Party. At dawn, if we had been successful, Golden, with the other squadrons of horse,

would enter, and the city would be under his command.
We were putting our lives on a throw; well, in Newgate,
I had not had a throw.

Having decided thus, we were going to rest, when an
officer came to in say that some scouts had come in with
a party of Matablancos. Now I had had dealings with
Matablancos, and knew that they were in feud with the
M'gai, so I asked if I might see them. I knew a few phrases
of their tongue. So we went down to the lower camp, and
there found these Matas under guard. Now to my surprise, I found that two of them were men who had been
slaves in the *Albicore*, and one of the two was my friend
Deray. Now I had not done much for these Matas in the
Albicore, but I had done a little, and had at least shewn
that I wished to do more. I was not prepared for the
extravagant gratitude with which they overwhelmed me.
Men have told me since then that slaves will ever remember gratefully one who does even a little for them.
I, who had been in Newgate, should have known this.
For a few minutes I was treated as though I had saved
their lives seven times over.

The news they brought was important. The Matas were
in force, expecting to attack the M'gai, but not while the
moon was ill; that was against their luck. They had heard
of the Kranish war with the M'gai and wished to share in
it as allies of the Kranois.

Golden was not well pleased with the news of more
savages moving up towards the Kranish lands. However,
I told him that these haunted near the Coast, and were in
feud with the M'gai. If they would help us against the
M'gai, any reasonable policy would keep them friendly to
the Kranois thenceforward. I said that two thousand
Matas coming in upon the M'gai rear, or moving against
their supplies, would be decisive helps to us. In the end,

I won them over to my view; the Matas were accepted as our allies. I persuaded Golden to let Deray come with us on our expedition.

Presently, we set forth to fling our throw. Ah, that night, which needs a book, almost, to itself; that was my night; mine in invention, mine in the doing. We went out in the swift dark night, and came to the blackness of the city, lit only in the towers and in lonely rooms far from the walls. The horse and the Matas scouted through the rocks for us; then we of the forlorn hope, with Deray, who would not leave us, came to the ruins, where we found the moving stones and so crept into the dark pit on hands and knees. We had rush-lights, which we managed to light; and holding these, crawled on into the darkness till presently we were in a most strange place, no doubt holy for its uncanniness; it was part narrow cavern, part a sort of crypt. As we went, I felt that strange rites, of an intense kind, had been practised there; no doubt the goddess had walked. Presently, we were in earshot of the singing women, and then slipped aside to an aisle of the temple, and so, by the temple door, into the Market-Square. We were in the city; now, if we failed, we should probably never get out of it alive.

We went into the Market-Square, I say, and so to the cattle. I scouted ahead and found an old chief of the Plainsmen asleep in his little den in the north wall. The King roused him quietly and bade him call down some of his men from their sentry duty; this he did.

With these, we walked through the city to the south gate; it was dead still, cold darkness; the city worn out and asleep; the night outside full, seemingly of a myriad of horse, trampling and jingling. The King called, 'Where is the Captain of the South Gate?' and on being told that he had been killed an hour before with a sling-

stone, said, 'Very good, then; open up here. The horse
are to come in.' The sergeant, seeing the gold on The
King's chest, opened up, not doubting; and a hundred
picked men filed in, picketed their horses in the Square
and prepared for what we meant to do.

What that was, we did. It was my thought, my deed.
We will not, therefore, speak of it. Someone has told us
that revolutions are caused by vanity. Think, therefore,
that this of mine was wrought from vanity; partly it was;
but partly, too, by love of Yvonne, by love of the
Quichets, who stood for Europe and thought against
these clotted and cruddled Old Swords; and partly by
the Newgate in me, which loathes that element in Man
which shuts a soul in prison and sends her out on Monday. We did it; we took the city of the Kranois, we freed
our friends, and had Old Sword out of it, with his
staff, on their way to the Big City, long before the sun
rose.

You must not think that I shall blow my trumpet
louder and longer. I had found what I could do. I could
work with Golden and The King, Yvonne and the
Quichets. We had saved them from death, now we could
work with them to save the city. I found the wagons in
the citadel yard. We had the guns out, and mounted during that morning. I had a couple of hundred Kranish lads
drilled in the cannon exercises within three days; nay, I
made those lads into light artillery, able to drag and
manœuvre their places, almost like horse artillery. They
had not fired; we dared not use our scanty powder, nor
lose the surprise we planned. We fired and surprised the
M'gai when the day came, be sure.

There is a phrase in a letter from some old soldier of
our Civil War: 'Our horse had the execution of them
almost to their camp.' Our horse, on the day of battle,

broke the M'gai, but the Matablancos had the execution of them. I am a doctor, and hate war and the killing of men; this great killing was largely my work. The Matas came in as I had bidden, and broke the Amalosa and the Umquilitzi, and brought the red and the black plumes into Kranish dust for ever.

It was a devilish deed, perhaps. It was my deed; and by it I broke the power of devils. You can settle the rights of it. I still glow with a gleam of the joy I felt on that day, when I looked on the victory and knew that we young men had broken the M'gai in pieces.

Five minutes after that triumph, intense as it was, I was saying to Edmond Quichet, 'Now the real test comes. Now we have to remake the Kranish state.'

I married Yvonne when I came back to the city with the army. I remade my state at least.

The war was over; and all admitted that we, the foreigners and Plainsmen, had won it, and gave us our due. At the same time, they became free, to say, that we were foreigners and Plainsmen who had taken liberties with the city's elected rulers. I will not weary you with all this. It is now a long time since these little squabbles in a small city in a distant part of the world. I triumphed, since I had medical skill, unique at that time in the land of the Kranois. But though I prospered and was happy, I longed, as Yvonne did, to clear my name in England and receive the Royal Pardon for the crime I never committed.

I knew how dangerous my coming to London might be. And yet, now that the first years of terror had passed, now that I had become another man, I could face that danger, and did face it, with a kind of anger of determination to crush the Fate that had so nearly crushed me.

Time had passed, which makes so much clear. Someone, by this time, might have let fall words, might have raised a doubt, might have set going an inquiry. My friends, Dr Copshrews and the others, all shrewd men, might have been busy on my account. Fate, too, the blind thing, which works with such apparent clumsiness, yet with such certainty, She, too, might have reckoned that the evil had had its hour, and that now evil should go down, and the wronged one be righted. And yet, I was cynical enough about that, too. I had been in Newgate, and took the Newgate view, that there is a lot more law than justice in this world. Yet I longed to try it, and to dare it. I had faced the armed array of the M'gai and had beaten them; I wanted to do the same by my old enemies, Murder, ill-luck, and that brutal rectitude, the Law, which might be wrong.

So I came to Gabo in state, with my rowers, with a blaze of new gold-leaf on my railings, and with my blue and white Kranish colours trailing from my flagstaff. As I drew in, I fired a salute to the Governor and dipped my colours to the Flag. When the Government boat came out to give me pratique, I sent in gifts of fruit, and asked for an audience. I waited with much anxiety, as you may imagine, for a reply. Presently, I was sent for by the Governor's coxswain, and went ashore to wait upon him. He received me in the cool, white-washed windward room of the Castle quarters, a very weary, white-faced man, from whom the climate had taken all vitality. He had a charming, limp manner.

'So, Sir,' he said, coming to me, and touching my hand with the wet rag of his own hand, 'so Sir, . . . Mr . . . ?'

'Mansell,' I said.

'Ah, yes,' he said. 'I have to thank you for this letter, and for the gift of fruits. You say, in your letter, that you

come from the cities of white people of whom tales sometimes come. You state that you have products with you
and that you can open a profitable trade with England.
That is very much the desire of our Government at the
moment. Can you now satisfy me as to the nature of the
trade?'

This I proceeded to do, for the next hour. I shewed my
specimens, and pleaded my cause and made my necessary
points, that the Kranois were to be protected from the
slavers. He was interested and impressed by what I said.
At the end, he said, 'The best thing that I can do, is to
send you home in the *Hannibal*, there, the frigate in the
road. She is sailing for home the day after tomorrow.
Captain Culham will give you and your wife a passage. I
will give you a letter to the Secretary; you will have no
difficulty in getting to him to state your case; he happens
to be my brother.'

So here I was received and honoured, sent forward
with a letter to a Secretary of State, in a King's ship. How
differently had I reached the Coast in the *Albicore*. To be
brief, we saw the anchor weighed and the Coast slowly
draw away from us as we stole to the windward. In no
long time, we were in the Channel, and so by degrees
came to Portsmouth, where we took post-chaise for
London and presented our letters.

It was a strange moment for me, when I saw again the
scenes of my old happiness. The journey had been by the
usual routes; I changed the last stage of all, so that I could
drive through Cholsington and look at some of the scenes
known to me. They say that nothing is ever really forgotten by the mind; probably nothing is. As we drove,
I would shut my eyes, tell myself what lay round each
bend before we came to it, then open my eyes to see the
familiar scene unfold.

I had last looked upon those fields in the autumn; now I saw them in early May with so little foliage on the trees that the growth was not marked; few things seemed changed except myself. There was the big house among its elms; there was the bend near which I had routed the footpads when they had attacked the Admiral; up there, to my left, was Hannibal House, and somewhere beyond it was the house where my Father had died. Yvonne watched me, knowing that I was deeply moved by my thoughts. Soon, we were going past the church, with that open space in front of it where I had bought the knife of Jane Jollycok. Presently the road swung, somewhat to the east for London town; before me, for all that I knew, lay my old friend and master Dr Copshrews. I longed to see him.

The lodgings that had been commanded for us were in the square in which I had lived with my parents, not one hundred yards from the door, though upon another side of the square. When I looked out from our sitting-room window, I could see the door to my left. Workmen were busy upon it at that moment, painting it blue and the iron railings near it white. I took this insistence on the Kranish colours as a good omen. I was there with Yvonne, and had much cause for gladness. I had also cause for alarm and for caution. Now that I was fairly back in London, I began to see clearly some of the dangers round myself. I knew now that I had become again a condemned felon, who might be denounced at any moment. How soon would the blow fall?

Well, blow or none, I had tasks to do.

My first task was to find if Dr Copshrews still lived. I could hope to discover this without running a risk of recognition. I had changed much since my troubles.

Then, I thought, after all, most people who remember

me at all wish to forget me, and will know, too, that I am dead. They will say, 'He is like that fellow who was hanged for the murder that time.'

I kept telling myself that my known death was my safe-guard, and boldness my shield. I sent for a glass coach or hackney-carriage, as they would now be called, and in this drove off alone through a part of London once very well known to me, till we were in the familiar street, and my eyes were fixed on the Doctor's house.

I saw at once, that his notice or placard was gone; we went past the familiar door, which had been new painted. Usually at that time in the afternoon our dispensary door had been thronged by the evening patients coming for our dispensary treatments. No patients were there now; the place was no longer a doctor's home. I called to the driver to drive me on to the church where Dr Copshrews had attended worship with me so many times.

In a grave beneath the floor of the church, lay the body of Josiah Copshrews, physician and churchwarden of this parish. He had died on November the twelfth, the year before, deeply loved and respected. I had expected something of the kind, of course, but I was deeply moved. I had so hoped to see him again and to thank him for all that he had done for me and to shew him that it had not been done in vain.

I looked at the tablet for a long time. The verger, seeing my interest in the tomb, looked at me curiously. I had looked at him, be sure, not less curiously, yet without recognition. He was not one known to me.

I said, 'Did you, by any chance, know the gentleman, the Doctor?'

'No, sir,' he said. 'I'm a newcomer here, sir. But I was here for his burial. It was like the burying of Royalty, sir; not a dry eye in the parish. He was a physician to the

Poor, sir. I suppose ten thousand persons came to the service.'

I was anxious to know if he had ever been in question about my escape, so I said, 'It is happy to think that such a man should live to a good old age and be loved to the last.'

'Yes, sir,' the verger said, 'he was happy in his life and in his death, which they say we might all be if we were as good as he.'

I asked if he had left any family.

He said, 'No, sir, I believe not, sir. His son died before him. They say, sir, he had a venture in Jamaica, I think it was, and died of the climate. We've a memorial to the son, too, sir.'

I had liked Dick; he had been very, very good to me. I could only say that it was sad, that so good a man had left no son. I gave the verger a shilling and went out, sad at heart, to find two of my helpers dead, never to be thanked or praised. At least, they had not suffered through me. I could thank God for that. But when I was out in the street, the tears ran down my cheeks, not for Dr Copshrews, he was with God, but for poor Dick. I had longed to see Dick again. He had been more than trebly good to me. What was this venture in Jamaica? I judged that it was some happy effort of friends, gay, charming and not very prudent.

I thought that perhaps he had looked out for me there. He might have asked, had any word come of a young doctor named Torrance? The young doctor might have helped him through the Climate, perhaps.

I took my glass-coach again and so drove home. I had steeled myself to drive back past St Sepulchre's and New-gate over my Via Dolorosa. We had gone along Holborn towards Snow Hill, when I noticed that the driver turned out of his way. I hailed him, 'Why are you not going down to Newgate?'

He said, 'I'd never get through, sir.'

Indeed, I could see that a mob of people blocked the way.

'They're all going to Newgate, sir,' my driver said. 'There's nothing like a good hanging to bring 'em all out; they'll sit up all night, the most of 'em, or stand where they are, rather than miss it. They've fine weather for it, but cold for the time of year; still, if it was snow, they'd stay, in a case like this. I suppose you've read it and followed it, sir?'

I remembered how many had come to see me in my misery and how I had longed that staring man might have but the one face, so that I might spit in it. I said, 'No. I've only just landed and know nothing about it. But I think I'd forgive any murderer rather than hang him.'

'Well, sir,' he said, 'you must excuse me; I'm all for the rope myself. I'd hang the murderer, then I'd be sure of my throat at nights. I've a weakness for my throat, sir.'

'Cherish it,' I said; and at that we parted.

I went upstairs to my rooms. It was early in May, and fair enough weather; but to us fresh from the Coast it seemed cruelly cold. I asked the maid, if we might have a fire? She said she would send up Harry. I braced myself against Harry; for though I had been out of London a long time, I had been known to a great many as Dr Copshrew's assistant. What if he should come up all eager to see the foreign gentleman, and at once recognize me as one who had poulticed his cut or bound his fracture? Harry came in with the firing, which he proceeded to lay and then to light. He had one or two glances at me as he worked. He was a smiling, good-humoured sort of man, of about thirty, as I judge.

'There's nothing like a bit of fire of an evening to cheer things up, is there, sir?' he said. 'London comes very cold, we always say, to them as aren't used to it.'

I thanked him and asked if he were used to it.

'Yes, sir,' he said, 'I'm getting used to it, but it's full of surprises, London; everyone has to admit that.'

I asked what the latest surprises were, since I had only just arrived from a far country.

'Why,' he said, 'why, sir, have you not seen an English paper?'

I said, 'No.'

'Why then,' he said, 'you've not seen that he's confessed?'

I said, 'I have heard hardly any news, save the foreign news, and that only as it affects the Navy and African trade.'

'You must excuse me, then, sir,' he said. 'A treat is in store for you. I'll bring you in the set. I've got them all laid by. It is one of the surprises of my life.'

The maid brought in the tea-tray, and as we settled to our tea, Harry brought the *Intelligencer* for the past few weeks: 'in case you should like to glance at them after your cup of tea, sir.'

We drank our tea; when Yvonne had gone to unpack, I took up the copies of the *Intelligencer*.

Harry had laid these papers for me in order, the oldest on the top; they had made his reading, perhaps his only reading, for some time, and had been a good deal worn. I read as follows:

STRANGE CASE AT CHOLSINGTON

Last week at the time of going to press, we promised our readers a full account of the astounding case at Cholsington. To those who by some mischance missed the opening scenes

of the drama, let us say that it began by the appearance of
Mr Dennis Rackage, at one time well known in sporting circles,
but latterly less frequent in his attendance, before Sir — with
a confession implicating his one-time servant — Henery in
systematic blackmail and himself in the double crime of
murder and permitting an innocent man to suffer for his crime.
Most of our readers will recall the murder of Admiral Cringle,
late of Hannibal House, in Cholsington. . .

Here was indeed matter to make me thrilled. I remembered the crowds outside Newgate and thought,
'Can it be, that those crowds are gathered to see them
hanged?' I felt faint for a moment, to think that somehow
those two had been the murderers of the Admiral.

. . . The Admiral was a crotchety bachelor, supposed to have
a sum of gold in his house. He had taken a fancy to a young
doctor, of the name of Mansell, who had saved his life from
footpads, and in gratitude for this valorous act had made the
young man his heir. Suspicion pointed to the young Dr
Mansell as the murderer, who was charged with the crime,
and convicted for it at the next Assizes, and though he
persisted in declaring his innocence. Mr Dennis Rackage
startled the magistrates by declaring, and with convincing
proofs, that it was he, not the young doctor, who had
murdered the Admiral. He had done the deed, hoping to lay
his hands on the large sum of gold said to be secreted in the
house, but was interrupted in his search, by the sound of
footsteps. He decamped at once, and left the house un-
observed. The steps heard by him were, by an unhappy
chance, those of young Dr Mansell, who was afterwards
hanged for the crime. Hannibal House, being devised to
Dr Mansell, was confiscated to the Crown on his conviction.
It was put up to auction, yet none would buy. It was true
that wealth was reported to lie hidden in it, but report soon
went abroad that it was haunted by the ghost of the Admiral
and by that of his unhappy heir. However, after it had lain
deserted for a year, it was bought for a song by Mr Dennis

Rackage, who had at that time lately sold his estate of the neighbouring Manor to the man Henery, sometime steward to the estate.

After a little while, it was noticed that the man Henery was frequently at Hannibal House, and that his coming was the signal for the locking of all gates and doors. It was supposed that the two were searching together. Certainly evidence of digging and destruction accumulated in the gardens outside the house. A householder of Cholsington told us that he had seen Mr Rackage, all white and sweating, digging in the garden far into the summer night. Others have said that he gradually gave up all intercourse with his fellows, and ceased to be particular in his dress. Instead, he appeared, if at all, in his shirt-sleeves often soiled with the dirt of the garden clay. He would not enter Cholsington, even to purchase the few necessaries, such as bread, beer and onions, which made the bulk of his diet. At the same time it was noticed, that his one-time servant, Henery, became more and more a figure in the world, drove his equipage, and dressed in an extreme of fashion, besides venturing with much acumen in the brick and gravel industry. It was easy to see that master and man had changed places. This state of things continued a long time, till it was at last understood that Mr Rackage had disposed even of Hannibal House, and now worked there as his steward's servant; indeed, some reckoned that the relation was more truly that of master and slave. But it is a well-known maxim, that murder will out and that the worm will turn. Mr Rackage determined to endure his conscience and his servitude no longer. He went, therefore, to the Rector of his parish and made a full confession. The Rector urged him to come at once to repeat the dreadful tale before the justice of the peace. This the unhappy creature offered to do and promptly did. He said that the man Henery had seen him near Hannibal House before the crime was consummated. However, it was not till after the execution of Mansell, that Henery shewed that he knew who had done the murder and was determined to be paid for his silence. In the shaken condition of nerves to which blood-guiltiness had reduced him, he weakly paid for the man's silence and surrendered himself to years of an extortion, at first not unreasonable, but growing with each fresh demand, until all that he had had gone into the leech's maw. He said, no doubt truly, that since the execution of Mansell he had known no single moment free from alarm and misery, till the happy day when the Rector urged him to come before the Justice. As the readers will by this time be aware, the man Henery was charged with being an accessory after the fact in the murder of Admiral Cringle. Being a ready as well as a resolute rogue he at first tried to brazen it out, with the expected defence, that the man Rackage was a poor creature not far above imbecility and not to be accepted as a witness. It was, however, retorted upon him that his wife, who some months before had gone out of her mind, had confessed to friends that Henery knew more of the Admiral's death than he let on to know at the inquest and the trial. This fact had so lain at her heart that it no doubt occasioned her unhappy insanity. From this point, the law was able to proceed by little and by little, with testimony from one and another to prove that Hencry had obtained power over his late master by the possession of a secret and had used this power to extort from him what he wished ...

The next copy of the paper gave a long account of the trial. The two criminals had been found guilty and sentenced to be hanged. The most recent of the papers said that 'the man Henery had made a full confession.'

The revelation was so unexpected, so complete, that I knew not well what to do first. But after a time, it seemed to me that the thing that I must do was to visit Newgate and somehow assure the two that they had not my blood upon their hands. I had always supposed that Henery had known of my escape from death, and had followed me to Liverpool. From what I read now, it seemed certain that both men thought that I was dead through their action. They were to die in a short while. I could perhaps get to the prison, and have access to them and assure them that that at least was not so. There was danger to myself in doing this; it might lead to my arrest. What though the confession of the men cleared me and amply cleared me; the old conviction held; and I knew enough of the Law to know that it was slow enough to move, slower to admit error, slowest of all to disgorge. It had gathered to itself a booty through my conviction; was it likely to welcome one who would demand restitution? Was it not far more likely, to hang me out of hand as a condemned felon, and seize upon whatever I had at the moment as a further payment for the trouble I had put them to? I did not trust our justice an inch. Still, I determined to get at these men, if it were possible.

I waited for a while; then, towards sunset, I went out and turned towards the city, down the hill up which I had once driven to my death.

I had felt sure that the coming of dusk would have taken half the sightseers home from the prison precincts, but as I went on, I found three hurrying towards the city, for every one turning away; long before I was in sound of St Sepulchre's bells, which I could tell from every other bell in Christendom, I saw that all that approach would be choked and blocked by sightseers. As there was no reaching the prison that way, I turned off to my right, and after a time reached Ludgate Hill, which I found choked and jammed like the other approach. I drew out of the press, and asked a decent fellow how one could get to the prison.

'Have you a ticket?' he asked.

I did not know well what he meant, but said, 'No.'

'Ah,' he said, 'I thought you couldn't have a ticket;

you've left it so late. The ticket-holders got there the first thing after church this morning; otherwise they'd have had no gettings in and lose what they paid. They pay for windows,' he added, with some pity in his voice for this stranger who knew so little. 'They pay to see the show.'

I asked, if he could tell me how to get a word to the Chaplain of the prison.

'Why,' he said, 'you couldn't do it from this side at all, not if his salvation depended on it. No man could pass these streets unless a troop of Horse-Guards rode along first and cleared the way.'

I found in a few minutes that the entire prison was surrounded. Throngs were filling all the lanes at the back of the prison quite as closely as they filled those on the west. What the crowds hoped to achieve by being where they were, I could not think. A good many were pickpockets and snatchthieves, who were there for business. A few were hawkers, selling or trying to sell broadsides and confessions, oranges, eel-pies, jellies and wisps of snuff. The main bulk of the company was made up of average stupid men. They could not hope to see anything or anyone even remotely linked with the events. They would stand all night, jammed in a pack in a lane, perhaps rained on, perhaps chilled by the cold north wind then blowing and unable to defend themselves if set upon by the gangs of thieves, who were already gathering to the prey. In the morning, if they could endure so long, they would at the most hear the tollings of St Sepulchre's and the horrible little bell of the prison, and might hear the yellings of the crowd stilled as the victims appeared. After this, they would be free to disentangle themselves from the mobs and make their ways to work. Yet they would be able to say, that they had been at the execution. Years later, when a famous rogue would hang, they would say, 'Ah, I was at the hangings of Henery and Rackage. That WAS a hanging.'

I reached home too weary to do more that night. I suppose that Dr Copshrews would have found the sheriff, obtained an escort, seen the Chaplain and given comfort to the dying. I thought of what he had done for me in a like case, and was sad to come so far short of a Christian's effort. I sat for a while looking out of the window at my old home. Lights shone from the windows. I wondered who was living there, and what they talked of. If they were talking at all, I knew that they would be talking of Henery and Rackage. I wondered if they knew that one of their victims had lived and been happy in their house.

I had meant to rise early, to pray for those two; but, lo, when I woke, it was after eight and they had trodden all the road that I had gone. The old Newgate phrase returned to me, 'We'll be out of it by Monday.' Here it was Monday and past the hanging time. By this time they must have ended, poor wretches, beyond any hope of a revival such as had come to me.

However, I was wrong about this. When I came to breakfast, Harry and the maid were both bursting with the news that the two had been reprieved for three days on the urgent recommendation of the Chaplain, who felt that they were not quite prepared for their fate. There was now a riot at the gaol, Harry said; people were so mad with disappointment at not seeing them hanged, after stopping up all night. Five had been hanged, but not these two. It was very much like waiting up to see Garrick act and then after waiting all day and part of the night, finding that he would not act for three days. I thought, 'Tomorrow, I will go to Newgate, to see those two.'

The newspapers were full of self-righteousness that

day, for the Christian kindness that had granted reprieves
to the two criminals, but I wondered whether the two
poor wretches in the Hold were not tortured the longer
by the mercy. They must have made up their minds to die
on Monday morning, and may even have contrived a
stupefying drunkenness to that end. When a man was reprieved, he always hoped for a second reprieve or alteration of sentence. They would cling to these hopes, no
doubt, and be frantic with hope, as I had been, and then
the hours would run and the hopes would dim, the bells
would strike the horrible hours and the clergyman would
tell us to hope for mercy. Mercy. I was sick with memo-
ries of my misery when I thought of those two there in
the Hold. Going out to inquire if there were any letters
for me, I heard Harry saying that he had been down to
the prison in his dinner-hour, and that there was a big
crowd, but the soldiers were keeping people moving. He
had the news that the gallows had not been taken down;
it was there still; 'So they will go out of it on Thursday,
sure to, or they wouldn't leave it up.'

But the next morning, some men came shouting about
the square, as they often did when there was terrible news.
The maid was sure from their cries that the French had
landed, but this seemed improbable. The yells of the men
were like the cries of wild beasts, but I made out the
words 'Escape from Newgate,' and at once guessed that
Dennis had somehow bribed his gaolers to let him get
away. As these men seemed to be selling newspapers, I
went out to buy one. One of the hawkers saw me come
from the house and waited for me. He said, familiarly, 'It
has come with a clap, sir. I thought when they granted
the reprieve there was something stirring. Money does
everything in the Newgate world, the same as in any
other.'

'Not quite everything,' I said. 'But how did they get away?'

'It's all in the paper, sir; if you'll excuse me, there are some wanting a copy.'

I opened the still damp sheet and read:

DARING ESCAPE OF RACKAGE AND HENERY

During the hours of darkness last night, the two prisoners who were to expiate their crimes on Thursday morning, contrived to make a daring escape. It is thought that the prisoner Henery received from some friend or sympathizer a set of files and picklocks concealed in a Bible sent in to him. It is learned that a Bible left in the condemned Hold was ingeniously contrived as a box, within which such articles may have been easily secreted. The escape must have taken place after the Last Rounds (at about 9 p.m.) of the Gaolers, who say that the prisoners then were quiet and securely ironed. Between that time and the morning visit the prisoners had ample time to remove their irons and pick the locks which stood between them and freedom. The prison officials preserve strict reticence as to the way by which the two left the prison. The fact remains, that they escaped, and are now at liberty. Be on your guard. Two murderers are now at large, and are not likely to have attempted to leave London.

That was the sheet; I have it still. I cannot begin to tell you what a storm was roused by the escape. Harry and the maid were both sure that the head-gaolers had received five hundred pounds each to let the men go. Money was everything in Newgate, they said; 'Nobody with money ever suffered.' The matter concerned me more closely than anybody, and I read all that I could find about it. The facts seem to be that Henery received the means of getting out. Who provided them was a point never cleared up. Strong suspicion was on two of the prison officers, that is, an almost certainty, but no real proof. Public feeling was that someone in the prison must have made their way smooth for them. They got out of the prison easily enough at last, by means of some builders' ladders on the roof at the back. Here again, someone in the prison must have helped for money down. Henery was rich, of course, and could have procured a good deal from some hidden source.

London never goes to bed, I suppose. A crowd, of sorts, will gather at all hours of the day or night, from nowhere, in any street. Yet it seemed that these two men had passed into the quiet streets at the back of the prison in the small hours of the morning unseen by anyone. There is little real darkness in early May; the milkmen must have been up and the bakers busy at the time; but the two had gone, and London had swallowed them up.

During that morning I received a letter from my Secretary, to tell me that he would be in London again in one week from then and would be happy to see me at his office in Whitehall upon such a day. As I had ten days to wait, I proposed to Yvonne that we should go into the country. It was fair spring weather, with England at her fairest, so we set out together by one of the famous coaches to Oxford and then away beyond to countries that Yvonne had never dreamed of, and all of them a wonder to her.

In the course of the next day we drove on, mostly by post-chaise, to the town of Condicote, where we put up at an inn. It horsed the up and down mail each day, each way, over one stage. It had therefore always a big and busy stabling and a strong smell of stable. The yard was busy with cocks and hens picking and scratching, ostlers passing with hay or straw, men polishing boots or harness, and now and then doing something to the feet of horses, or pulling out some trap, cart or chaise to wash its wheels. When I looked out upon it now, I saw a famous thief-taker in talk with two whom I supposed were sheriff's officers. They had some horsemen with them, waiting on their pleasure, and a glass-coach was being prepared for them. Word of something had gone abroad, for they were being watched by a little crowd, which was increasing.

Now this man was well known to me, who saw him in Newgate daily while I was there. I suppose that no one once pursued by him, or in danger from him ever forgot or could forget him. His face with its inhuman mask of indifference was like a cat's face; it had the same sort of smile of cruelty and of power. Nor had I forgotten him. I had thought of him often and often; he had been in my nightmares and my terrors for months together.

I had a sinking in the heart of think that this thief-taker whom I had done my best to avoid had come to the very place to which I had come and may well have been staying in the inn there with me, unsuspected by me; yet making all inquiries as to who I was and what I did there. He may have had many a good look at me, and must no doubt have thought, 'He looks very like that young doctor we dealt with, the murder case, the man they thought got spirited away; however, this fellow is said to be a foreigner, married to a French wife.' However, there he was, talking quietly to these two men, giving them last instructions. Soon, all three of them moved over to a window-ledge at the side, and loaded and primed their short pocket pistols. This last task was watched with intense interest by the little crowd. When the pistols were loaded, the three turned and walked with decision to the coach and climbed in; the door slammed fast on them, the coachman called up his team and they drove out of the yard under the arch into the street, followed by the atten-

dant horsemen, who led a spare horse or two. As soon as
the horsemen had passed, the little crowd turned after
them and followed, running. I went down to the inn
office and asked what the disturbance was. 'It's the murderer,' the girl said. 'They think the murderer's come
here.' From the inn office I could see through greenish
window-panes the street of the town. All who could run
were running after the horsemen, those who could not
run were gathering at the cross-roads to discuss.

I felt that I would not be about when the thief-taker
returned to the inn with his victim. It would be wise for
me to get away while the interest was on someone else;
so I bespoke my chaise. Just as we started off, we saw
surging round the corner towards us a running, shouting
mob of boys and young men, with some frightened or
excited women among them, swept up probably by the
crowd's approach and unable to get away. With these
came the glass coach, with the outriders on each side of it.
They were coming pretty fast; our driver had to pull to
a side and stop to let them by. They came surging and
whooping past us. I had a glimpse of Henery wild-eyed
and white sitting next to that impassive awful man, whose
face was a cat's face. I imagine that Henery was hand-
cuffed to him, and the cat was smiling at having caught
his mouse. I have often wondered at the man. He was
born with this aptitude of following trails and catching
people; he was not more virtuous, probably, than the
men he brought to the gallows; but chanced to be born
on the right side of the prison bars; he was the son of a
turn-key; he was born against the mice and had continued
in that way.

Well, he was past in a flash, staring, smiling, straight
ahead of him, thinking of his triumph at the Newgate
regale, and the payment of the reward; his calculations

had come off, he had perhaps won some side bets as well as the reward. He went past the victim who might have won him a little more glory. Ah, if he had but looked at me with recognition at that instant, what a triumph his had been. However, he was looking ahead, smiling at himself; and in an instant he was past and round the bend upon the directest road to London. The boys and young men called and booed at us, in their noisy way, and then we were through them and away.

At Oxford, the next day, we had a London paper that told us that Dennis had been taken. He had, it seems, set fire to Hannibal House, in some crazy hope of finding the hidden treasure in the ruins. The house had burned to the ground and he himself had been taken while digging in the ruins with a stick. No treasure had been found, the paper said. We delayed at Oxford a little while, and while in our lodgings there we learned of the safe arrival of both prisoners in Newgate. They had been carried before the magistrates for formal evidence of identity: after which both had been very heavily ironed and taken to the Hold, where it was made impossible for them to escape again. They were to be hanged immediately. There had been some little delay, it seemed, for the man Henery had offered to reveal some important fact, if his life might be spared. What the fact was he would not say; but he let it appear that it had to do with the bringing of somebody to justice. This staggered me, for I was in an uneasy position. I knew very well how swift and flashing a perception may be in times of distress. What if Henery had had glimpses of me as I drove past in the road? He may have recognized me, and at once known that I was a returned felon. I was scared, I own, and yet, what had I to fear, you will ask? I had everything to fear. I was a condemned man. I had been hanged once for a crime I didn't do, and could be hanged under that sentence until I was dead, and had no doubt that I should be so hanged, even though another man had confessed to the crime, and a witness had brought evidence to confirm the confession. I had had enough of our justice to know that it was pretty merciless and by no means likely to examine into my case. I should be hanged out of hand and inquired about later. You say that this was crazy of me. Well, wait till you have been in Newgate: then you may know a little.

So I drove on to London, sick at heart at what I was to bring to Yvonne. As we turned into the Square, we were delayed for perhaps twenty seconds, by a carriage in front of us, which, after making the turn, stopped to set down a passenger. In the little halt I looked out idly on the pavement, and saw two men standing at the corner, both looking into my carriage. They were mean and shady-looking men, with looks at once furtive and resolute. As I looked, I saw one of them nudge the other with his elbow, and make a sort of signal with a jerk of his thumb to a third man standing farther into the Square. It was after sunset, but the light was full and glowing. I thought idly that the men might be snatchthieves, who came to arriving coaches, and under cover of helping to unload would pass some package to a confederate. I said something to Yvonne about London having always its pickers and stealers, then we set forth again and drew up at our door.

As the horses stopped, the maid and Harry came across the pavement to us, opened the door and helped Yvonne down. The maid went in with Yvonne; Harry took my mails and I stood for a moment to pay the driver and to thank him. I had not thought of the two men at the corner, but I now saw them coming swiftly to me from the one side, while the third man came from my right. I looked at them sharply. The two men were not known to

me, but the third man was the thief-taker, the cat-faced
man, whom I had seen so recently sitting smiling beside
Henery in the road of that country town. He said, 'You
must excuse me, Dr Mansell. I have my duty to perform.
I must ask you to come with me.'

'Certainly,' I said, with my heart all gone to water.
'But come where, and why?'

'To the Bailey, sir,' he said, 'if you please.'

I was stunned and without defence or wit. I had a
glimpse of Harry staring from the door of the house, and
one or two people staring. I think they thought that I was
a young debtor caught by sheriff's officers. A glass coach
appeared and I was in an instant in it and we were moving
off: I have no recollection of getting in or being pushed
into this carriage. I know that there I was, with the cat-
faced man beside me, and one of the other men opposite
to me inside, staring hard at me, 'learning my face,' as
they called it, in case I should ever escape. The third man
was on the box with the driver. They had been very quick
with me. I had a dreadful minute thinking of Yvonne.

'Mrs Mansell will be all right, sir,' the man said kindly.
'We arranged for her to be seen to.' 'Seen to'; what
amount of seeing-to would help a widow in a strange
land? For the first few minutes of the drive, I suffered as
I suppose few can have suffered from the blackest of grief
and despair. We were driving very fast, and nothing was
said. I was in no condition to speak. I became conscious
of many people in the street and of the cat-faced man
calling to the driver through the hatch to give up the
thought of it and get in by Poll Maggot's, so we turned
into some by-road or lane and so by lane and lane till we
were in a dark alley at the back of the prison. I suppose
no daylight could ever get into the lane even in summer.
It was in dark twilight when we stopped; two or three

men were loitering in the lane, seemingly waiting for our arrival; our driver whistled and they closed in. At the same time a door opened and sent a great glow of light on to the pavement. The place seemed full of light and people; I heard laughter and the clinking of glass. This was no doubt the warders' regale before the famous hanging; they were entertaining the great, no doubt; turn-key and title alternating with song and sentiment. But it was not quite that. A great gentleman, somewhat flushed from his punch, was coming towards me. 'Dr Mansell,' he said, 'you have nothing to fear. We know all about you. Come in and join the party. We are going to repair the wrong done to you. You'll get your pardon tomorrow, for the crime you never did. Now here are all the warders; some of them remember you, and the rest are all your friends. Now we all want you to shake hands.'

I was in the room of the regale. It smelled very strongly of punch; there were fourteen or fifteen people there and they were at their second or third bowl. They had all risen, who could rise at all, to greet me, and shake hands. I said something about, 'Am I not a prisoner, then?' The cat-faced man said, 'No, sir.' The great gentleman said, 'Now, gentlemen, we have got Dr Mansell here. Charge your glasses and let's drink to him.' They were all unsteady and uproarious, except those who had come in with me. The great gentleman said, 'You may think we're Bedlam, but nothing of the kind; absooty nothing of the kind.' I said, 'I must ask to be allowed to go back, to reassure my Wife.'

'That is done. My Wife is there to do that,' the man said. 'I've been asked by the Ordinary to bring you here. He begs that you will have the charity to see the prisoner, Dennis Rackage. He was the main cause of all your trouble, of course, but he asks to speak with you.'

'I will see him,' I said, 'but tell me the truth. You are not going to shut me in the Hold?'

'No,' he said. 'On honour, no. Let me explain, though. You were recognized at the inn yard by our friend here, who followed the case when you were supposed to have escaped that time. Our friend here, as it happens, suspected that you were innocent from the first. He believed that Rackage and Henery between them had put the Admiral away. He had his eyes upon them for a long time before he could deal with them. When he saw you at the inn yard he let me know. You will have your pardon tomorrow, and no further trouble at all. I understand that you will be with Mr Secretary tomorrow. But come now to the Ordinary; you shall be off home as soon as you have seen the prisoner.'

I hardly knew if I were living or dreaming. I was not sure that I was not a prisoner and that these men were too drunk to be sure of it. However, there was an Ordinary, whom I well remembered. 'Dr Mansell,' he said, 'you did not care for what I offered in the past, but perhaps you may reflect, after tonight, that the case for guidance is stronger than you supposed.'

The prison smell was as before. The stone corridors stank and echoed in just the same way. The old terror of that awful place stuck in my throat as we trod towards the Hold. In the darkness of the night outside a church bell struck the hour. It was St Sepulchre's. No need to tell me what that bell was. Near the Hold I heard again the loud mad whimpering of the despairing women who were under sentence and the yelling of the main prison from all the men who had the fortune to be drunk. It was terrible to smell the Newgate stink and hear the Newgate snarl and yell. The great locks clicked and the heavy doors rolled back. The Ordinary whispered that they had put the two in separate cells, lest they should destroy each other. It seemed to me that they had done that completely as it was, but the mercies of Newgate were ever odd to me. 'Mr Rackage,' the Ordinary said, 'I've brought Dr Mansell to you.'

I believe that the Ordinary had not seen Dennis for some hours. In the interval some kind warder had brought a can of brandy; Dennis was by this time pretty drunk.

'This is Dr Mansell,' the Ordinary said. 'You wanted so much to see him, to tell him something.'

Dennis stared through the fog of the prison brandy at me, and asked, 'Who is he?'

'Dr Mansell,' the Ordinary replied. 'Young Dr Mansell.'

'Tell that to the godly,' Dennis said. 'Don't tell it to me; for I'm an unbeliever; see?'

'Come, come,' the Ordinary said, in pleading tones, 'Come, Mr Rackage; recollect yourself, and where you are presently to appear. You were going to tell Mr Mansell something; something that might be of value to him.'

'What was it?' Dennis said, supping his brandy.

'Something perhaps about money,' the Ordinary said.

'Money?' Dennis said. 'If I'd money I wouldn't be here. What does a man of your cloth want with money in this carnal world? I've done with money. The only comfort money's been to me is this. With this I can forget. This time tomorrow I'll be given a golden harp and set to sing. Any harp that's given to me I'll pop for brandy any time, and so I give you warning. Have a sup with me for old sake's sake.'

He held out the brandy to the clergyman. He was heavily ironed, so that even a simple movement needed an effort.

'Rackage,' I said, 'I am Edward Mansell. You came to

see me here in this very place. Whatever bitterness has been between us, let us put an end to it now, for God's sake. Let us shake hands and be done with that. I am grieved indeed that we were not better friends in the past.'

'Friendship goes by destiny, my joker,' Dennis said. 'You say you are Ned Mansell, as your filthy father called you. Well, you always were a fool and won't mend that by keeping. See here, you who are come to see this Christian die, this fellow, if he's Ned Mansell, thought he'd done for me with the Admiral; thought he's feathered his nest; got the old boy to make him his heir. So he had done, and got me put off the course; all his way was as smooth as soap; he'd only to keep treading water and he'd have been in the Admiral's shoes, house and lands and blunt. He'd as good as landed his fish. Then what happened? Little Dennis stepped in. He had a row with his Admiral. I heard it. I heard lots of what went on. So I thought, this is the chance. This is the time.

'I had only to go in and stick a jemmy in the panel and out the gold would fall, or so I thought. I was wrong about that; only papers were in the panel and the Admiral came in as I was making sure. That was the silliest thing the old cock ever did. I stuck him with this poor fool's knife, the one he'd just bought as a fairing. He didn't take a second stick, only one was needed; down he went and out went his candle. And then in came this Edward Mansell, the heir, by the back door.' Here he turned to me and added, 'If you ever have the spunk to kill a man, outside your doctoring, do it when there are fools about; then they'll be hung instead of you.' He took more brandy and began to sing a low song.

'Rackage,' the Ordinary said, 'we have the man Henery here. We want you and he to shake hands with Dr Mansell and with each other. You both stand in need of forgiveness.'

'Am I going to be forgiven, old cock?' he asked. 'You know quite well I'm not. I'm for the public show tomorrow. Hark at the audience already, the dirty dogs. That's the measure of forgiveness you're giving me. Don't think that I'll give you, or any one, a penny better love than you give me. As for that dog Henery, I'd like to bite his throat open with these teeth.'

'I'm here, Master Dennis,' Henery said. They had brought him there from the next cell at the Ordinary's request. 'I'm here, Master Denn, and I want you to forgive me, so as I may come to God forgiven.'

'Forgive you,' Dennis said, 'no, you come to the wrong shop for forgiveness, my cock. You thought you'd set up for being a Lord Henery, Baron Cholsington, no less, and to that end you rode me like the Dick's Bay Horse; ah, you leech and suck-blood. But the worm turned and bit you dead at last, didn't he? You won't be Baron, just yet, I gather. Ah, and when we were here together all bound for the cold-meat-cart, who put you up to making an escape and bribing a way out? Little Dennis Rackage, that was. And when we were out, who thought of being King's evidence and getting a pardon? Henery that was, but little Denn got the better of him. I saw your game, you twister, and I put the cross on it. I knew where you'd make for, as soon as leg would get you there. I might get away or I might not, but you weren't going to get away. I had you watched for, you great looby, and in you walked to the trap, you so smart and so cocky. I didn't get far myself, but I had my run for my money. I'm drunk now, drunk and dying. And I'll be drunk till I'm dead now, but I'll not be so drunk as not to know I've done for you. The rope's all knotted for me; so's yours, my Lord, and I'll see you in it, drunk as I'll be. I, whom you squeezed dry, have got you so you'll be squeezed dead.'

He lapsed into an outrageous song, so loudly that the men outside the prison in the lane heard it and laughed and joined in it. There must have been twenty thousand men outside the prison, all somewhat touched with drink; they sang the filthy tale to its end, with disgrace notes of howls and cat-calls. Dennis, who became drunker momently, sang with them and swayed to the sound. It was pretty dark there; they had a lantern in the yard outside the Hold, and a couple of lanterns, one a small one brought by the Ordinary, where we were. Dennis swayed as he sat, being ironed to the floor. Henery stood with the irons hanging from him, like draperies on a bronze. Henery was weeping with grief, rage, fear and misery. I was weeping from the thought that I was freed from my terrors, and that I had been in that Hold, expecting Death remediless, and that by miracle I had been brought out of it to life; the Ordinary was weeping, from the thought that the hours would soon strike, and that those souls, but for him, might fall to a fearful fate. When the song died away into yells, screams and howlings, the crying of fried fish and eel jelly, the shouts of encouragement and obscenity, I said, 'I don't think even I could be quite such an iron thing as to send anyone here, after being here myself.'

'No, sir,' he said, in his servant's voice, 'no, sir; I suppose not, sir.'

'Tell me, can't I do anything outside for you?'

'I daren't ask it, sir,' he said. 'I've hated you too cruel.'

'That's done,' I said. 'I've not liked you, but that's done, God knows. What can I do?'

'There's my poor wife in Bedlam, sir,' he said. 'I've let

her go in on the poor side, to save expense. But the
keepers stir them up for sixpence on the poor side, to
make them rave to visitors. If she could be put on the
paying side, where they are all spared that; or are said to
be, sir, it couldn't be for very long.'

'I will see to that, I promise,' I said.

The great gentleman (I call him this, because that was
his position, if not his nature) whispered to the Ordinary,
that we had better go from there. I think that he needed
more punch. The warder motioned Henery back to his
den.

'Time to go home,' he said.

'Good-bye, Henery, and God bless you,' I said.

'Time to go home,' he muttered bitterly. He seemed to
droop down into his irons and shuffled and clanked into
his lair. Dennis had forgotten all things except that there
was no more brandy, and even that he was too stupid to
feel acutely. He, too, was collapsed into his irons, and was
repeating some nonsense to himself; I have thought since
that it was the jargon of some gambling card-game of a
kind simple enough for him to follow. He was repeating:

'Spider, fly . . . fly . . . fly . . . spider, fly, web, web.'

'You had better come away, sir,' the Ordinary said. 'I
will return to him later, when he is in more of a mood to
listen. I thank you, sir, for coming to them.'

'Good-bye, Dennis,' I said, 'good-bye.'

'Don't interrupt the dealer,' he said savagely. They
were plucking me by the sleeve to go; I was eager to be
gone. In a moment the door had snicked-to with that
clickety-clock of the well-oiled, beautifully made great
door-lock, that triumph of skill, which helped to end
what man had neglected till too late. I was outside the
Hold, and he was shut up within it. I saw a glare above
the wall, from the lights outside where people were yell-

ing their wares, of last dying speech and confessions and the like. I found myself with the turn-key following the party. 'Look here,' I said. 'Will you promise to do something for those two men?'

'Yes, sir,' he said, 'on the usual terms.'

'Well, then,' I said, 'here are two guineas. Promise that you will get to them as much brandy as will make them both senseless, if they wish that, before they go out.'

'I'll promise that,' he said, 'but the brandy'll be a guinea extra.'

'Here it is, then. God help you if you fail,' I said.

'We never fail, sir, where the money doesn't fail.'

'I believe that's true,' I said.

The carriage brought me home to Yvonne. The house was brightly lit; the great gentleman had sent his wife there to comfort Yvonne during the hour of my absence. She swept out, gracious and glittering, as our carriage drew up, and was swept into the carriage as I came out of it. She looked at me, but did not speak to me. I knew that this was because I had been hanged. That would not be forgiven me, whatever pardon might come.

'You will hear from us tomorrow,' the man said, 'and he is expecting you at Whitehall at eleven.' The carriage drove on.

What more shall I say? Those two went out of it the next morning. All the reports note that 'both prisoners seemed unaware of their condition.' My turn-key kept faith it seems.

At eleven I was at Whitehall, arranging that the land of the Kranois should begin a trade with us. This has continued ever since, with good and evil fortune. One good thing had come from it, that the slave-trade has been shut from that part of Africa. My pardon was handed to me before our business talks began. The Lord who handed

it to me said, that of course no one, and no thing, could
atone to me for what I had suffered. What reparation
could be made, would be made, the site of Hannibal
House would be mine, and some sum would be offered
for the Admiral's house-property, now long since sold,
and not to be recovered. He said that all had agreed, and
perhaps I should agree, that the matter should be kept
quiet; he was sure that both I myself and my wife would
prefer that. He was a man of charming manners; he began
then to talk about the weather, and about the possible
origins of the Kranish people, and of the beauty of the
new theory of disease which had been put forward in a
remarkable book.

After that, with some more compliment and the ex-
pression of obligation, he left me, with my pardon and
my title deeds and a note of money.

The Fortune, who gives, is ever prodigal. Some time
later, when we were about to sail for Sixteen Peaks, I
went out to Cholsington, to look at the site of Hannibal
House. It was a fair summer day. Since the fire, the place
had been deserted. Being now full summer, the weeds
had taken charge in such strength that even the curious
had ceased to trespass there; a few boys after birds' nests,
perhaps, no others. The blackened walls partly stood.
The roof had collapsed into the shell, all the windows
had gone; the starlings, which once nested in such
strength in the roof, now nestled in the ruin, they were
very busy, whistling, chuckling and bringing food.

All was thickly grown with nettle, some of it four feet
high. Going round, I came to the track made by some
animal. I followed it with difficulty, beating down the
nettles till I was inside the house, by what had been the
back door, through which I had been taken to Newgate.
The door was gone, of course; I clambered over fallen

roof and wreck to where a little dog was scuffling and snuffling. He was in the central part of the house now, scratching at a rabbit-burrow. The floor had been burned or stolen; I was on the earth on which the house had been reared, in what had once been the dining-room, a very beautiful room, where the Coroner had once committed me for trial for murder.

The little dog paused from his scuffling, put his head upon the ground and tried to clear the moist clay from his nostrils. As he could not do this, I did it for him. Bending down there, I thought that I saw something in the burrow, and putting down my hand touched metal; something hard was stuck in the earth there; some post or column of iron, it seemed; I could not budge it. It flashed into my mind that it might prove to be the Admiral's treasure chamber, and so it proved to be.

In a narrow space he had contrived to pack, muzzle up, nine of the small guns which had been the armament of the *Hannibal*. He had used each one as a strong box. Eight were full to the muzzle with notes and golden guineas, the ninth half-full. Each was carefully stoppered with a metal tompion, puttied in. This wealth had been kept from all till a little dog led me to it.

So there I was, with Wife, Friends and Fortune, the Rose revived, Ned alive and the bright road clear before me.